THE GREEN CORN REBELLION

THE GREEN CORN REBELLION

A Novel by
William Cunningham
Introduction by Nigel Anthony Sellars

UNIVERSITY OF OKLAHOMA PRESS · NORMAN

This book is published with the generous assistance of the Wallace C. Thompson Endowment Fund, University of Oklahoma Foundation.

Library of Congress Cataloging-in-Publication Data

Cunningham, William, 1901–1967.
    The Green Corn Rebellion : a novel / by William Cunningham.
        p.   cm.
    Originally published: New York, NY : Vanguard Press, c1935.
    ISBN 978-0-8061-4057-5 (pbk. : alk. paper)
        1. Farmers—Fiction. 2. Insurgency—Fiction. 3. Oklahoma—History—Fiction.
    I. Title.
    PS3505.U455G74 2010
    813'.52—dc22

2009029266

The paper in this book meets the guidelines for permanence and durability of the Committee on Production Guidelines for Book Longevity of the Council on Library Resources, Inc. ∞

INTRODUCTION

The Deep Roots of an American Rebellion

NIGEL ANTHONY SELLARS

The tenant farmers of the Green Corn Rebellion are all too often either characterized as ignorant, backward, and foolhardy yokels or instead, as in William Cunningham's novel, romanticized as proletarian heroes in a tragic but heroic struggle. In fact, they were impoverished, necessitous men who, finding their efforts and trust in political reform repeatedly frustrated, turned to a long, and very *American*, tradition of resistance to oppression and injustice.

Make no mistake—this was indeed class warfare. That this warfare took the form of barn burnings, night riding, and destruction of property does not make it any less a class struggle than that of revolutionary industrial workers storming the barricades. Such rural uprisings against heavy taxes, burdensome rents, and political institutions controlled by uncaring elites dot the landscape of the American past. From the colonial era to the twentieth century, these rebellions reflected deep class-based antagonism.

The pattern of agrarian unrest dates at least as far back as Nathaniel Bacon's 1676 rebellion in Virginia and the colony's subsequent 1682 Tobacco Plant Cutters' Riots. From 1699 to 1700 and again in the 1740s, New Jersey's small farmers rioted and took over courts in land disputes with the colony's wealthy landholding proprietors. North Carolina suffered serious anti-quitrent and anti–land tax riots in 1737 and 1759, while tenants in upstate New York engaged in riots and protests first from 1751 to 1757 and then in 1766 to protest oppressive rent increases. Those protests continued with the Anti-Rent War of 1839–46, when the tenants won a rare victory.[1]

In the 1771 Regulator War in North Carolina, small farmers and landless tenants from the colony's western highlands, styling themselves "Regulators," protested high taxes, corrupt and extortionate sheriffs and court officials, and legislative abuses by the wealthy Atlantic Coast planters. When their petitions for relief were rejected, the Regulators took over courthouses, intimidated judges, and destroyed property. After a colonial militia defeated the Regulators at the Battle of the Alamance in 1771, the authorities hanged several Regulator leaders. Surviving Regulators fled across the Appalachian Mountains and settled in what became Tennessee.[2]

Strict foreclosure laws and disproportionate taxes after the Revolution led to Daniel Shays's Rebellion of 1786–87 in Massachusetts and the Whiskey and Fries's rebellions of the 1790s in the Pennsylvania backcountry. While these rebellions all collapsed, they did create a fear of popular revolt among the conservative landholding class. The government created by those elites under the new Constitution quickly asserted its authority, claiming that as its power came from the sovereignty of the people, any challenge to its authority—even by the people themselves—was treasonous.[3]

Descendants of these rural rebels eventually migrated west, settling in Tennessee, Missouri, Arkansas, and the northeastern region of Texas bordering Indian Territory. Even as they sought land of their own, these small farmers soon learned they could escape neither the control of large landholders nor the tenant farming system, not even in Indian Territory.

The use of tenants to farm cotton in Indian Territory began in the 1880s as mixed-heritage and intermarried white citizens of the Five Nations (the Cherokees, Chickasaws, Choctaws, Creeks, and Seminoles) converted tribal land to large-scale agricultural production. Tribal laws forbade directly leasing land to noncitizens, so tenants were defined as "agricultural workers," who could work under permit. The tenants, mostly white, and former African American slaves worked the land for a small elite of landlords, just as had their ancestors in the seventeenth and eighteenth centuries.[4]

After 1890, large numbers of whites from Arkansas and

northern Texas joined smaller numbers of African Americans in moving to Indian Territory. Most hoped to claim homesteads after the Indians' lands were allotted, as had happened in Oklahoma Territory to the west. The 1898 Curtis Act, however, allotted all the land to tribal citizens—including intermarried whites and African American freedman and their descendants—and left no surplus land for homesteaders. In addition, wealthier whites and mixed-heritage citizens used an array of devices, including outright fraud, to gain control of the bulk of allotted land, often for speculative purposes.[5]

As in the colonial era, land speculation proved more profitable than growing any crops. Oklahoma land was worth an average $6.50 an acre in 1900. By 1910 it had risen to $22.49 an acre, a 246 percent increase. Such profitable investments for speculators meant that land prices were beyond the means of most tenants.

Numbers of tenant-run farms in Oklahoma ballooned between 1900 and 1910, especially after the Panic of 1907. Tenants operated 47,250 out of 108,000 farms (44 percent) in 1900, but 104,137 farms of 190,192 (55 percent) in 1910. Only the large number of owner-operated farms in western Oklahoma kept the state from having the nation's highest tenancy rate.[6] Overall, Oklahoma tenants were young; white; of old English, Scots-Irish, or German stock; and unlikely ever to own farms. Of Oklahoma farmers under age twenty-five, 76 percent were tenants, as were 55 percent of those between the ages of twenty-five and thirty-three.[7]

The largest percentages of tenant farms lay in the southeastern quarter of the state. Tenants ran 60 percent of the farms in the three counties of the Green Corn Rebellion: Hughes, Seminole, and Pontotoc. In Pottawatomie County, where Cunningham sets most of his novel, tenants ran half the farms by 1910. Other counties had rates as high as 75 to 80 percent.[8]

The cash-poor tenants of southeastern Oklahoma also suffered under an in-kind rent system that took one-quarter of a cotton crop and one-third of a corn crop—or more. With crop prices regularly depressed, the earnings from rents barely covered most landlords' taxes on the land. Land speculation, therefore, became the landowner's real moneymaker, especially if the tenants made capital improvements to the property. The landlords were not obligated to compensate tenants for improvements if they left or were forced off the property.[9]

The tenants also relied heavily on town businessmen—"furnishing merchants"—for credit or loans, using their crops or what livestock they owned as collateral. Interest rates on loans were exorbitant: 20 percent was common on personal security loans, while the interest charged on a chattel mortgage ran from 20 to 200 percent. Compounded, some rates reached 2,000 percent interest. Rates were especially high in Hughes, Seminole, and Pontotoc counties, where by 1915 the tenant farmers were paying some of the highest interest rates in the nation. Such usurious rates meant tenants could never be free of debt and were effectively laborers earning a subsistence wage.[10] Although the Oklahoma legislature passed anti-usury laws in 1910 and 1916 that set interest rates at 6 percent without a contract and at 10 percent with one, the laws proved toothless. Tenants knew that suing a bank meant being blacklisted by all other creditors. Desperate for funds, the tenant had to accept the illegal rates.[11]

Even reasonable interest rates could hardly have improved the poor quality of southeastern Oklahoma's soil. Spending fourteen to eighteen man-hours per acre, Oklahoma cotton tenants worked as much as Mississippi or Louisiana sharecroppers—and on more acreage per farm—and still had poorer yields. A tenant's entire family had to work constantly from planting to harvest, so his children spent little time in school. Many tenants still had to take seasonal jobs in the oil and mining industries or the wheat harvest just to get by.[12]

Such bleak prospects undoubtedly drew many tenants to socialism. Continuing in the tradition of the Populists, the

Oklahoma Socialist Party called for expanding the public domain for tenants' use, a graduated land tax to end cutthroat land speculation, and a cooperative marketing plan. These programs were especially appealing in counties with high rates of tenancy, where Socialists saw enormous electoral gains by 1912 and even as late as 1916—this despite the landlords' practice of evicting Socialist tenants.[13]

Socialists also developed self-help organizations such as the Oklahoma Renters' Union. Organized in September 1909, the Renters' Union demanded "three-room tenant houses with glass windows and wooden floors, two-room school houses with six month terms[, and] payment for the improvements made on the landlord's property in case of surrender or eviction." Tenants who belonged to the Renters' Union, however, were all too often evicted by the landlord or simply refused a new lease, rendering the union largely dead by 1914.[14]

Despite such setbacks, tenants and the Socialist Party (SP) formed other organizations. Choctaw County tenants formed a Growers' Protective Association and sued banks violating the 1910 usury law. Members of the more radical, or "Red," wing of the SP organized the Farmers' Emancipation League in Pittsburg County and also planned to sue banks and to force rent reductions. The fortunes of such groups, however, depended on sympathetic judges, a rare commodity. By 1915 many tenants had grown frustrated with the ballot box and the courts and returned to traditional forms of protest such as night riding and barn burning.[15]

That frustration found another outlet in the Louisiana-born Working Class Union (WCU), headquartered just across the state border in Van Buren, Arkansas. The WCU grew from the bitter labor wars fought in the Texas-Louisiana piney woods between the anti-union lumber companies and the Brotherhood of Timber Workers (BTW), an affiliate of the militant Industrial Workers of the World (IWW). Former BTW members such as John E. "Hobo" Wiggins and Cash M. Stephens organized heavily in eastern Oklahoma, where they were joined by Henry Hamilton "Rube" Munson. The WCU eventually claimed 20,000 members in the state.[16]

While the vast majority of WCU members were white, a significant number were African American and American Indian. The black tenants, like their white counterparts, had come to the former Indian Territory in search of land, but found hostility not just from whites but also from those African Americans descended from slaves owned by members of the Five Nations. Land was especially important for African Americans, as the number of black-owned farms in Oklahoma Territory demonstrated. In the rebellion counties, entire extended families often occupied a homestead. In Indian Territory, African American tenants found frustration for the same reasons as did white tenants.[17]

Yet the Working Class Union proved capable of overcoming the prevailing racism of the era, even if for only a short period. While the WCU was hardly an enlightened organization on the matter, the locals in the rebellion counties did include black members. At least two, Price Street and Ira Hardy, were sufficiently high up in the WCU leadership to be involved in planning the rebellion. Street's prominence seems due in part to his being a Spanish-American War veteran and thus the only WCU member with any military experience. That, however, did little good when, as a "Captain," he was placed in command of one group of rebels and some white members refused to take orders from a black man. They did listen to him when he ordered them to disperse in the face of a sizable posse on horseback. Both Street and Hardy, a twenty-year-old who had joined the WCU only in late June, were arrested and, along with the other WCU leaders, received lengthy prison sentences in the federal penitentiary at Leavenworth.[18]

More problematic was the participation of some members of the Snake faction of dissident Creeks. Led by John Harjo, a relative of the late traditionalist Creek leader Chitto Harjo, the Snakes seemed unlikely allies of black and white tenants as the traditionalists had twice, in 1901 and 1907, revolted against both the allotment system and the leasing of any tribal land to tenants, black or white. These Snake faction participants, including a few Creek freedmen who were arrested, refused to talk to the authorities, and not one even hinted at why he took part. It appears that the WCU leaders, at least in Seminole County, believed they needed the Snakes as allies, so much so that they may have delayed the rebellion in order to accommodate the Snakes' Green Corn Ceremony at the end of July.[19]

Tenants were drawn to an organization that, while its demands differed little from those of the SP or the IWW, did not reject violence as those two organizations did.[20] That violent tendency manifested itself in 1915 when the state imposed a cattle-dipping program to stop the spread of "Texas fever" among Oklahoma herds. County sheriffs, charged with enforcement, could seize the livestock of uncooperative farmers. Those farmers, however, asserted that the arsenic-based dipping solution was toxic to cattle and that, for them, even one dead cow meant economic disaster. In September, night riders—mostly WCU members—dynamited dipping tanks in Pontotoc, Sequoyah and Muskogee counties; burned barns belonging to county commissioners; and flogged tenants who rented from landlords blacklisted by the WCU. Despite denunciations from the press and local officials, the night riding had one positive effect: it encouraged the legislature to amend and strengthen the existing anti-usury law. Afterwards, night riding and extralegal violence declined dramatically.[21]

Violence returned in 1917 after Congress authorized American entry into the Great War in April and President Woodrow Wilson signed the Selective Service Act on May 18. Historically, military draft laws had hit the rural and urban lower classes hardest. During the Civil War, in addition to the infamous New York City draft riot, regular draft resistance arose regularly in both the North and South. Confederate conscription officials were particularly hard-pressed by resisters in northern Texas and the Ozarks. When tenants later migrated to Oklahoma, they brought both a tradition of draft resistance and a system of passwords and rituals, which many of the Working Class Union locals adopted. Perhaps most significant, they brought a draft resister's slogan used across the Confederacy: "Rich man's war; poor man's fight."[22]

Once war was declared, the WCU responded, relying on the leadership of Rube Munson and his lieutenant, Homer Spence. A former lead and zinc miner and tenant farmer from Missouri, Munson was actually the black-sheep son of a well-to-do Kansas pharmacist. By 1917 Munson had organized for the WCU for two years, and he alone apparently conceived the plan of moving the WCU toward militant draft resistance. A persuasive orator with a gift for speaking to the uneducated, Munson used scripture to make points and often brought his children along to sing labor songs. But some individuals who knew him believed Munson was at best a semiliterate braggart.[23]

In April and May, Munson and Spence warned WCU locals that all able-bodied men would be sent to Europe, and their families forced onto large farms for the war effort. Munson and Spence claimed that two million men from forty-eight organizations—including the IWW and the railroad brotherhoods—would march on Washington, D.C., force "Kaiser" Wilson from office, and end the war. More than a few WCU locals agreed to stockpile weapons, dynamite, and poisons in preparation.[24]

Tensions grew during May and June 1917, when President Wilson signed the Selective Service Act and the Espionage Act, the latter intended to suppress dissent. For many farmers, these laws likely confirmed that what Spence and Munson said was true. Most WCU locals actually planned only to shelter and protect draft resisters, as their Civil War–era forebears had. But along the South Canadian River in Seminole, Hughes, and Pontotoc counties, the lodges burned with the fires of rebellion. Regardless of whether members were white, black, or Indian, they all distrusted the draft system, which they saw as dominated by small-town bankers and merchants. The farmers believed those men harbored strong class and racial biases that favored their own interests, meaning farmers or their sons would be drafted while shop clerks, bank tellers, and the sons of the prominent men received exemptions or special treatment.[25]

The situation worsened throughout the summer. On June 7 Seminole County authorities arrested five men on draft resistance charges, and they implicated the WCU. Also on June 7 some WCU members dynamited a water storage tank at Dewar. That same day, federal authorities arrested both Munson and Spence on charges of conspiracy to obstruct the draft. Spence was soon released on bond, but federal authorities kept Munson in custody at Muskogee. A week later, Holdenville police arrested a local WCU leader for distributing antidraft literature. Authorities arrested more WCU members after gas explosions at Kusa and Henryetta, although both were probably accidental.[26]

In July, federal authorities arrested eight members of a Pottawatomie County WCU local that planned to hide draft resisters. Soon reports of unrest came from places as far away as Enid, Coalgate, Tishomingo, Shawnee, Wewoka, Holdenville, and Pontotoc County. On July 26 Konawa authorities arrested two more WCU members on draft resistance charges. In the meantime, Homer Spence went from local to local, warning members to be ready to rise up.[27]

Then, on August 2, 1917, a handful of African American WCU members gathered near the Little River and fired on the Seminole County sheriff and his deputy, slightly wounding the deputy, as the pair investigated claims of a rebellion. Within hours there was one, as WCU raiding parties cut telegraph and telephone lines, set fire to railroad bridges and trestles, and attempted to dynamite oil pipelines. Other members gathered on a ridge on the Little River near Sasakwa in Seminole County. There they prepared for the revolution that never came.[28]

The revolt collapsed when many rebels saw that they faced hastily formed local posses—consisting of neighbors, not the federal troops they had expected to engage. Minor clashes occurred over the next few days, leaving four men dead. Sheriffs and deputies arrested 458 men for allegedly participating in or supporting the rebellion. Another 16, including the man who fired on the Seminole County sheriff, were never caught. Most of the arrestees were soon released, but 86 men ultimately pleaded guilty and received prison terms of from one to ten years. Twenty-eight men of these, including Munson and Spence, were imprisoned at Leavenworth, Kansas, while the other 58 served time either in federal jails in Oklahoma or at the state penitentiary at McAlester. One reporter described men as "haggard and broken" when they left the court after sentencing. Most were freed after just a few months, but some remained in prison until 1923.[29]

Those not convicted, facing landlords who refused to rent to rebels or sympathizers, simply moved on. A number settled in western Arkansas near Mena, where William Cunningham, then teaching at nearby Commonwealth College, later interviewed them for his novel. The rebellion also proved disastrous to the Oklahoma Socialist Party, which, after having achieved so much for the state's tenants, disbanded in 1918.[30]

In the end, the Green Corn Rebellion was merely the last in a long line of courageous struggles that America's landless poor, regardless of their race, had waged since the day the first English colonists set foot on North American soil at Jamestown. Theirs was a deeply and profoundly American struggle, despite its eventual futility. As the Socialist organizer and newspaper editor Oscar Ameringer wrote, "Illiterate, poorly schooled, doped with all the mental poison their 'betters' could pour into them, yes; but ignorant, no." Ameringer's friend the great Socialist and IWW writer and poet Covington Hall later noted the draft resisters acted on simple, Jeffersonian principles: "They actually believed they had some rights that the government was bound to respect."[31]

It is those Jeffersonian principles, infused with a strong dose of Marxist political ideas and sex, that is at the center of William Cunningham's novel. *The Green Corn Rebellion* is an episodic novel, with sections that often loosely link to the main story. In that respect, it bears a resemblance to Steinbeck's *The Grapes of Wrath*, though that work deals with tenants in a later decade, after years of oppression, poverty, and drought. Cunningham's novel, in contrast, is about those years of oppression, poverty, hope, and failed revolt. Despite the title, *The Green Corn Rebellion* is less about the rebellion than it is what motivated men to take up arms in the first place and the price they paid in the aftermath.

"The artistic representation of history," Cunningham once noted, "is a more scientific and serious pursuit than the exact writing of history. For the art of letters goes to the heart of things, whereas the factual report merely collates details."[32] This approach to writing fiction may explain some of the novel's more unusual aspects, particularly Cunningham's decision to set the novel in Pottawatomie County, which saw little, if any, actual fighting, rather than in one of the three counties where the main part of the rebellion occurred. The county was, however, home to the so-called Jones Family—a number of WCU locals that government informants and provocateurs had infiltrated. In fact, like most WCU locals outside of the rebellion area, the "Jones Family" had planned only to help young men hide out from conscription officers or to help them reach safe areas, especially Mexico. This practice mirrored that of WCU locals in Arkansas. Cunningham may have chosen to set his novel near Shawnee, precisely because it was not near the actual fighting. This certainly allowed him greater leeway in telling his own story, unhampered by the real events. Another aspect of the novel involves scattered references to wheat harvesting. The rebellion area was almost exclusively cotton-growing country, but Cunningham was both born and raised in the wheat-growing regions of the state, and he may simply have been more familiar with wheat agriculture.

Despite the apparent artistic license, *The Green Corn Rebellion* also reveals the considerable research Cunningham put into the novel. He portrays a rural Oklahoma as it was before 1920, a world comprising the poorest farmers in the state, mostly tenants "who could not borrow money at the banks because they had voted the Socialist ticket. Some of them were Negroes; a few were half-breed Indians, half white or freedmen" (121). He successfully brings these people to life, people who recalled ancestors forced to fight in endless wars. They had good reason to suspect the motives of the "electric light towns" and cities and to distrust any ruling group, especially the large landholders and their banker and merchant allies, as well as a government that they viewed as more interested in protecting large corporations than in helping small farmers.

Many other details, as well as the inspiration for several characters, came from Cunningham's tenure at Commonwealth College, a Socialist school in Mena, Arkansas. While teaching there, Cunningham met and interviewed a number of people who actually took part in the rebellion. The most important appears to have been Clyde Washington, a square-dance caller and farmer from the hills near Mena. Although Washington had been a deputy helping to track down the rebels, he seems to have provided Cunningham with much information about the rebellion and its aftermath.[33]

While at Mena, Cunningham also met Rube Munson. Munson arrived at Commonwealth from Sallisaw in the summer of 1927 as a poultry expert—skills he evidently learned while incarcerated at Leavenworth—and brought with him several crates of his own strain of Crown Comb leghorn chickens. Munson's stay at Commonwealth was brief. Contentious and disruptive as ever, he was soon leading an opposition movement against the college's administration. After a strike he organized failed, Munson left with several others, not including Cunningham, by fall 1927. Still, Munson did influence the novel, as it appears that Cunningham based the character of Mack McGee, Jim Tetley's father-in-law, at least in part on the old radical.[34]

On a literary level, Cunningham shapes characters who possess a working-class essence as opposed to a middle-class resignation to commercial drudgery. The novel expresses this working-class-ness both politically and sexually. Jim Tetley's desire for his sister-in-law Happy is a natural product of his class-consciousness, whereas his businessman brother, Ted, with his crippled body and casual anti-Semitism, frequents prostitutes and views sex merely as a business transaction.[35]

Politically, Cunningham has Tetley—probably more an autobiographical character than a historically based one—ruminate on whether to lie to his wife about taking part in the rebellion, and come to the conclusion that competition breeds lying and theft. The big capitalists grow wealthy on such lies and larceny, he realizes, while they also reduce honest people—who, like his wife, Jeanie, buy into the idea that hard work leads to success—to desexualized drudges. "Any way you looked at it, it was this damned competitive system that made people liars and thieves" (120). Although this part of the novel is often seen as expressing Cunningham's own personal views, it bears a striking resemblance to the stump speeches and revival-style rants of actual rebels like Homer Spence and Rube Munson.[36]

Throughout the book, Cunningham also captures, in little episodes, the sense and feel of important events in the farmers' lives. Early on he portrays a Socialist Party meeting featuring a German-born organizer who can communicate and joke with the tenant farmers despite his thick accent. The character, for whom Cunningham shows obvious affection, is based on the Austrian-born Socialist, humorist, and journalist Oscar Ameringer. Cunningham knew Ameringer well, having worked on two Ameringer-edited newspapers, the *Illinois Miner* and *Oklahoma Leader*.

In addition, Cunningham has Tetley influenced by a black tenant farmer named Bill Johnson, whose class-consciousness and commitment to the tenants' common cause remains strong despite his having suffered far more than any white tenant from the added burden of racism. While Cunningham was certainly aware of such figures as Price Street and Ira Hardy, he probably invented Johnson as a composite of several individuals. He clearly saw Johnson's character as a means to emphasize the role that African Americans as a group played in the rebellion.

The rebellion itself is ultimately another character in this novel, which is really about how taking part in collective action can bring about personal redemption. Jim's life changes only after he is transformed from a narcissistic, adulterous, ne'er-do-well farmer, whose lack of ambition will trap him forever in a loveless marriage and perpetual poverty, into a man of the people: a true revolutionary who sees clearly that only by rebelling against the existing state of the world can the fruits of that world be equitably distributed to people like him. Early in the novel, Tetley has an epiphany after reading the patriotic editorials in the local newspapers. "The rich sons-of-bitches start a war," he realizes, "and make things so that a lot of poor people are starved to death—let alone millions that get shot—and then talk about God still reigning and about the obligation of the rich toward the poor" (94–95). That, finally, is what this too-long-neglected novel is really about. I can only add that it is a joy to see it back in print after more than seventy years, for new generations to discover and, we may hope, to ponder.

NOTES

1. Edward Countryman, "'Out of the Bounds of the Law': Northern Land Rioters in the Eighteenth Century," in *The American Revolution: Explorations in the History of American Radicalism*, ed. Alfred Young (DeKalb: Northern Illinois University Press, 1976), 43, 45; Richard Maxwell Brown, "Violence and the American Revolution," in *Essays on the American Revolution*, ed. Stephen G. Kurtz and James H. Hutson (Chapel Hill: University of North Carolina Press, 1973), 117–18.

2. Marvin L. Michael Kay, "The North Carolina Regulation, 1766–1776: A Class Conflict" in Young, *The American Revolution*, 71–123.

3. David P. Szatmary, *Shays' Rebellion: The Making of an Agrarian Insurrection* (Amherst: University of Massachusetts Press, 1980); John A. Garraty, "Rebellions," in *The Reader's Companion to American History*, ed. Eric Foner and John A. Garraty (Boston: Houghton Mifflin, 1991), 915–17.

4. Robert L. Owen, Superintendent of the Five Civilized Tribes, to the

Commissioner of Indian Affairs, September 20, 1886, in *Report of the Commissioner of Indian Affairs for 1886* (Washington: Government Printing Office, 1886), 146–61; W. David Baird and Danney Goble, *Oklahoma: A History* (Norman: University of Oklahoma Press, 2008), 210.

5. U.S. Bureau of the Census, *Thirteenth Census of the United States, 1910*: Vol. 7, *Agriculture*, 352, 357; Southwestern Bell, *Economic Survey of Oklahoma* (St. Louis: Southwestern Bell, 1929), 104; Baird and Goble, *Story of Oklahoma*, 310, 312–13; Arrell M. Gibson, "The Centennial Legacy of the General Allotment Act," *Chronicles of Oklahoma* 65 (Fall 1987), 239–40, 247–49; Angie Debo, *And Still the Waters Run: The Betrayal of the Five Civilized Tribes* (Princeton, N.J.: Princeton University Press, 1940; repr., Norman: University of Oklahoma Press, 1984), 53–58.

6. *Thirteenth Census*, Vol. 5, 125–26; U.S. Bureau of the Census, *Fourteenth Census of the United States, 1920*: Vol. 5, *Agriculture* (Washington, D.C.: Government Printing Office, 1922), 484–85; E. A. Goldenweiser and Leon E. Truesdell, *Farm Tenancy in the United States, Census Monograph IV* (Washington, D.C.: Government Printing Office, 1924), 148–49; W. W. Pannell, "Tenant Farming in the United States," *International Socialist Review* 16 (January 1916), 431–32; William Bennett Bizzell, *Farm Tenantry in the United States* (College Station: Texas Agricultural Experimental Station, 1921), 118–19, 156–57, 159; William J. Spillman and E. A. Goldenweiser, "Farm Tenantry in the United States," in *Yearbook of the United States Department of Agriculture* (Washington, D.C.: Government Printing Office, 1917), 337.

7. Bizzell, *Farm Tenantry*, 156–57; Charles Holman, "The Tenant Farmer: Country Brother of the Casual Worker," *Survey* 34 (April 17, 1915): 64.

8. *Thirteenth Census*, Vol. 7, 375–77.

9. Goldenweiser and Truesdell, *Farm Tenancy*, 15, 19; Oscar Ameringer, *If You Don't Weaken: The Autobiography of Oscar Ameringer* (New York; Henry Holt, 1940), 253; John Thompson, *Closing the Frontier: Radical Response in Oklahoma, 1889–1923* (Norman: University of Oklahoma Press, 1989), 42; *Harlow's Weekly* (Oklahoma City), December 22, 1916.

10. *Harlow's Weekly*, October 30, 1915; C. A. Thompson, *Factors Affecting Interest Rates and Other Charges on Short Term Farm Loans*, United States Department of Agriculture Bulletin No. 409 (Washington, D.C.: Government Printing Office, 1916), 2.

11. *Revised Laws of Oklahoma, 1910*, Vol. 1, 269, No. 1004; Senate Bill No. 3, *State of Oklahoma, Session Laws of 1916: Extraordinary Session, Fifth Legislature* (Guthrie: Co-operative Publishing Company, 1916), 24–28; *Harlow's Weekly*, March 11, March 29, May 21, 1916.

12. Ellen Rosen, "Peasant Socialism in America? The Socialist Party in Oklahoma before the First World War" (Ph.D. dissertation, City University of New York, 1975), 153; Bizzell, *Farm Tenantry*, 156–57, 232–33, 260; Holman, "The Tenant Farmer," 64; Pannell, "Tenant Farming," 431–32; Oran Burk, "From a Cotton Picker," *International Socialist Review* 14 (May 1914): 690; Edward N. Clopper, "Causes of Absences from Rural Schools in

Oklahoma" (National Child Labor Committee, September 1917), 17.

13. James R. Green, *Grass-roots Socialism: Radical Movements in the Southwest, 1895–1943* (Baton Rouge: Louisiana State University Press, 1978), 244–48, 291, 352–53; Donald Kenneth Pickens, "Principles and Programs of Oklahoma Socialism, 1900–1918" (master's thesis, University of Oklahoma, 1957), 106.

14. *Oklahoma Pioneer* (Oklahoma City), March 2, 1910; Green, *Grass-roots Socialism*, 81, 108.

15. Green, *Grass-roots Socialism*, 301–302, 324.

16. Covington Hall, *Labor Struggles in the Deep South & Other Writings*, ed. David R. Roediger (Chicago: Charles H. Kerr, 2000), 187–88; "WCU membership card," in Box 36, Folder 2, Redmond Cole Collection, Western History Collections, University of Oklahoma, Norman (hereafter WHC/OU); untitled and undated WCU flier issued from National Headquarters, Lock Box 72, Van Buren, Arkansas, in Correspondence Binder 1-216, p. 103, Box 36, Folder 2, Redmond Cole Collection, WHC/OU; *Daily Oklahoman*, August 8, September 25, October 7, 1917.

17. Bonnie Lynn-Sherow, *Mechanization, Land Use, and Ownership: Oklahoma in the Early Twentieth Century*, Land Tenure Center Paper 155, University of Wisconsin–Madison, June 1996, para 20 (online edition at www.ies.wisc.edu/ltc/ltc1#9A4ED).

18. Agnes "Sis" Cunningham and Gordon Friesen, *Red Dust and Broadsides: A Joint Autobiography*, ed. Ronald D. Cohen (Amherst: University of Massachusetts Press, 1999), 131–33, 329, 330; "Statement of Ira Hardy. August 13, 1917," 4-page typescript, in Case File No. 39665, Investigative Case Files of the Bureau of Investigation, 1908–1922, Record Group 65, National Archives and Records Administration, Microfilm edition, reel 388; Gene Lantz, "History Lies about Heroic Oklahomans in the Greencorn Rebellion!" *Labor History from Texas* (online article), www.labordallas.org/hist/greencor.htm. Lantz interviewed the descendants of two rebels, one black and one white, who repeated the story regarding both the refusal to take orders from Street (whom they called "Straight") and the flight from the posse.

19. Debo, *And Still the Waters Run*, 154–56, 294–96; Green, *Grass-roots Socialism*, 359. For an example of the Snakes' refusal to cooperate, see "Statement of Cowradochy (Wildcat)," 1-page typescript in Case File No. 39665, Investigative Case Files of the Bureau of Investigation, 1908–1922. Ethnologist John R. Swinton, in his study of Creek religious and medicinal practices, quotes extensively from Creek official George Washington Grayson's account of attending a Green Corn Ceremony at the Tukabahchee campground, where a John Harjo— possibly but not likely the John Harjo of the rebellion—provided a pallet in his tent for Grayson. At the least, the timing of the Green Corn Ceremony coincided with the initial date for the rebellion, and the ceremony ended just before the uprising actually occurred. This might explain the delay. See John R. Swinton, *Creek Religion and Medicine* (Lincoln: University of Nebraska Press, 2000; reprint of "Religious Beliefs and Medicinal Practices of the Creek Indians," *42d Annual Report of the Bureau of American Ethnology* [1928]), 574–76. In her autobiography *Red Dirt: Growing Up Okie*, historian Roxanne Dunbar-Ortiz relates two incidents twenty years apart when she meet American Indians, one an elderly Seminole in 1994 and the other the late Muskogee medicine man Philip Deere in 1974. Both were alive at the time of the rebellion and describe the event, which Deere believed, incorrectly, was Indian conceived and led. See Roxanne Dunbar-Ortiz, *Red Dirt: Growing Up Okie* (New York: Verso, 1997; repr., Norman: University of Oklahoma Press, 2006), 15.

20. Hall, *Labor Struggles in the Deep South*, 187–88; "WCU membership card," in Box 26, Folder 2, Redmond Cole Collection, WHC/OU); untitled and undated WCU flier issued from National Headquarters, Lock Box 72, Van Buren, Arkansas, in Correspondence Binder 1-216, 103, Box 36, Folder 2, Redmond Cole Collection, WHC/OU; *The Daily Oklahoman*, August 8, September 25, October 7, 1917.

21. Green, *Grass-Roots Socialism*, 338–40; *Harlow's Weekly*, January 15, December 13, 1916; J. Stanley Clark, "Texas Fever in Oklahoma," *Chronicles of Oklahoma* 24 (Winter 1951–52): 429–43; *Muskogee Daily Phoenix*, January 6, 1916; Case No. 1553, *U.S. v. Isenhour et al.* trial notes, in Correspondence Binder 1-216, 47, 52, 79, 129, Redmond Cole Collection, WHC/OU.

22. Selective Service Act (1917), 40 *U.S. Statutes at Large* 76; Robin Brooks, "Domestic Violence and America's Wars: An Historical Interpretation," in *Violence in America: Historical and Comparative Perspectives*, revised ed., ed. Hugh Davis Graham and Ted Robert Gurr (Beverly Hills: Sage Publications, 1979), 311–12; Georgia Lee Tatum, *Disloyalty in the Confederacy* (Chapel Hill: University of North Carolina Press, 1934), 24–25, 36–46, 54–72, 90–91, 143–55.

23. Norma Jane Bumgarner, "The Milton Colony: From Utopia to Ghost Town, 1913–1916," *Chronicles of Oklahoma* 78 (Spring 2000): 74–75; "Cross-Examination of Tobe Simmons," trial notes, "Jones Family," in Box 36, Folder 2, Correspondence Binder 1-216, 94, Redmond Cole Collection, WHC/OU.

24. *Wewoka Capital-Democrat*, May 31, August 9, 1917; *Seminole County Capital* (Wewoka), May 31, 1917; *Ada Weekly News*, May 31, August 16, 1917; *Shawnee Daily News Herald*, August 5, September 25, 1917; *McAlester News Capital*, August 18, 1917; *Daily Ardmoreite*, October 31, 1917; *Daily Oklahoman*, September 25, 1917; "Testimony of William Hoobler," in Transcript of Record, *Clure Isenhour et al., plaintiffs in error v. United States, defendants in error*, June 1, 1918 (U.S. Circuit Court of Appeals, Eighth Circuit, No. 5170), pp. 362, 413 (copy in Manuscript and Archives Division, Oklahoma Historical Society, Oklahoma City); "Direct testimony of George Ingraham, Konawa," in Case No. 1553, *U.S. v. Isenhour et al.* trial notes, Box 36, Folder 2, Correspondence Binder 1-216, 55, Redmond Cole Collection, WHC/OU.

25. Selective Service Act (1917), 40 *U.S. Statutes at Large* 76; Espionage Act (1917), 40 *U.S. Statues at Large* 217; Jeanette Keith, "The Politics of Southern Draft Resistance, 1917–1918: Class, Race, and Conscription in the Rural South," *Journal of American History* 87 (March 2001): 1338, 1341.

26. *Daily Oklahoman*, May 30, June 4, 1917; *Shawnee Daily News-Herald*, August 5, 1917; *Wewoka Capital-Democrat*, June 7, 1917; *Holdenville Democrat*, June 14,

1917; *Norman Transcript*, June 7, 1917; *Norman Democrat-Topic*, June 22, 1917; *Enid Daily Eagle*, September 24, 1917; Reports of Bureau of Investigation agent T. F. Weiss, Oklahoma City/McAlester, dated September 18, 24, 27, 1917, in Randolph Boehm, ed., *United States Military Intelligence Reports: Surveillance of Radicals in the United States, 1917–1941* (Frederick, Md.: University Publications of America, 1984), reel 6, frames 279–83. This microfilm edition includes material from National Archives Record Group 165, File Series 10110 and 10058; "Federal Arrest Warrant for H. H. Monson, Alias Rube and H. C. Spence, Sallisaw, Case No. 435, May 28, 1917," in Record Group 21, United States District Courts: Eastern District of Oklahoma, Criminal Case Files Nos. 2633, 2650, 2651, 2652, Box 125, in National Archives and Record Administration, Southwest Branch, Fort Worth, Texas (hereafter NARA/SW).

27. "Indictment against Clure Isenhour, Obe Isenhour, Daniel Isenhour, J. L. Bohannon, Tobe Simons, John Shirey, Walter Phillips, French (alias "Daddy") Henry, Frank Banning, J. R. Sparkman, C. W. Morris, Earl Whitten, Clarence Roberts, William Ellis, and John Snyder, Defendants, for Violation of Sections 4 and 6 of the Federal Penal Code, July 31, 1917," in Record Group 21, United States District Courts: Western District of Oklahoma, Criminal Case Files 1553, Box 79, Folder 1, in NARA/SW; *Shawnee Daily News-Herald*, July 22, 1917; *Norman Transcript*, August 1, 1917; *Cleveland County Enterprise* (Norman), August 2, 1917; *Norman Democrat-Topic*, August 3, 1917.

28. *Shawnee Daily News-Herald*, August 6, 1917; *Wewoka Capital-Democrat*, August 9, 1917; *Ada Weekly News*, August 9, 1917.

29. *Muskogee Times-Democrat*, December 1, 1917; William Preston, *Aliens and Dissenters: Federal Suppression of Radicals, 1903–1933* (New York: Harper Torchbooks, 1966), 263–64; "List of Pardons, Commutations, and Respites Granted by the President during the Fiscal Year 1923," in *Annual Report of the Attorney General of the United States for 1923* (Washington, D.C.: Government Printing Office, 1923).

30. *Norman Transcript*, December 7, 1917; Cunningham and Friesen, *Red Dust and Broadsides*, 329.

31. Hall, *Labor Struggles in the Deep South*, 189; Ameringer, *If You Don't Weaken*, 350.

32. Cunningham and Friesen, *Red Dust and Broadsides*, 133.

33. Ibid, 130–31.

34. William H. Cobb, *Radical Education in the Rural South: Commonwealth College, 1922–1940* (Detroit: Wayne State University Press, 2000), 80.

35. Barbara Foley, *Radical Representations: Politics and Form in U.S. Proletarian Fiction, 1929–1941* (Durham, N.C.: Duke University Press, 1993), 340–44.

36. Other ideas expressed in the novel, however, are more reflective of Cunningham's personal opinions than Tetley's soliloquies and are perhaps a bit unfair, especially for placing much of the blame for the rebellion's failure on the Socialist Party. This, however, is probably more a result of the antagonism between the Socialists and Communists of the 1930s than a historical argument.

The Green Corn Rebellion

ONE

"WELL, the best horse I ever seen was when I was a boy when I first come out to Kansas," Mack said. He twisted the stem from his pipe and looked at a drop on the end of it. But he wasn't seeing anything. The current was shut off inside him for a little while.

Jim Tetley had time to think about how the old man was running down. These little dead spells were long enough with him that you noticed them. Everybody has little flickers of death, but with an old person the blank spaces are long and apparent.

"The first horse I ever got on. Old Dixie."

Mack whipped the drop off the end of the stem and his milk-stained coat sleeve flapped. Then he blew into the stem and there was a rattling sound as the juice sprayed out.

"For cryin' out *loud*!" Happy shouted. "You're squirtin' spit on me. This here is the only dress I got!" She was a lank, pretty girl with a small nose that was still too red from the summer sun.

"What's that!" the old man said, startled. "Well, you hadn't ought to wear your high-school dress around home."

"Well, we got company. An' you want me to run around naked?"

Jim got uncomfortable, thinking how she would look naked. She was a taffy-blonde. It's a good thing that nobody can know what you're thinking.

The old man wiped the stem of his pipe on his faded overalls, leaving brown streaks.

"Daddy, that stain won't wash out easy," Jeannie Tetley said. She was Jim's wife, a gnarled older sister of Happy.

"Aw, leave the old man tell his story," Happy said. "It must be a new one he thought up yesterday, plowin'."

Mack looked indignant. "Well now, maybe *some* fellers can think up stories and tell 'em like they was true. But I ain't no hand at that. If a thing ain't the gospel I don't never tell it."

Ted Tetley, who was company, got over the sick feeling he had when Happy talked about running around naked, and he laughed. "This here story is true, ain't it, Mack?" he gasped. "It really happened—when you was a kid up in Kansas?" Ted was Jim's crippled brother, almost a monstrosity with his big head and dwarfed body. But he was well dressed. He laughed a while and then cleared his throat and spat into the draft of the stove.

"When I first went out to Kansas with my dad," Mack said, "we got jobs on a sheep ranch. Well, I wasn't much good, but the first morning they put me on old Dixie and told me to go out and round up a little herd about a mile away and run 'em into the corral."

The old man lapsed again, and wrinkled his forehead, that looked blood-red under his white hair, as if he were concentrating on the exact truth. Jim saw a brass safety-pin in Happy's garter. She was careless about her dress' getting up. The pin looked like gold in that light, and her bare leg above the garter looked golden too. She was golden, Jim thought, and wondered if anyone could tell what he was thinking. Sometimes in scuffling with her, brother-in-law fashion, he had touched her warm, golden-rubber legs, and he remembered the feel of her skin over the moving muscles. He didn't want to think about it. It was a hell of a way to do.

Mack got going again. "The boss told me that old Dixie would round up everything in sight, and all I needed to do was to stay on. He told me that Dixie would turn so quick that if I didn't pull leather I'd go off and bust my tail. Well, I hung to the saddle-horn, and me and Dixie rounded up the herd and got 'em in the corral.

"But it took a long time, and when I finally got through and went over to where the other fellers was workin' Dixie was sweatin' perty bad, and the boss looked surprised and he said, Did you have trouble or somepin'?' And I said, 'Well, the sheep didn't give me no trouble, but some of them lambs was a lot of bother.' Well, the boss thought that was mighty funny and he went over to the corral with me and he started to laughin' and I guess he laughed off and on for a week. But finally he explained to me that them critters with long ears was jackrabbits."

Ted laughed loudly and the others grinned.

"Aw, dad, I heard that before." Happy said sorrowfully.

The old man looked stern. "I ain't through."

"Aw' right. Now le's hear what you thought up yesterday, plowin'."

Mack's face looked like a rain-worn bank of red clay. He didn't know he was getting old and slow, Jim thought, so what difference did it make? He could still push in the collar. Like a horse with pumpkin-seed teeth, there was still a lot of work in him.

"It was too bad about Dixie, the way he ended up."

"Somebody go on and ask him how Dixie ended up," Happy suggested. She smiled, stood up and stretched, ruffled the old man's hair, and went into the kitchen for a drink. Bubbles had formed on the side of the bucket just under the water line. The water was stale. Little ravelings of dust had settled on it and, without getting wet, were making dents in the smooth tough skin of the water. When the dipper banged on the side of the bucket the sound was dead and thick. Happy hated stale water but it was a long ways to the pump. Right now the water was worse than usual because there was a dead toad or something in the well, probably lodged against the sand-point. To clean it out you would have to get the well-digger and his outfit out from town, and that cost more money than they had right then. In a week or two the toad would be all washed away and the water would be all right. When it was right fresh you didn't taste it very much, but when the water stood a while it was bad. Little rainbow-colored spots of oil floated on the surface, probably grease from the dead toad.

Disgusted, Happy blew into the bucket and the little dust particles and oil spots were overwhelmed and driven back by the storm. She plunged the dipper into the dustless spot and brought it up quickly before the dusty skin could flow back over it. As she drank she leaned forward so that the little streams from the bottom of the leaky dipper would not get on the front of her high-school dress. She breathed through her mouth for a while so she wouldn't have to smell the water she had swallowed. She went back to the front room and flopped down on the bed and noticed that her dress was up and Jim was looking at her leg. She pulled down her dress for fear Jeannie would notice. Her father was just getting his story going.

"One thing about Dixie was he was always careless about the way he stood . . . the way he stood, with his hind feet and his front feet too far apart. You see, a critter has to be careful to keep his hind feet a certain distance behind his front feet, and likewise to keep his front feet the same distance in front of his hind feet. If he don't he'll stretch himself.

"Well, one day Dixie got out into the roastin' ears, which he always was a fool about roastin' ears, and he filled himself up. Then he come up to the water trough, and he was thirsty and it was a hot day, and he must of drunk a tubful before anybody seen him, and all the time his hind feet was too far behind and his front feet was too far in front.

"Well, somebody seen him and yelled at him, but it was too late. All that there weight in him had bent his back so he was the worst sway-back I ever seen. It was too bad, because we all thought a lot of old Dixie. He wasn't no good for a saddle horse no more because his belly hung so low that if he trotted he would kick the wind out of himself."

The phone startled them. It rang five longs: the general alarm.

The bed thumped as Happy leaped off it. She ran to the phone and took down the receiver. She turned, facing them, the receiver pushed tight against her ear, and her mouth opened slowly as she listened. Jim watched the tip of her tongue moving over the lower front tooth that was crowded out of line. They all stared at her open mouth as if they were trying to hear through her bright head.

Then she pulled her mouth shut and smiled and began to twitch her shoulders rhythmically. She stepped back from the phone and did a half-whirl.

"Say, whata' you sashayin' for?" Mack demanded.

Clasping a hand over the transmitter, she explained. "It's Uncle Billy and Johnny playin' on the wire," she said. She pointed the receiver at them and they could hear, thin and far away, a lively dance tune.

"*Hur*ree up, *boys*, you're *mightee slow.*

"You *ain't* goin' *now* like you *was* awhile *ago*," Happy sang softly.

Jeannie looked tired. Everyone knew she didn't approve very much. She was still a little bit religious, like her mother had been.

"Jist like that old cuss to be a playin' dance music of a Sunday afternoon," Mack said.

They settled to listen. Dance numbers were long. Happy's arm got tired holding the receiver and she rested it on the shelf of the phone. The music was so thin that she got to thinking of other things.

She had been looking at the side of Ted's face. If you looked just at his face and forgot everything else about him you saw that he wasn't weak. He appeared middle-aged and hard. Then suddenly he jerked his head around and caught her looking at him. One of his long hands jumped out of his lap and wrapped around the cigar in his mouth and there was a shower of ashes over his coat and vest. Happy's face felt hot, and she looked at a strip of dusty paper hanging from the ceiling.

TWO

SAM GLADSON had been sheriff for a good many years, and he made a good sheriff because he had plenty of sand and was as honest as a man could be and hold office. He was an old-timer and had been raised in the Indian Territory. He didn't talk much about himself, but sometimes he told about the time he ran away from home, when he was eleven, because he didn't want to clean out the chicken house.

Sam was born in Texas and his mother died down there. Then his dad brought Sam with him up into the Indian Territory, and the old man married an Indian girl and got three hundred and twenty acres of land because he was a member of the tribe. He leased more land and fenced it in and started raising cattle, but when Sam was about ten the old man decided to raise a few chickens like they had down in Texas. Sam got to hate chickens. He was old enough to ride fence and carry a gun, but he had to take care of the chickens. The Indian woman the old man had married put on clothes and lived at home like a white woman, but Sam didn't like her.

One summer the Indians camped down on the river not far from the Gladson place for their harvest dance and Sam liked to go down there. Under a brush shelter some young bucks would dance all day and night without eating until finally they dropped down. Along toward the last they got yellow, and all they did was stand and jerk and blow little whistles in time with the drum, until finally they dropped down.

In summer the Indians didn't wear anything at all except clouts and moccasins. The men wore hats, too, or sometimes war bonnets. When the old squaws leaned over to poke sticks under the pots their breasts would hang down almost into the fire. The kids ran around naked and splashed in the river. When they found a turtle they took it to one of the squaws to cook.

Man-on-the-cloud would sit in his teepee and make arrows. Little Hand would walk around making speeches that nobody listened to. Sam wondered what he was saying but didn't savvy enough Indian to make it out. Sam liked to play around at the Indian camp. He thought the Indians lived a lot better than the white men.

One morning he was fixing to go down to the camp when his dad told him to clean out the chicken house. Sam said he didn't want to. The old man got white under his whiskers. He grabbed a quirt and got Sam by the arm and began pouring leather. He didn't know when to stop. Sam yelled at the top of his voice and tried to get away but couldn't. Finally the old man gave him a shove and curled the quirt right around Sam's neck. The lash cut his lips. He went down and rolled around in the sand, gagging because it hurt so much.

When the old man rode off to the brush pasture Sam set the chicken house afire and lit out. He worked here and there and got along fairly well, although sometimes between jobs he was so hungry he had to beg. He went to New Mexico for a while but came back. He intended to marry into the tribe and get three hundred and twenty acres, but they put a stop to that by charging a thousand dollars for a license.

He made the race and staked down a claim and farmed for

a while, but he didn't like farming. He lost his farm in a poker game, but got elected sheriff. The boys voted for him because he had plenty of guts.

Whenever an outlaw holed up in a cave in the hills it was Sam who smoked him out. He got six gunshot wounds that way.

Sam didn't talk about his early life after he was grown, but the old-timers told lots of stories about him.

One fall there was a bad Indian scare. The government had been giving the Indians their beef on the hoof, and the Indians would drive the steers out on the prairie and stampede the herd. Then they would ride among the steers and shoot them down, as they used to shoot buffaloes. The squaws would follow with butcher knives and do the butchering right there. It was a big celebration. All the Indians, old and young, would fill up on warm blood and whiskey, and then they would dance all night.

But some of the white settlers objected to this and used their influence to put a stop to it, and that fall the beef came to the Indians already dressed. The Indians didn't like it of course. Some bucks got drunk in a saloon and told the saloon-keeper that the Indians were going to kill every white in the country.

The saloon-keeper was pretty scared, and he sent his brother out on a horse to tell all the whites to meet at Fleming's grove if they didn't want their throats cut before morning. He also sent a man to the nearest fort to get a company of soldiers.

All that night the settlers came galloping into the grove, on horses and in buggies and wagons. One fellow was so excited that he didn't wait to put collars on his horses but buckled the hames around their necks. He ruined a good team that way.

Several old veterans were there and they tried to take command, but they were so scared that they didn't know what to do. Sam rode into the grove about daybreak and told them there was nothing to worry about. He was so drunk he could hardly stay in the saddle, and his horse was shot up and died that morning.

They found out later what had happened. When Sam heard about the scare, instead of going to the grove he rode into the Indian camp in the middle of the night and started shooting. The Indians didn't know what was going on and thought hell had busted loose. They started yelling and shooting, and the whole tribe took to the sticks. Three of them were killed.

The soldiers arrived about noon and the whites went back to their shanties.

But not long after that Sam pulled a bonehead that nearly ruined him. A telephone line had just been put in and not very many people knew about it. Sam got a call from a town about twenty miles away that Yager and Black had just robbed a bank there and killed the cashier and were headed toward the county seat.

Yager and Black were pretty bad. They had killed a dozen men and posses had been out looking for them many times. They shot on sight.

There was a country store half way between the two towns and Sam decided they would drop in there as they passed. They didn't know about the telephone line and wouldn't be expecting anyone to meet them. It was getting dark and there was no time to wait for a posse to collect. He started out and made the store in record time.

He explained to the storekeeper what had happened and hid in the back of the store. A few minutes later a man walked in with a shotgun and poked it at the storekeeper. Sam dropped him where he stood.

The man Sam killed was a young school teacher who was going to a school house not far away to make a political speech. He was a candidate for a county office. He had a shotgun along to kill a mess of quail, and had decided to leave it at the store while he was at the school house for fear it would be stolen.

Sam was tried and turned loose because the jury happened to be on his side, but feeling ran pretty high against him. The community was getting more settled. Just before election some political enemy of Sam's got out an anonymous leaflet calling him "quick-triggered Gladson, who shoots respectable citizens from ambush?" The leaflet also accused Sam of having had "sectional intercourse" through the bars with women prisoners in the jail. Every sentence ended with a question mark because it was generally believed that libel laws did not apply to sentences punctuated that way.

Sam would have been ruined politically except that a revival meeting started about that time and he got converted. He gave up his wicked life and the Lord forgave him everything. He was elected, and not long after got married and settled down.

After that he was sheriff most of the time, except for a few years when he tried sheep raising again in New Mexico. He didn't like the way things were going. He was always on the side of law and order, but as he got older and the country got more and more settled things got worse and worse with him.

There were two kinds of people: bad characters and good citizens. In the early days it was the horse thieves, the Republicans, and the loose women you had to look out for. Now it was the bootleggers, the Republicans, and the niggers.

It got so an honest citizen, if he wanted to keep in office, had to make deals with bootleggers and with Republicans in the bank, otherwise a Republican would be elected and then the county would go to the dogs.

Lately a lot of riff-raff, poor farmers mostly, had got to be Socialists. Socialists were worse than Republicans ever dared to be. They wanted to take all the money away from honest citizens and divide it up with fellows who were stinkin' lazy and never saved a cent. A Socialist had run for sheriff the last election, and for a while it looked like he might be elected, or anyway get so many Democrat votes that the Republican would get in. To stop this Sam and some other county officials had to make a deal with the banker, had to fix up some road work like the banker wanted although it was crooked. The banker then wouldn't loan a cent to a Socialist. Socialists had to have money to carry them over the winter because most of them were renters. That winter, by God, they went hungry, and their kids went hungry. Some of them were clearing out, and the rest would be gone before election, except a few who owned land and could hang on. Sam hated to fix up a crooked deal with the banker, but that was the only way you could drive these dirty Socialists out of the county.

Strictly speaking, Sam was honest, because he never took a cent except his salary. He and Emily, his wife, seemed like they couldn't save anything.

Sam had fought bad men for thirty years and risked his life, and still he didn't have enough money to be independent. If he couldn't get elected again and save every cent so that he could start a little sheep ranch he and old Emily would end their days likely at the poor farm. Already he was too old and sick to be sheriff and he was scared somebody would find it out. If somebody found out how sick he was and spread it around somebody else would get elected, and then him and Emily would have to go out to the poor farm and set on a bench beside good-for-nothin' trash out there. If the Republicans got in they might even put niggers out there and poor old Emily would have to pass her last days in nigger stink. That's the way it looked to Sam, although he wouldn't say so to anybody but Emily.

Sometimes in the middle of the night Sam's leg would start hurtin' and he would wake up and start thinkin' about all these things and get scared like a kid. He would toss around and wake Emily up, and then they would both worry and talk about it half the night.

It took all the fight out of a man the next day. You couldn't stand up and face anything, thinkin' of the nigger stink in the poor house. Your guts all caved in, and you shook.

Sometimes when a bad nigger broke away from arrest and started runnin' and you pulled your gun to plug him—sometimes you thought of all this and your hand shook, and you missed the bastard. Then the fellows around the court house would be sayin' the old man was slippin'. Missed a nigger today.

Sam got grouchy and short-tempered at home and had fights with Emily. One morning they had a bad fight.

When Sam woke up his leg was hurtin' worse than it ever had. He groaned and yelled, and Emily came in from the kitchen. "It's worse than it ever was," he said.

"Git up and warm it now," she said. "I got a hot fire in the heater."

Sam stuck his foot out from under the covers. It was blue and yellow. He sort of slid out of bed, trying not to bend his left hip. Cold sweat popped out on him.

"I'm gonna faint," he said.

"No you ain't," Emily told him.

She wasn't any too well herself and had a big goiter under her chin about as big as her head. Her eyes looked like they would pop out. She couldn't breathe very well.

Sam finally got out of bed and stood up. He took his cane in one hand and holding to Emily with the other hobbled into the front room. He kept saying he was gonna faint and she kept telling him he wouldn't if he quit thinkin' about it.

"Yeah—quit thinkin' about it. If you knew how it felt—"

"I mean quit thinkin' about faintin'," she said.

When they got to the front room Sam stood close to the fire and pulled up his flannel night-shirt and let the heat hit the bare skin. His leg was knotted and had blue veins, some of them as big as your finger. The heat turned his leg red as a beet, but it eased the pain. Finally he could lower himself into the rocker.

"Sam," Emily said, "you ain't goin' to the office today."

He didn't answer her for a long time but stared at his leg like it was a snake. Then he yelled out that he was, by God!

"Don't swear at me, Sam," she said.

"Take that cane out of here," he said. "Do you want somebody to come in here and see it?"

She took the cane out, and by the time she was back he was swearing again. "This damned rocker is scorchin'. I can smell it," he said.

She grabbed hold of the rocker arm and tugged. He lurched, and this way they moved the rocker inch by inch.

She brought him a cup of coffee and he tried to drink it. Then he saw on the center table a farm magazine open to an article on chicken raising. She had been reading it.

"Well, for Christ's sake!" he yelled. He hopped up, standing on one foot, grabbed the magazine, and slammed it into the stove. "You jist let me ketch you with one of them damned things around again———." He groaned, and slapped his hand on his hip, and crashed back into the chair. "Ah-a-a-," he gasped. "Oh, *my God!*"

Emily hobbled out of the room as fast as she could and went into the bedroom. He knew she was bawling. "Oh, God!" he groaned over and over again.

After a while she came back, red-eyed, and brought him his flannel underwear, his pants, his high-heeled boots, and a clean shirt. She helped him put them on and neither of them said a word.

When he was dressed she said feebly, "Sam, you want some breakfast?"

"No I don't."

He went to the sink and washed the matter out of his eyes, put on his cartridge belt, and looked at his pistol. Then he put on his coat and overcoat and hat and limped to the stove. He pulled up his overcoat to get his pants leg good and hot so his leg wouldn't hurt so much when he hit the north wind. As he went out he told her to be sure and keep the cane out of sight if the nigger wench came to clean that day.

Soon as he was gone she started crying again and got down on her knees and prayed to Jesus to help her make him realize that he was too old to try to run a sheep ranch and that he ought to get a little chicken farm on the edge of town.

 THREE

HAPPY MCGEE was going to town high school, but she wondered sometimes what good it did anybody to work algebra problems and read history lessons. If you got an education you could get ahead in the world, she had always heard, but how did you get ahead by knowing a little about ancient Athens? The high school kids made fun of everything they were supposed to learn in their classes. What good would it ever do them if they hated it?

Once Happy talked about it to her father. "What good does it all do?" she asked.

"Well, I reckon it makes you parlor-broke," he said. "Now me, I ain't parlor-broke, and you lead me into one of these swell places and I'm likely to git scared and snort and break wind and knock over somepin' and jump through one of them bay windows and go gallopin' off with my tail in the air. You can't trust me around folks that don't smell like cow manure."

He told Jim and Jeannie a story on her which wasn't true but made a good story. Of course they knew it wasn't true. The old man would never think of deceiving anybody, except maybe a green town kid who deserved to be codded.

"Gladys," he said, "don't much like to help with the milkin' in the mornin', but when she does she comes in and washes her hands and smells of 'em, then she washes 'em again and has me smell of 'em, then she washes 'em again and we both smell of 'em, and then all day up to high school she is afraid some feller will come up to her and say 'hist.' "

Happy's real name was Gladys, although only her father and Jeannie still called her that. When she first enrolled in town high school there was a joke going around among the boys about a girl named Miss Happybottom who was called Gladys for short. Only the boys knew the joke, and even Happy didn't know why they gave her the name. She was walking past a bunch of them one day at noon and one boy called out, "Howdy, Happy." The others kept still to see how she'd take it. She didn't know very much about town boys then and she just smiled and walked on. They all laughed and decided she was fast. The name stuck, and even the teachers got to calling her Happy.

She wanted so much to be popular that she was always friendly, and this of course gave her a "reputation." The boys snickered when she passed sometimes, and once one of them goosed her. She didn't know exactly what to do, and didn't care very much. They talked around about what you could do if you walked home with her. She lived more than a mile out.

Living on a farm she couldn't really get to be popular. Country kids were gawky and didn't have decent clothes. The town kids paid no attention to her socially when they were planning parties or thinking of dates.

Older men were attracted to her, and one day she had a horrible experience with one of her teachers, Mr. Hardman. She had stayed after school to write a history paper which was due, and when it was finished she stood for a while outside the door of the study hall trying to get up enough courage to interrupt him.

He was playing his queer classical music on the piano. The music thundered but didn't seem to have any tune that she could follow. The janitor had just finished his work in the study hall and came out carrying his brooms and hobbled downstairs to the lower rooms.

The wind was howling outside, and Happy stood for a while looking out the window at the fields where the tumbleweeds rolled and piled against fences. The sky was a reddish-yellow, which meant there would be more wind and a real dirt storm to fight against on the way home. Her father would pull his old joke about seeing a ground squirrel ten feet in the air digging to get to the ground. Hardman might play for another hour, and Happy had to start home soon.

Always when she had an idle moment she worried about her clothes, and she looked down at her faded pink dress and run-over shoes. If she didn't look so funny she could get up more courage, she decided.

Then she stepped forward and stood in the doorway for a while, hoping he would look up and see her. But he went on playing, unconscious of her presence.

His face reminded her of a bowl they had at home, round and not much chin. The big boys had a theory they could run him out of the building any time, but they were not sure because they never quite got around to trying it. Sometimes they got him on the ragged edge, red-faced and uncertain. They talked of pulling knives, and one suggested that if you popped him in the mouth you could knock his two front teeth down his throat because they were false, and he would look funny as hell with his two front teeth out.

He was of medium size and plump at the top, but his legs were spindly. He wore rimless glasses clamped to his nose, and they trembled sometimes but never quite came off. He was just young enough to wear his hair in the latest style, clipped very close on the sides, rather long and pompadour on top. Almost always one strand stood up like a little hook, and the kids wondered if you could hang him on a nail. He wore a high, stiff collar and the knot in his necktie was very long and slim. His shirts were silk and very expensive.

Happy watched him playing and wondered what he was really like. In his English class he sometimes pointed out the "particular beauty" of a passage in one of the classics, and when he did this he looked particularly fierce to keep the boys from giggling. In Happy's mind beauty had become associated with fierceness. The boys sometimes called him "Particular Beauty" behind his back.

Happy shifted from one foot to the other and he caught sight of her out of the corner of his eye. He stopped- playing and stared at her as if he were still in a fog.

"Did you want to see me, Happy?" he asked. His eyeglasses were flashing the yellow light of the afternoon sun and she could not see his eyes.

"The history paper. You said we must get it in today and I didn't have mine, so I stayed after school and here it is."

"Oh, yes."' cleared hs throat. "Let's have it," he said, standing up.

He opened it and read the first paragraph, but the paper was shaking. "It's very good, I think," he said, and then repeated "I think" for no reason.

He folded it and put it in his pocket and stared at her. She could not leave without some permission, from his eyes at least, and he did not dismiss her. "You're a very good student, Happy," he said.

She blushed to the color of an Indian, so that her hair seemed almost white. He giggled nervously. "You're blushing, Happy— and it becomes you—you are a very pretty little girl—" He took off his glasses and his eyes seemed to pop. He pinched her cheek and let his hand drop to her shoulder. She looked at him in amazement, and then he began to croak her nickname over and over: "Happy! Happy!"

Suddenly he threw his arms around her and pressed his mouth against hers with bruising force. She had never been kissed this way before. If it had been anyone except a teacher she would have resisted instinctively, but she had been trained to fear teachers and now she stood trembling and paralyzed while he covered her face with kisses.

He clamped himself against her in a sudden frenzy and pulled up her dress. When she felt her ragged underwear being torn she realized that something horrible was about to happen, even if this was Mr. Hardman, and she began to fight. She did not scream or faint because she was used to fighting country boys in contests that had nothing to do with sex.

She was very strong and when she gripped Mr. Hardman's hair she forced his head back. She got her foot between his legs, and if he had not suddenly relaxed his hold they would both have crashed to the floor.

She jumped back. She was free now to run, but she was no longer afraid of him and was almost in the mood to attack him with her fists.

"Happy," he gasped, clenching a desk, "I'm sorry. I lost my head. I'll kill myself—but don't tell—I would be lynched—please." He started to cry.

She looked at him in astonishment for a moment. "I won't tell anybody—ever—if you won't ever try anything again."

"I swear—I'll never come near you," he promised.

Her underskirt dropped suddenly down around her ankles. She glanced about. Hardman darted past her and across the hall to his office. She pulled the underskirt up and fastened it, tugged at each stocking, inspected her dress, and hurried down the stairs and out into the storm.

As soon as the excitement was over she became very weak and sat down for a while to rest. She thought about it and decided that nothing had really happened and she wouldn't have a baby.

Mr. Hardman came to school as usual the next morning, but he didn't look at Happy nor even ask her a question in class for a long time.

 # FOUR

As Ted Tetley, linotype operator at the *Star*, left the shop that afternoon he got a distant glimpse of Happy coming out of the school building, and became suddenly excited. She was almost a woman now and looked a little like her older sister, Jeannie, had looked years before. Ted had been silently in love with Jeannie, but his own younger brother, Jim, had married her.

Where only men were concerned Ted could be hard and shrewd, but he could never have any confidence with women. Lately he had been dreaming about Happy. He was making good money now and getting ahead, and he would make a good husband, he told himself, but he could find no opportunity to get better acquainted with her or even to talk to her seriously about anything.

He thought about it as he flapped awkwardly along the street toward his boarding house. He was very short, with a head too large for his body, and he leaned far back as he walked, his high, narrow, square shoulders making a wide pendulum swing with each step, and the soles of his shoes slapping the sidewalk.

He turned in at the gate and pounded up the steps of the boarding house. This was a cheap place and Ted was saving money by staying here. He sat down for a moment in the front room, trying to decide whether or not to smoke a cigar. Mrs.

Conklin, the landlady, came in from the kitchen, sniffed a blue wet nose and said to him, "They's hot water tonight. I thought you might want to know."

"Huh!" said Ted. His mouth snapped shut and his face went livid except for two red splotches on his cheeks. The two stared at each other for an instant, but the landlady's eyes dropped. She sniffed again and left.

Ted gripped the handles of his rocker until his knuckles were as white as his face. "Huh!" he said again. "I'll tell the old bitch if I want hot water."

He arose and paddled up to his room, slammed the door, opened the screen and spat out on the lawn, dropped down on the bed and lay still for a long time.

Any suggestion of bathing irritated Ted, and a hint that he should take a bath put him in a fighting mood. About once a month he got drunk and then usually took a bath. Only when he was drunk could he strip himself and bathe his queer body.

He had hated bathing since he was a boy, and the reason was that his brother Jim, two years younger, had always made fun of him when they had had to take a bath Saturday afternoon in the kitchen. Jim got even with him that way.

Ted could always lick Jim in those days. He would bloody the younger boy up on the way home from school. The other kids who walked out that way with them would start the fight by saying that they had heard Jim say he could lick Ted. Jim wouldn't deny saying it and the fight would start. Jim wouldn't give in but would fight until he was too bloodied up to see what he was doing. This happened about once a month. The folks would never punish Ted because he was a cripple.

But Jim would get even when they took a bath. He would look at Ted's crippled back and funny legs and laugh. The folks finally got to locking him out of the kitchen when Ted had to bathe, but Jim would look in at the window and grin, or just stay outside and laugh loud enough to be heard inside. Ted never got over these experiences. Every time he took a bath, even after he was a grown man, he would imagine that the people downstairs or in the next room were thinking how funny he must look without anything on and were laughing among themselves.

After he had been in his room a while there came a tap at the door. "Come in," he shouted.

Mrs. Conklin stuck her wet nose in and said, "Mr. Tetley, I list wanted to tell you that you better find another place. My other boarders is complainin' about how you smell when you come to the table, and if you won't take a bath—"

"All *right,* by God!" he yelled, leaping up so suddenly that Mrs. Conklin was frightened and shut the door and hurried down the hall. Ted yanked his suitcase from under the bed and opened it. From various drawers he pulled garments and stuffed them into the suitcase, but in the bottom drawer of the dresser he found his fruit jar full of corn whiskey. He shook the stuff and watched the charcoal swirl. Then he unscrewed the lid and took a drink. Shuddering, he sat down on the bed.

A half hour later Mrs. Conklin down in the kitchen heard the water running in the bathtub and heard Ted singing in a loud flat voice.

FIVE

ONE BRIGHT MORNING of the early spring Jim Tetley was thinking that he would like to do something a little bit different that day. It was Sunday. He had been working hard ten to fourteen hours a day for a month or two. A cow needed to go to the bull. As Jim was finishing his breakfast he suggested that Jeannie go with him to take the cow to her father's pasture.

"You ain't gonna clean out that barn today?" she asked. "It's awful. I never seen the flies so bad this time of year. And that outhouse!"

It made Jim mad. "You know that cow's got to go," he said, "or wait a whole month."

Jeannie sighed. "Well, there's no reason why both of us should waste the whole blessed morning." She was hinting for Jim to take the cow over and hurry right back to clean out the barn.

The flies were pretty bad. Two of them were in Jim's plate, and when he waved his hand they went buzzing off, fighting at each other in the air. But he just didn't feel like doing a damned thing that morning, especially cleaning out the barn.

He tried to think of something that he really did want to do. He thought of going over to Oklahoma City, like he had once before he was married, and going to a moving picture show where they had vaudeville. The sunlight coming in through the window reminded him of the spotlight they threw on the girls.

At first the girls had on long dresses that were real thin so you could see their legs through the dresses, and while they danced there was a searchlight up above the gallery someplace that threw different colored lights on them. Finally they threw off their dresses and their legs were bare clear up to their crotches, or looked like they were. Probably they had on silk tights or something, because it must be against the law to show bare skin, but it looked just like bare skin.

After the show Jim and the boy he was with, a neighbor boy, went to their room and tried to sleep, but Jim couldn't sleep much because an electric sign across the street kept going until midnight and reminded him of the colored lights and the girls' legs. And the street cars kept going by.

Jim and the other boy felt so damned mean that they almost got up enough nerve to call the porter and ask him to send some girls up to their room, but they knew it was dangerous, because they might catch something, so they just tossed around in bed and talked about girls. The next day they were so sleepy they slept on the train coming home.

If a fellow could go to the city and fool around like that every once in a while, two or three times a year, it wouldn't be so hard to work like a horse the rest of the time. Today, for instance, he wouldn't mind cleaning out the barn if he knew that next week he could go to the city.

But when you work day after day at the same old things you have done since you were a kid you get damned tired of it, and finally you get mad and you just want to lay around and read and do nothing, until you get ashamed of yourself.

Jeannie looked so old and brown. There was not a damned thing nice about her. When she stooped over to get some cobs to put in the stove he saw the calves of her legs. Her stockings were twisted and wrinkled. All she thought about was work and getting ahead.

"Well, I'm gonna take that cow over," he said. "I don't give a damn if that barn never gets cleaned out."

He thought about the things that ought to be done. The roof of the house ought to be fixed because there was a leak and the plaster on the ceiling was coming off. The floor was sagging because the sand had blown out from under the foundation and there ought to be a lot of dirt hauled in and put around the house. There ought to be a window pane put in the north window.

He went outdoors and down to the barn. The windmill ought to be greased, and one of the tanks leaked. He would have to put cement in the bottom of it. The hen-house door was banging on its hinges and would be clear off in another month. The shed roof ought to be braced or one of these days it would be so bad it couldn't be fixed. The corral gate was falling to pieces. Some night one of the cows would rub it down and then he would have to spend a half day looking for the herd.

The cow that needed the bull had been shut in the corral, but the others were out in the pasture. She kept bawling and slinging slobbers. Jim opened the gate and walked across the corral to her. It was hard not to step in any of the fresh cow manure. After a rain you bogged down to your ankles. All this manure ought to be dug up and hauled to the north eighty. It was a month's job.

There was enough work for ten men and only one to do it, and nothing to do *with*. And what did you get for it all? Right now if it hadn't been for Ted Jim and Jeannie would be going hungry.

The bank had quit loaning money to the farmers that voted the Socialist ticket. Jim had voted for some of the Socialist candidates and because of that couldn't get a damned cent to buy seed wheat with. But Ted had money and Jim had to borrow some from him, much as he hated to. Ted had it lucky. He worked from eight in the morning until six at night and made thirty-five dollars a week, nearly six dollars a day, and didn't even have a wife to support.

Jim yelled "Hi" at the cow and flapped his arms. The cow looked at him wild-eyed and then started off, shaking her bag. A cow always acted wild when she wanted a bull.

There was an old rooster in the barnyard that had rheumatism so bad he could hardly walk. His feet were big knots. He ought to be killed and taken off some place. Jim ought to kill him right now and carry him along and throw him somewhere in the pasture. But it would take time to grab him and kill him and then the old cow would climb through the fence and run over to her own herd, though she knew there wasn't any bull there, and it would take a half hour to run her back and get her started down the road, and you couldn't run a cow very well when you had a damned old rooster to carry. Jim decided to leave the rooster live; pretty soon he'd die and then he'd *have* to be taken off and buried.

The cow ran off to the potato patch that had grown up among the gourd vines and she stopped there where there was a little straw mulching and stuck out her tail and urinated. Jim had time to catch up with her and head her off toward the road. She walked along with her tail still stiff and pulled up a dead sunflower stalk and waved it. Jim knew she didn't enjoy a dead weed like that and wouldn't eat it if you gave it to her in the corral.

Jim took a chew of tobacco. The plug was pretty old and dry and tasted more like alfalfa than tobacco. The cow climbed up a sand bank at the side of the road and went over to where the fence was, hidden by the weeds. She stopped there and looked over toward her own herd. Jim didn't want to go after her because there was a patch of sandburs at the edge of the road that got in your pants legs. He looked around for something to throw at her and found an empty extract bottle that some passing Indian had thrown down. He picked it up and bounced it off her hip and she trotted on, finally scrambling back into the road.

Jim was thinking that he was not a bit better off than he had been a year before, and it wasn't because he laid off once in a while for an hour or two to read the *Appeal to Reason*. A fellow could work twenty-fours a day and still never make anything. Jeannie's mother used to say "Read, read, read! I never seen a *Read* yet that amounted to anything." But it wasn't just reading that kept people poor. In fact, if they read a little more maybe they'd get sense enough in their heads to wake up and change things a little bit.

Jeannie was like her mother. But Happy took after her dad: easy-going and liked to have fun. Jim thought about Happy for a while and hoped she would come over that day.

Jim was ashamed of it, but sometimes he thought he had got married too damned soon. But even if he had put off marrying until now he couldn't very well marry Happy rather than Jeannie because of the good times he had had ever since he could remember with Jeannie, out on the river, in the sand, at barn dances. Remembering all the fun he had had with Jeannie it made him feel funny to want to have Happy now instead of her.

Once he had asked Jeannie why in the hell she couldn't stop pushin' in the collar once in a while long enough to have a little fun with him like they used to, and she had said to him the meanest thing she'd ever said. "If I didn't work any harder than you do this house would be as filthy as that barn of yours."

By God, that made him mad. He worked ten hours a day, and more, all week, and then when he wanted her to take Sunday off and go fishing with him she screwed up her face and said something like that.

It made him mad, and he went out and worked all day Sunday cleaning out the barn. He swore he'd never take another day off as long as he lived.

Then, that afternoon, Ted came out in an automobile. Ted was dressed up in white pants and a white shirt. He looked in at the barn door and grinned. "Kinda ketchin' up with the work, eh?" Ted said. Jim felt like sticking his dirty fork into him.

But it wasn't Ted's fault. Their father had mortgaged up the place to send Ted through high school and then to a Linotype school because Ted was crippled and couldn't do work on the farm. Jim was one of the strongest fellows in the neighborhood and it wouldn't hurt him a damned bit to work on the farm, the old man said, just like he'd always had to do.

One way of looking at it, though, Jim should have gone to school rather than Ted because Jim was a natural student and always better in his studies than Ted. Of course, Jim would finally have left home and worked his way through school, he wanted an education that bad. But then his mother died and his father got sick. Ted didn't have a job yet and couldn't support the old man, and you couldn't let the old man starve to death.

By the time the old man died Jim was grown up, and he wanted to get married so bad that he could taste it. So he got married and settled down on his half of the farm. Ted got a good job then and began to save money.

It couldn't have happened any other way. When they'd got married they thought Jeannie had a kid inside her. But she didn't. Now she had one sure enough. That's just what Jeannie'd wanted, and Jim hoped she'd got a belly full.

Jim had to let down McGee's fence and then run up the road and head off the old cow. It was hard to get the damned fool to go through the fence although she was crazy to find a bull.

He put the fence up again and decided to follow the cow to be sure she found the bull. He didn't have to pay for the use of the old man's bull. The old man was mighty good about everything.

The pasture was no good, of course, this time of year, but Mack didn't have any wheat pasture to speak of. The winter had been too dry for wheat. Mack had to feed his stuff.

The cow bawled every few steps and Jim heard the bull answering her in falsetto not far away. When they got to the herd one of the McGee cows started pushing with Jim's cow, but the bull separated them and then tested Jim's cow, screwing up his face and pointing his nose at the sky. Meanwhile McGee's old brindle cow, who had been hostile at first, took a friendly interest in the new-comer, and topped her. The brindle's bag flopped impotently, and Jim wondered what she got out of it. Wishes she'd been born a bull, he thought.

The bull, having finished his test, seemed to be impatient of this female foolishness and pushed the brindle off and took her place. The process was quick and decisive. The brindle, no longer interested in the love-making, started grazing. Jim's cow stood with her back arched and her tail sticking stiffly out.

Well, he made her hump, Jim thought, and maybe that would do the trick, but there was no separating them then without a good corral to shut the bull in. Jim ought to go back now and clean out the barn, and come after the cow that night, but it was a beautiful day.

A bull calf that had a slight cold smelled the milk and came around and tried to suck Jim's cow, but she forgot her hump long enough to kick at him. Then he tried to imitate his father, made a heroic leap, and fell backwards. "That ain't for you, sonny," Jim said, "and you should have been cut before this." The bull seemed lost in thought, but he came out of it now and served again.

A bull was lucky. He didn't have a thing to do and wasn't bothered. He had plenty of wives. If he got tired of the old cows there were always heifers growing up.

If a man lived with one woman and took care of her as best he could, and was always friendly to her, why was it such a God-damned crime to love up some other woman once in a while?

Jim was young, twenty-five, and just getting to be a real man. Women liked him because he was bigger than most other men, and smarter than a lot of them. He was just at the age to enjoy life and really have a little fun, but there wasn't a damned thing that he could do that he wanted to do. He was like a stallion hitched up to the plow, except that any stallion would kick over the traces if a mare came around that smelled like she needed him. Even a gelding would squeal and fight if he had been cut proud or had been kept for stud for a while. Jim had to act like he wasn't even cut proud.

His wad of tobacco didn't have any more taste now than a wad of hay but he kept chewing it not to waste any.

He wanted to stay in the timber a while because of the smell. He dreaded the stink of cleaning the barn, although he knew that he wouldn't mind it much after he got started and got used to it.

If a fellow was unlucky enough to be poor he had to get used to stink. He was a stinker when he was a baby, and just as soon as he got old enough to know better than to dirty his pants he started sweating, with no time to clean up, and went right on stinking until he died, and then they buried him in a hurry to keep him from stinking worse than ever. But all this stinking was unnecessary, except the last big stink, which didn't matter because you were underground. The working class would have time to keep itself from stinking as soon as the stinking capital-ist system was put underground. That's what the Socialists said, and it sounded pretty reasonable.

Then Jim remembered the war and decided that maybe he was lucky after all. All the sweat and manure in the world couldn't smell as bad as a thousand corpses hanging in the barbed-wire entanglements, and maybe he'd be smelling that stink in a year or two. Or adding to it, while the blow flies laid eggs on his tongue.

And while the maggots were squirming under his toenails the sweet-smelling fat boys who'd sent him over there would be squirming in bed with their pretty women.

With all this to look forward to he was cussing himself for taking ten minutes off to smell the pasture air.

Something banged him on the elbow and he jumped and let out a grunt of surprise. A hedge-apple bounded in the dry grass, and there was a gurgling shriek behind him. He whirled and saw through the shrubbery the seat of a pair of overalls jerking out of sight. "By God!" He grabbed up the hedge-apple and hurled it and missed. Then he spat out his tobacco and sprinted in that direction.

He knew who was inside the overalls before he got the sight of taffy hair. It was a real race. Happy's legs were long and strong, and her wind was good. When he was within a few feet of her she squealed and ducked and he went lumbering past, clutching her shirt and tearing it half off of her. He caught a suspender on the next turn and then the seat of her overalls, and they went down in a tangle, gasping for breath. Jim pinned her down and spanked her until she quit struggling.

"Pick on somebody your size, you big steer," she panted. She lay back on the grass, red-faced, and stuck her tongue out at him. One of her small breasts was shining in the sunlight.

"You'll never be a good milker," he said. "Your tits ain't big enough."

"You dirty devil!" she said, pulling the torn shirt over the goose-flesh. "You tore my shirt—" She slapped him.

This started the wrestle all over again, and suddenly Jim lost control of himself and began kissing her as hard as he could. She relaxed slowly and put her arms around him for a moment.

But she tried to push him away after that. "Jim," she said, "we can't do this way. I ain't a baby any more."

He released her and sat up. "I know it—but you know I won't really do anything—really hurt you. I just get kind of hog-wild when I play with you."

"Suppose somebody would see us!"

"I know. I'm a damned fool."

"I was goin' over to see Jeannie, but I guess I can't now."

She stood up, stooped suddenly and kissed him on the mouth, and then ran off toward home.

He sat there for a while and swore at himself. Then he took another chew of tobacco and got to wondering how he would feel if he caught somebody kissing Jeannie as he had kissed Happy.

SIX

"Ah ben hyarin' about this sway-back hoss you used to have up in Kansas," Uncle Billy Turner said to Mack, "and how you fixed him up right smaht, an' Ah got 'nole plug like that, an Ah wondahd jes' how you-all up in Kansa fixed up that ole hoss." Uncle Billy looked solemn, but Johnny Fane, whose teeth stuck out in front, grinned. There was a little ridge of tartar across Johnny's big front teeth marking the line where his upper lip reached. His teeth below the ridge were always exposed to the weather.

Mack's stories about the sway-backed horse were famous and fellows were always asking him to tell about it. He always had a new version.

Uncle Billy was a fiddler and a sharecropper. He had grown up in Arkansas.

It was afternoon, and they were sitting in the grandstand at county fair grounds waiting for the big Socialist meeting to begin. Fred Niek was going to speak.

"Well now, I reckon you mean old Dixie that got sway-backed from eatin' too much roastin' ears and drinkin' a lot of water," Mack said.

"Yeah, that's the hoss."

"Well, he wasn't no good for a saddle horse," Mack began, "but we figgered that if we fixed him up a little he could do a little light plowin', so we rigged up a pole and put the front end on his shoulders and the back end on his rump, then we took some sursingles and put 'em over the pole and under his belly and tightened 'em up and pulled his back up straight.

"Well now, one thing we forgot. When he was rigged up that way he couldn't turn a corner but had to travel in a straight line, and he wasn't no good plowin' because when you got to the end of the furrow and wanted to turn around, there you was. We took off the pole and fixed a hinge in it, bendin' sideways, so he could bend his back enough to turn a corner. Well, that seemed like it would work, and it did for a while, maybe an hour, but you see we had ganted him up so there wasn't much weight in his belly, and we hadn't thought how weak his back was from bein' bent once and then straightened. I was plowin' along and the old fool he forgot himself and pushed harder with his hind feet than he pulled with his front feet, and all at once his back arched up like a cat's and there was that darned pole 'way up in the air. Well, I unhitched him and took him to the barn, and we got a ladder and took the pole down.

"We couldn't lead him into the barn because he was too high in the middle, so we tied him outside and fed him a heavy meal and his back gradually settled down till it was as swayed as before."

Mack's story was cut short by a stir down in front. Fred Niek had climbed on the platform and was shaking hands with the men there. Niek was a pleasant-looking fellow, kind of fat.

"He's a Gehman, ain't he?" Uncle Billy asked. "Lookin' at him it's kind of hawd to believe that them Gehman soldiers cut off women's breasts and stick bayonets through the kids."

"Well," Jim Tetley said suddenly, "even if they do, which I doubt like hell, they ain't no worse than Americans. I seen a crowd of fellers cut a Negro once. If German soldiers do as bad as that then French and English soldiers do the same things."

"Yeah, and us Americans is gonna have our chanct to cut a few off over there," Mack added.

"Hit shore looks lak we was headin' into that waw," Uncle Billy said, "and Ah cain't think of no reason neither."

"The reason is," Mack said, "that this here war is fought for profits."

"Well, Ah ben votin' the Socialist ticket," Uncle Billy observed, "because Ah think the Socialists is a lot nearah right than the Democrats. But the trouble is the old pawties will take a lot of Socialist planks an' git the votes and not do anything about hit."

"They's only one Socialist plank," Mack said, "and that's govament ownership, and the old parties won t take that."

"Well, hit's hawd to believe some of the things you Socialists have ben sayin'. You say that ev'body will jes' have to woak five owahs a day. That means that if you stawt to woak at five o'clock in the mawnin' you would be through at ten in the mawnin' hinstead of ten at night, and eve'day would be like Sunday. Hit sounds crazy."

"Maybe so," Mack agreed. "Maybe it sounds crazy, but it can be figgered out. Brainy men can figger it out and nobody can show where they're wrong."

"Well, that mot be," Uncle Billy admitted. "But maybe Socialism won't woak. Maybe ev'body'll git shif'less. Now Woodrow Wilson is a brainy man and a college pafessah, and he ain't a Socialist."

"No, he ain't a Socialist," Mack said, "but he's a crook."

Jim looked around over the crowd. The place was packed with farmers and poor people from town, and you could tell it was going to be a good meeting, because everybody was excited. The banks had quit loaning money to Socialists, and the business men in town had talked about running every dirty Socialist out of the country. But the farmers didn't feel like taking talk like that. They were sore. Jim had heard fellows say they ought to go to town and horsewhip a few guys. And now when it seemed that the young men might have to go to war there was talk that the American people wouldn't stand for it, that the farmers and working men everywhere would get out their shotguns and see to it that no damned capitalists and politicians would send boys to Europe to be killed.

There was a lot of clapping when Niek got up to talk. Most of the people there had heard him before and liked him. They felt like he was on their side.

He talked with a German accent. He told the crowd about his old German mother and his brothers in the German army, and after you listened to him a while you knew damned well that the German people were just like the American people and didn't want this war.

Fred Niek could tell a lot of funny stories and get you to laughing, then change his tone and before you knew it you wanted to cry.

He said some things that made you think. He said that people in this country starved to death because there was too much food, and went half naked because there was too much to wear. "Dit you effer hear of a betbug," he said, "that starved to det because there vere too many lumberjacks in the bunk? Or a jackass that went hungry because there was too much grass in the pasture? Vell, you fellers ain't got the brains of a betbug or the sense of a jackass."

Jim nudged old Uncle Billy and grinned. Old Uncle Billy after hearing this speech would have to admit that Socialism would work better than capitalism.

When the speech was over a lot of the farmers went up and shook hands with Niek and others stood around a while and talked. Jim heard some of them talking about the Working Class Union. They said they would order ammunition from Montgomery Ward, and the first son-of-a-bitch that tried to make them go to war, well, we might as well have the war right here close to home.

SEVEN

AFTER THINKING IT OVER a long time Ted Tetley formed a plan for beginning his courtship. It came to him as he was setting up an item about the senior play, and it excited him so much that he got up and walked around the shop and smoked a cigar. It was simple and it had to work.

Happy had about a mile to walk along a country road from the school building to her home. She left the school a little after four o'clock every day. Ted could pick her up as if by accident, saying he was going out to Jim's place, and naturally they would talk about the senior play. Ted could say, as if he had just thought about it, that he was coming out on the night of the play to take Jim and Jeannie in and Happy might as well go along. Save her the walk.

After the play, of course, he would take Jim and Jeannie home first and that would give him a chance to be alone with her. He thought about it all day and the plan seemed to be all right.

The next afternoon he got off work early, went to his room and put on a clean shirt, tied his tie very carefully and looked at himself in the glass. Then he went out to his car, adjusted the spark lever and the gas lever and switched the key over to "Bat." He pulled on the hand brake to be sure the automobile was out of gear, then he flapped around to the front and hooked his finger in the gooser.

It was a hot day and his shirt stuck to his back. He braced himself and spun the motor. It started with a roar and he hurried as fast as he could around the fender to the door that wouldn't open, pulled down the spark lever and pushed up the gas lever. He floundered over the door and into the seat, turned the ignition key to "Mag," released the hand lever, pushed the clutch pedal, pulled down on the gas. His head jerked back as the car leaped forward.

The street was full of chucks and each chuck had fine dust in it. Whenever a wheel dropped into one of these dust pools the car bounced and Ted was bounced up, the tools under the back seat were tossed up, and the back cushion was thrown forward an inch. After a dozen such crashes the cushion was on the floor.

The dust that was splashed out of the chuck holes swirled under the car, mixed with the exhaust gas, rolled up in a cloud twice the size of the car. Some of it sucked over the folded top and into the back seat, into the front seat, and settled on Ted's wet shirt and in the corners of his eyes.

He was early and had to bounce along the streets near the high school until he saw the students come out and saw Happy leave the crowd and walk toward the edge of town. He went around a block to kill time.

Ted usually kept the top of the car folded. The car could go faster, he thought, without the top to catch wind. But he knew that women mostly wanted the top up to keep off the sun, even if it did catch wind like a sail. Little they cared. A man with a wife usually had to keep the top up. You could just about tell whether a man was married or not by looking at his top.

The windshield was sticking up at right angles to the ground. Ted pulled the top half of it back to an angle of forty-five degrees. This gave the car more dash and less wind resistance. Ted saw Happy on the road ahead of him. This was his lucky day. Everything was working out.

When Ted honked Happy looked back but didn't recognize him. She stepped out among the sandburs and walked carefully, pulling her skirt up a little.

The car stopped beside her and she looked up. The sun was in her eyes. Underneath her chin was a bright red light reflected from her dress.

"Want a ride?"

"Oh Ted! I didn't know it was you."

He opened the front door and she got in. He pushed on the clutch pedal. The car jerked and stopped. Killed the engine. Ted stared at the floorboards for a while, trying to collect his thoughts.

"Killed the engine!" he said.

"Yeah," Happy agreed. She was impatient. "I'll crank." She started to climb out.

"No, don't you git out." He grabbed her arm. "You watch the spark."

Ted leaned forward over her knee and switched the key to "Bat." He lifted one of his legs and hung it over the left door that wasn't made to open. Then he wiggled and flopped over the door, got overbalanced and made a little run out into the sandburs to catch himself.

He went around in front and made two or three quarter turns.

"Goose it," Happy suggested.

Sweat was running down Ted's nose. He spun the engine and it roared. Happy shut it down expertly. Ted struggled around the fender, holding to it to keep his balance, and wallowed back into the seat. He laid his ribs on her knee again to reach the switch.

Happy's nose curled up because of his stink and her eyes got big with horror. She moved over to the right as far as she could.

She had developed a loathing for Ted before she was six years old. He and Jim used to walk past the McGee place every evening on the way home from school, and usually several other country boys were with them. One day they came past fighting. The other boys were egging them on. Ted was pounding Jim, knocking blood out of him. For a long time after that she always ran when she saw him coming. She still wanted to run, but she was grown up and couldn't.

Ted's big head snapped back again as the car jumped. The ruts jerked the wheel out of his grasp. She decided he was the worst driver she had ever seen.

"You like the top down?" he asked.

She hadn't thought about it. It didn't make any difference. They would be home in three minutes. She wondered if he would be fool enough to get out and put it up.

"Yes. Sure. I like it down."

"A lot of women don't like it down."

"I like it down."

"A lot of women don't like it down at all."

"I like it."

"You're not like a lot of women."

"I'm not a woman. Not yet." For some reason she remembered that she had told Jim, one day in the pasture, that she was grown up. When Jim was loving her. It would be terrible if Jeannie ever found out, or anybody else. It was awful the way Jim kissed her sometimes. It wasn't Jim's fault. It was ber fault. If she didn't like it he wouldn't do it.

Would Ted maybe be like Jim if he hadn't had that disease? She couldn't imagine Ted being like Jim. Ted was awful. Like a spider. It wasn't his fault he was like a spider, but you couldn't help hating to have him close to you. It was his fault that he never took a bath. You wouldn't mind him so much if he ever took a bath.

"Yeah, you are. I think so," he said.

"Are what?"

Ted was growing desperate. He would have to get the conversation around to the senior play or they would be at Happy's place and it would be too late. "I mean you're grown up. Say, you going to the senior play Friday night?"

Happy was scared. It might possibly happen that he would ask her for a date.

"Yes," she said quickly. "I've got to go real early, because I'm going to be an usher. I won't come home in the evening after school. Won't have time." She had just decided not to come home after school.

He looked at her then and she was sure what he was thinking. He was disappointed and hurt. Happy unlatched the door. They were almost opposite her house.

Ted had time to make another vague plan, but not time to broach it carefully.

"I'm goin' myself," he said. "And after the play there's no use of you walkin' home—"

She pretended not to understand him. "Oh, yes. After the play Bud Filmore is havin' a dance over at his house, and I'm invited—" She opened the car door before the machine stopped and got out on the running board.

The mention of a dance paralyzed Ted's brain. He could not dance and therefore hated dancing as he hated bathing.

Happy jumped from the car and ran headlong through a patch of weeds. Ted was trying to stop, but the car rolled on for several yards. By the time it had stopped Happy had recovered her balance and was crossing the road toward her house.

"Much obliged," she called.

Ted twisted his neck and stared after her. There was nothing he could say or do, but he sat frowning until she reached the front steps. Then, because there was still nothing he could do, he turned his head and looked at the dash board, trying to remember how to start.

# EIGHT

B U D F I L M O R E was one of the best football players in high school, but he never would apply himself to his studies. He was naturally a bright boy, his mother said, but he wouldn't get down and study. This was because of the teachers he had; they never did give him the high marks he deserved, his mother insisted.

Now Bud's old woman was a tightwad, Bud said. She had money. Three farms that the old man had left her. But she wouldn't turn loose any of her money. They could afford to have a car, and not a Ford either but one with a self-starter and an accelerator, a Maxwell.

Bud's old man had been in real estate and was pretty slick. He would fix things with the Indian agent to get an Indian declared competent, then he would mortgage the Indian's land for maybe a thousand dollars. The Indian couldn't pay the mortgage, usually, and the old man would foreclose and get a farm worth five or six thousand. But there were some pretty nasty people around town that had it in for the old man and they finally fixed it up so that he was arrested. Old Sam Gladson the sheriff arrested him, and Sam hadn't been any angel himself in the early days. Bud's old man hadn't done anything that a dozen other fellows didn't do, but he was the only one they picked on. It looked for a while like the old man might have to go to prison, but he was cleaning a gun one day and it went off and shot him in the side and killed him.

The trouble he had got in cost a lot of money, so there wasn't much left but three farms, and the old woman wanted to be sure she'd have enough to live on the rest of her life. That was why she was so tight. But she could have afforded a car if she'd only wanted it.

Another thing Bud didn't like was their front-room furniture. The furniture itself was all right. It was mission style, real heavy, and looked good. But it was nigger furniture.

For a while there was a fellow lived in town who was real rich. He built a house, and the house alone, not counting the furniture or anything, cost ten thousand. Back of the big house was a small one for a couple of nigger servants. They were real high-class niggers especially trained to serve rich folks, and they made good money. In these servants' quarters, as they called them, there was high-class mission furniture, better than almost any white people in town had. Well, the big house burned down and the fellow that owned it left town, but what did Bud's dad do but buy this nigger furniture for little or nothing. They didn't tell where they got it, of course, but Bud and Bud's mamma always felt like people knew where they'd got it and talked about it. Bud wanted the old woman to sell it and get some more, but she was too tight, so Bud was a little bit ashamed to have young folks come in.

Bud had planned with his mother to have some high-school kids come in for a little party after the senior play, and everything went all right until the day of the play when Bud brought in some phonograph records he had borrowed. The old woman put one of them on and it was dance music and she asked Bud why he brought records like that into her house. She was mad.

Bud told her, "Well, Mamma, the kids will want to dance a little tonight."

The old woman's nose got white, and she said, "Not in my house, because I'm not gonna have my house used for *criminal* purposes."

That made Bud mad, and he didn't say anything to her but he went around and told everybody he had invited that there wouldn't be any party. After the play Bud's mamma hurried home, with a neighbor lady that she had in to help her serve, and the two of them sat around until after eleven waiting for Bud and his friends to show up and they never did. Bud got in about midnight and his mother raked him over the coals good and plenty, but she didn't find out where he had been.

As it turned out Bud wasn't sorry that he couldn't have a dance, because he had more fun that night than he would have had at any party. At the dress rehearsal in the afternoon he got to fooling around with Happy McGee, a junior girl who was one of the ushers, and got her around behind the scenery and loved her up. She was a country girl and didn't have a real good reputation, although the boys didn't really have anything on her. But anyway Bud knew he wouldn't dare to ask her to his house because his mother would throw a fit, but he knew that Happy kind of expected to be asked, and he wanted to stay in good with her to see what he could get. So he got out of it all by telling her that he had planned to have a little dance at his place after the play, and wanted her to come, but his old woman was so darned old-fashioned that she wouldn't let them dance, so he'd called the whole thing off—and could he take her home that night after the play?

"Why, I live out in the country a *mile*," she said.

"I know it," he said. "But I guess I got legs."

She was real excited. "Well, all right, if you think it won't be too far for you to walk," she said.

Bud really didn't know much about women. The only experience he'd ever really had was on one of the football trips.

The team had to stay all night in a town of about ten thousand, and one of the fellows said he knew where there was a whore house. He wanted Bud and another fellow to go with him, and finally they sneaked off and went to this place. When they got there it was just an ordinary house.

They knocked and went in and talked to the landlady, who was about forty. She said there were just two girls there that night but that if one of the boys would like her, she was pretty good. The other fellows said they'd take the girls and they told Bud to take the landlady. "She's real good lookin' for an old lady," they said.

Well, Bud finally took the landlady, and the next day the other two kidded him about it, but the joke was really on them because they both got doses and Bud didn't.

But even though Bud hadn't had any experience to speak of he could talk just like the fellows who had. He heard one of the older boys say once that after you had got to a girl you ought to get up and kick hell out of her so that if she got knocked up she wouldn't want you to marry her. Well, that sounded good to Bud, so he said he always done them that way. He heard another fellow say that if a girl made you use one you could punch a pin through it right at the end and it would bust and not bother you and the girl would never know any difference, so he told the boys that he always done that.

The night of the play he met Happy on the stage behind the scenery, and after the crowd had left they went out the back door. He knew she was real excited, because he was one of the most popular boys in school. He didn't try to love her up in town, for fear somebody would see them, but when they got out on the country road he started loving her. She acted like she was real scared, but she let him go a long ways. He told her she was the sweetest girl in the world and that he loved her.

Finally he said, "Let's go the limit, darling," and she didn't say anything. He didn't know how far to go, but he thought, hell, why not go as far as he could and see what happened.

He went on with it and she didn't stop him. He was so excited it was all over in a minute and didn't amount to much after all. She cried and seemed to be in pain. She asked him if he still loved her, and before he thought he said sure he did. That was wrong, of course; he ought to have kicked hell out of her. But it wasn't likely she was knocked up, and maybe it was better this way, because he could come back later.

But he didn't want her to think that he was crazy about her, so he said it was late and his old woman would raise hell, and if she wasn't afraid to walk the rest of the way alone he would go back. She said she wasn't afraid. He kissed her again and then walked back toward town.

He was feeling a little bit sentimental, but he knew that wouldn't do. Some damn fools got to fooling around with that kind of a girl and then fell in love with them and married them. Jesus! It was all right to fool around with one, but when Bud got married he didn't want none of this two-bit lovin'. He wanted to be sure his boat was the first one up the stream.

When he got home he took his tongue-lashing and went to bed. The old lady was still bawling around when he went to sleep. When he woke up the next morning she was in his room fooling around and he saw she was still bawling and he thought he was in for some more, but when she saw he was awake she said, "Honey, why didn't you tell me you wasn't feeling well last night?"

He didn't know what the hell she was driving at, so he just grunted. She said, "You must of had a terrible nosebleed, like you used to have when you was little and got real nervous." Well, that scared him plenty, but he kept still and she said, "Now you go on and rest, honey, and mamma won't bother you."

That was a narrow squeak with the old lady, and, God, he ought to of thought of it. He was surprised and mighty pleased.

Later that day he met one of the fellows, Weenie, downtown, and Weenie said, "Say, I seen you sneak out of the Opery House last night with that jane, and how was it?"

"Why, I got me a maiden-head," Bud said.

"Aw, you're a damned liar," Weenie said.

"Naw, listen. It was funny as hell. Boy, did she yell. But the worst of it was that I damned near got caught. My old lady come in the room this mornin' before I woke up and she was gatherin' up dirty clothes and she found a bloody handkerchief in my pocket, and she said—listen, this is good—she said 'I didn't know you was feelin bad and had the nosebleed last night.' "

Weenie said, "Hot damn!" and laughed and laughed.

"It's a good thing I slept in my underwear," Bud said. "I got it here in my pocket, and I got to find some place to wash it out and dry it."

For a while that spring Bud got in the habit of sneaking off and taking Happy home, but finally his mother found it out and gave him such a bawling out that he knew he would have to quit. Of course the old woman didn't know what was really going on. She kind of half-way promised to buy him a Maxwell if he would never have anything to do with the girl anymore. So he sort of broke it up, although he kept on good terms with her and saw her once in a while and kidded with her. He knew she was still crazy about him.

Hot weather came, and his mother would not buy the car. Bud finally told her that she would either buy a car that very day or he would leave home.

The old woman started crying and put her arms around him like he was a baby. He shoved her off. "Honey," she said, "you know I'd buy you a car, but you would have a wreck and kill yourself, and then what would I do?"

"All right," he said. "I'm goin' out to McGee's place and get a job in the harvest. They need a hand."

"Bud!" Mamma started yelling at him. "You been goin' with that McGee girl again."

"Well, what of it?" he asked. "She ain't poison."

"All right," Mamma said. "Go on and leave your mother, who's worked her fingers to the bone for you, for that shameless—that—"

"Now look here," Bud said. "You don't know nothin' about that girl." He picked up his straw hat that he had bought the day before, and walked out. The last thing he heard was the old woman bawling as loud as she could.

NINE

THE FIRST HEAT of the spring kept Ted restless. Sometimes it was a clean romantic restlessness that made him love Happy McGee, but one Saturday morning when a dirt storm blew up he began to want something else. The swirling dirt in the street made it impossible to see more than a few yards, and Ted felt free. People couldn't watch him from windows across streets and feel sorry for him. He was hidden in a little space of brown dust, and yet in this obscurity he was lonesome.

He unlocked the shop and went inside, blew his nose, and looked absent-mindedly into the muddy handkerchief. When he closed his mouth he could always hear the grinding of sand particles between his teeth. The atmosphere was tan, and the smell outside was of the horse manure that had been dried and ground to dust in the street, but inside this was mixed with the odors of ink and oil and fresh paper. As he generated the burner under the metal pot he added the smell of wood alcohol—enough like the smell of corn liquor to make him think of hell-raising. As the metal got hot there was a new smell of the burning scum on its surface.

Ted stood at the window a while and stared at the sun. It was a harmless yellow disk hardly visible. People who passed had their eyes squinted, and they pulled up their upper lips, instinctively trying to protect their nostrils with mustaches they didn't have. Eyelashes were muddy. Ted thought of pulling a woman up close to him in some dark brown room and gritty bed.

Edwards, Ted's boss, came in and went to his desk, and struck angrily at the dirt on its surface with a folded newspaper.

"I gotta go to the city this afternoon on business," Ted told him. Ted was important enough in the shop that he did not have to ask permission.

Edwards was rolling a cigarette, and he bared his long yellow teeth to say, "Fine. That'll make a fine personal. 'Ted Tetley, well-known linotype operator at the *Star,* made a *business* trip to the city Saturday night and come back the next day with his *business* all done.'"

Ted wheezed with indignation, but he had to take it. There was no way of concealing from Edwards the fact that he was going to the city, since the editor met the trains, but on the other hand there was no danger that a personal item about Ted would actually appear in the paper, for Ted did the setting-up and the printing.

He also did the writing. Edwards could not write a grammatical sentence. The editor's function was to talk merchants into inserting ads and to keep up with what was happening in town. From Edwards' scribbled notes on local events Ted wrote the stories which appeared in the *Star.*

"I can give you the address of some five-dollar business if you'd ruther have it than this loose two-dollar stuff," Edwards went on. "Now, the way you're built, I don't see what good a horse collar does you. And at the price you pay you can't even get a collar for a shetland pony."

"God-damned little you know about horse collars," Ted replied bitterly. "It's mule racin' you're interested in."

"Well," Edwards observed quietly, "it ain't every feller at my age that can git a mule into a lope."

Ted went to work, glad that this business was over. Maybe someday he would pi a form over Edwards' head and go to Mexico to live. It wouldn't be a bad sight to see Edwards lying on the floor, the chase around his neck and his head in a bloody litter of type, furniture and quoins.

In his room that afternoon Ted took a drink of corn whiskey and tucked a large medicine-bottleful of the stuff in his inside coat pocket.

When he got on the train he went to the smoking car. He was more comfortable where there were no women to glance at him or kids to stare open-eyed.

Ted blew a layer of dirt and cinders off the leather seat. The window ledge had a layer also which swirled up in a blinding fog when he raised the window. Some of the men in the car were so begrimed that you could not tell whether they were Indian or white.

As Ted sat down his heel clinked against the spittoon and he shoved it as far as he could out of sight. It's slowly stirring contents made him a little sick.

He was going to the city to have a good time, so he leaned back and looked up at the shiny green ceiling of the car and pictured there a green girl naked on a green bed.

Cinders came in with stinging force and the little valleys on his coat sleeves soon filled with them. He put the window down and began to sweat.

Facing Ted, two seats up, was a man with a glass eye. The eye was large and watery and not quite the right color, and the side of his face which held the eye was ridged and worried with the problem of keeping the eye in its socket. That side was dull and blind, but the other side of the man's face was alert and good natured.

A young man across the aisle stood up and took down an old-fashioned ear trumpet from the rack overhead. He looked into the trumpet and then poured a little stream of dirt and cinders out of it.

Thinking about having a woman in a few hours, Ted squirmed in his seat and crossed his legs. Cinders got under his collar and scratched his neck. He would have her take off everything. A man ought to have it every once in a while or he might go nuts. That made him think of a damned good joke about a Jew on a train and a crazy man with his hands tied behind him. Ted thought it was so damned funny that he chuckled out loud, then he remembered that people might think *he* was crazy laughing to himself, so he kept the laugh inside him. The corn liquor and the rolling of the train made him feel good and the laugh kept piling up inside him until he thought he'd yell out and make everybody look around.

The conductor came through and punched his ticket and put a slip in his hat band, and if the conductor hadn't been busy Ted would have told him the story. He would have to remember to tell it to the woman. You can tell a story like that to a woman like that.

There was a sheriff with a crazy man, and the Jew said to the sheriff, he said, "Vat's de matter vit det men vit his hends tied behind him?" Well, Ted wasn't very good at talking like a Jew, but he could tell the story anyway. And the sheriff said "Bugs." And the Jew didn't understand, and pretty soon he tapped the sheriff on the shoulder again and said, "Vat did you say vas de matter vit him?" And the sheriff said kind of loud, "Nuts." But the Jew still didn't understand, and pretty soon he tapped the sheriff on the shoulder again.

Ted was feeling pretty gay and happy. Maybe he'd drunk too much of that corn and would get sick on the train. He'd better sit real quiet and not think about the joke or the woman or he'd get sick. He looked out the window and got a glimpse of a horse galloping off into the storm. He never really had done anything although he was almost thirty years old. It was going to be different this time. Once a woman told him to take off his clothes, and another one said he ought to take a bath. After this he would just tell them to go to hell, and not pay any attention but go ahead and do as he pleased. A man had a right to have some fun even if he was a cripple. Ted hardly ever thought about being a cripple any more, although when he was a kid it used to bother him a lot and make him feel like killing himself. That was when he got over being religious and decided that maybe there wasn't any after-life.

He would be better off maybe if he was sure that after he died he could have a big strong body, but if he believed that, he couldn't ever get drunk or go and see a woman.

If he only had some way of telling what women really thought of him—if he could only find out some way that Happy liked him, then he could go ahead and ask her for dates and overcome her shyness. Nothing could possibly be as nice as having her all the time.

The Jew didn't understand and he tapped the sheriff on the shoulder again. "Vat you say vas de metter?" And the sheriff turned around real sore. The joke swelled up inside of Ted and made him feel like he was going to bust. It was the liquor rolling around inside him and making him feel like his head was full of fireworks. He kind of wondered if the joke was really as funny as it seemed. He'd have to remember to tell it to the woman. He didn't want a blond woman because this was a nasty business and he couldn't help feeling that blond girls were sweet and pure.

When he walked out of the station at Oklahoma City he found himself at the top of a little flight of stairs. On the street below him were people milling around or hurrying past, and he could look down on them, see the tops of men's hats. He always liked to be higher than other people and look down at them.

Then other people came out of the station and crowded past him and the feeling was lost. The sun had just gone down. The dirt that whirled up and struck Ted's face seemed black and sticky, not like the dry dirt from the fields. A piece of newspaper with transparent greasy spots popped against Ted's shin, wrapped itself around his leg, and clung there. He kicked and turned around to dislodge it and wondered if anyone was laughing at him, but people were bent against the wind and didn't look up.

Then Ted felt his hat slip and grabbed his wild hair. "Whoa!" he yelled angrily. His hat was gone. He saw it sail into a woman's face, and she slapped it away instinctively. He started to run, whacking the sidewalk with his awkward feet. The hat went to the ground. A man stepped on it, kicked it off his foot as if it had been an animal attacking him, and then, seeing what it was, grabbed at it and missed. Ted's haylike hair drove into his eyes. The hat went two stories high and Ted, watching it, crashed into a Negro woman. It dived to the broken bricks of the railroad right-of-way and rolled against a telephone pole. For a moment he gained on it, but it climbed the pole a couple of feet and then hurtled off again. A tall man leaped up and caught it in midair, and grinned when he handed it to Ted. The grin was meant to be friendly, but Ted was red-faced and angry. He jammed the hat on his head and paddled along with the wind as if he had been going in that direction all the time.

He walked for a while until he had recovered his breath. His lungs felt raw from breathing dirt so fast. He shouldn't have run. Better let the damned hat go to hell. Hundreds of people saw him and were now going along grinning to themselves, like the fellow who caught the hat, over the funny little guy running after his hat. They'd tell about it on the street car or at the supper table.

He had intended to go to a show and then to a hotel, but now he wasn't interested in a show, or a woman either, for that matter. This was a damned silly and expensive thing to do, to come to this filthy town. He decided to get a cheap room and get a good night's sleep. He didn't want to go to any hotel where he'd been before.

He smelled food and went into a little restaurant. A cheese sandwich and a bottle of near-beer made him feel better. A door next to the restaurant had a sign over it: "Rooms 75c and Up."

He went up a brass-trimmed stairway, and a Negro met him on the second floor. "Yass, *sah!* Got a nice room Ah c'n let you have f' six bits." They climbed another flight of stairs. The Negro pushed open a rickety door and Ted looked into a dismal room. "You wanta see a nass gal?"

"Naw," Ted said. "You ain't got no good-lookin' women here."

"Listen, boss. Lemme show ya. C'meah."

"Naw. Not now."

"Maybe latah. Suah. Maybe half owa."

Ted grunted and looked at the bed. The edges of the quilts were black with human grease. The rim of the sheet had a layer of dust on it. "Where's the bathroom?"

"Right across the hall, two dowas down. Yass, sah. 'Bout half owa."

Ted turned around to argue but the Negro was gone. He took off his coat and the bottle clinked against the bed post. He pulled it out and took several gulps, shuddered violently. His breath caught in his throat and he twisted his face until the liquor quit hurting.

When he rolled up his sleeves to wash he saw that his arms had a black coating of dirt and soot. The bathroom was across the hall. The burning inside him cooled to a pleasant warmth, and then he remembered that a girl once, in a place like this, had told him to take a bath.

There was a layer of dry dirt in the bottom of the bathtub, and the first water he ran made a swamp which he had to push down the drain. He looked around the room for peepholes in the wall ; then he took a bath.

The joke about the Jew and the crazy man came to him suddenly and he chuckled as he got into his clothes. He went back to his room and threw himself down on the bed and laughed. He was still there when a tap came at the door. "Huh!" he said startled. A girl walked in.

She was real skinny, with kind of a pink dirty dressing gown on. She was blond, and her face was painted up. It looked good.

"You want a nice date, don't you, daddy?" she said, sitting down on the bed. If he didn't get up she couldn't tell he was a cripple.

"Say," he said, full of mirth. "You heard this one? There was a Jew and a crazy man on the train and there was a sheriff taking the crazy man to the bug house. So the Jew says to the sheriff, he says, 'Vat's de metter vit det men?' I ain't no good at talkin' like a Jew, but you know how they talk. Well, the sheriff he turned around and he says 'Bugs.' And the Jew he didn't know what he meant, so pretty soon he says again, 'Vat's de metter vit det men?' And the sheriff he was kind of sore, and he says, 'Nuts.' And the Jew he still didn't understand, and pretty soon he tapped the sheriff on the shoulder again and he said, 'Vat did you say vas de metter vit det men?' And the sheriff was real mad and he says, 'He's crazy.' Well, the Jew he says, 'Vel, it's no yonder he's crazy, vit bugs on his nuts and his hends tied behind him—.' Aw I forgot to tell you this crazy man had his hands tied behind him. I spoiled it."

The girl lowered her head. "I don't like dirty stories," she said. "Ain't you had somepin' to drink?"

"Yeah. It's right there in my coat pocket, the inside pocket."

"Naw thanks." She leaned close to him. "How about that little date you was gonna have?"

She began to touch him, but he grabbed her wrist. "Hey! Look out! I didn't tell that boy I wanted a date. Why don't you have a little drink?"

"Would you like me better if I had a little drink?"

"Yeah, sure. Have one."

She took a couple of swallows and replaced the bottle. Then she coughed and lay back on the bed. He wondered how she would look without any clothes on and tried to open her dressing gown, but she clutched it tightly.

"Ain't you gonna pay me, honey?" she asked.

"What you charge?"

"Two dollars."

"It ain't worth it," Ted said sadly. "You'd rush right off and then I'd be lonesome again."

"For three dollars, honey, I'll stay as long as you want me to. All night if you want me to."

Ted was feeling good. What was the use of coming all this way for nothing? He pulled some bills out of his pocket and gave her three dollars. Then he took another drink.

"Listen, honey," she said, "if you git sick on that stuff for God's sake go to the bathroom to puke because I got to clean up this place."

"Aw, I won't git sick." He got close to her. "How did you git into this business?" he asked.

"My husband died, and I got a baby to support, and there ain't nothin' else a girl can do nowadays."

He thought about it a while. "Aw, you ain't got no kid."

"The hell I ain't! Look at this here." She pulled the dirty silk from her abdomen and showed him jagged red marks like flames. "That rotgut makes me feel good." She sat up and took another drink. "You got any kids, honey?"

"I ain't married," he said.

"Well for God's sake don't never git married then, or if you do don't bring no kids into the world."

He pulled her gown open again and saw little muddy streaks running down from her arm pits where drops of sweat had plowed through the layer of dust on her skin.

All this corn liquor was ruining Ted's kidneys. No use trying to put off going to the bathroom. He got up and waddled out.

When he returned the woman was sitting up. She stared at him, and she was scared. He saw her and the room and himself, all very plain and clear, the room and the woman sitting up in bed, but it was all a show. Not a very good show, and he didn't care how it turned out.

"You ain't got syph,—have you?" He heard her very well. Her voice made a big noise in his ears; but it was all very far away. He felt himself being surprised and wondering what she was talking about, but he wasn't there at all. It was as funny as the story about the Jew and the crazy man, but if he tried to tell it he would spoil it.

"What you talkin' about?" he asked. "They ain't nothin' wrong with me—." He laughed, and he knew she wouldn't understand why. He remembered how sober people felt. She was still sober.

"Because I knew a fellow," she said, "who had syph real bad, and he walked like you, and, honest, I'm scared to death of it."

He felt himself getting sore, but he didn't care. "You git the hell out of here," he yelled. "I been this way since I was a kid, and naturally I don't like for people to talk about it. I didn't tell the nigger to send you in here, and I'm not gonna do anything to you. I don't think I could because I'm too awkward. I didn't want nothin' from you except to talk to you a while because I was lonesome. Now you git the hell out and leave me alone." He got the bottle and took another drink. He wasn't sore at her. She meant well.

Her eyes got full of tears and he mussed up her blond hair with one of his long hands. Then he tumbled down on the bed and told her to get out before he batted hell out of her. He felt good. It was worth it, no matter how sick he was the next day. She stayed around a while and said something or other. She was sorry, but what of it?

Then he was alone and real sick, but what difference did it make? He mustn't puke in the room because she would have to clean it up. Someplace inside him he had a little stomach which was deathly sick, but it didn't make any difference. It was all so damned unimportant.

Holding to the foot of the bed he got up. The room dipped. He got his eye on the door and went for it and found it, and found the bathroom in the same way. In a dirty little hotel in Oklahoma City a God damned cripple was going to the bathroom to puke, but it wasn't important. If it wasn't for liquor a fellow might never find out about things. He discovered the toilet seat and seated himself on the floor in front of it and put his chin on the enameled seat and turned everything loose. Seemed like his guts were coming out.

When everything was out of him he rolled around a while and then got up and went back to his room. . . . Somebody was inserting a knife blade into one of the joints of his skull and was patiently trying to crack his skull open by pumping the knife handle back and forth. It was daylight and he was alone in the room, so he must have been asleep, and it was his heart that was trying to bust his head. He might die of thirst before he could get up and find some water.

He sat up and the heart-beats came faster. He put his hands on his head and pushed, trying to hold the sides of his head together. He remembered where he was, and he remembered where the bathroom was. He caught hold of the bed post and got up and leaned toward the door and caught it, then leaned across the hall to the bathroom door and caught it on his knees.

Inside he leaned over the bathtub and turned on the faucet and gulped the water, sat down on the stool, got very sick, and spurted the water he had just drunk into the dust that had collected in the bottom of the bathtub.

A half hour later he was back in his room. It was not so hard to stand up now, but the skull-popping was still going on. Maybe it was about time for the morning train. He put on his hat and coat and looked around the room. On the table were three one-dollar bills.

He looked at them a long time, and then remembered and put them in his pocket. He was surprised. Honest whore. But his head hurt too much to think about it. The trip wouldn't cost as much as he'd thought it would. He pulled his hat down tight on his head for he could see out the window a fog of dust and cinders.

TEN

MCGEE HAD JUST STARTED heading his wheat and he
needed another hand. A header crew has a header driver, four
barge hands, a stacker, and a scratcher. Generally the scratcher
is an old man. His job is to scratch up the loose grain around
the stack and shape up the sides of the stack now and then. He
hands water up to the barge hands and puts up the ladder for
the stacker when the stack is finished.

But McGee's crew was short and so the old man who had been
hired for scratcher worked in a barge with Jim Tetley. The old
man drove all the time and let Jim do the loading, and in throwing off he didn't do his share, so that Jim was doing the work of
a man and a half.

When Bud Filmore showed up at noon McGee hired him and
put him in the barge with Jim, but before they had been at work
a half hour it was plain that Bud was worse than nothing at all.
While the barge was filling he could neither drive nor load. If
he tried to drive he either crowded too close, standing the elevator straight up and forcing McGee to run the header out into
the grain, or he drove too far away so that McGee had to follow
him out into the stubble and cut only half a swath.

If he tried to load he floundered, getting wheat down his back
and bull-nettles up his legs. Once in his agony he lost his fork

and the whole outfit had to stop while it was being located.

At throwing off he wasn't any better. He either tried to pitch the grain he was standing on or stood on the grain that Jim was trying to pitch. When he did get a forkful clear he spooned it against the side of the stack so that most of it dribbled back into the barge. Bud's face was soon as red as a beet. Big blisters formed on his hands. Wheat beards gnawed at his feet and back and wrists so that he smarted all over.

Meanwhile Jim chewed tobacco and grinned and did the work of two men. The day was scaldingly hot so that every man and every horse was dripping wet. Bud started getting a little bit sick. He wondered what time it was. Already he had found out that he couldn't make a hand. These men worked in the wheat twelve hours a day, seven days a week, during harvest time. Before he had worked two hours Bud knew that one day of this would kill him. He wondered if he could possibly hold out until sundown.

At four o'clock Happy appeared driving a very old horse hitched to a rickety buggy. In the buggy was lunch—fried chicken, gallons of cold tea, bread and butter, dill pickles, cake and pie, and potato salad. McGee always fed his harvest crew well, even if he and Happy had to go without later on.

Jim climbed out of his barge and went over to help Happy carry the lunch to the shade of the stack. Happy looked excited and pretty.

"How's he gettin' along?" she asked in a low tone.

Jim felt like codding. "Meanin' who?"

"You know who I mean." Happy was a little bit resentful.

"I reckon you mean that college athalete. Well, he's winded. He's petered out, and so far he's done absolutely nothin'—worse than nothin'. He don't know nothin', and you can't learn him nothin'—that's the hell of it. When you put him drivin' he goes to sleep and starts off down to the creek. If you put him loadin' he slings his fork away and starts swimmin' like a puppy dog to keep his head from bein' covered up. And pitchin' off, by God, he's worse. He stands on every wad I try to throw off so that three times I threw him up on the stack by mistake."

"I think it's darned mean of you, Jim, not to have no more patience with him when he's learnin'."

"Oh, you're talkin' about patience! Looka here." Jim pulled up his pants leg. From a tiny wound in the calf of his leg there was a broad band of dried blood running down into his shoe. "That's where he got me once, and I didn't even mention it to him. If you give me my choice I'd ruther have a rattlesnake in the load with me."

"Aw, Jim," Happy said. "I'm sorry. You're a good sport. Here, let me wrap up your leg with somethin'."

"Naw, it's quit bleedin', and your rag wouldn't stay on. It's all right."

"Jim, you're a good guy. I'm sorry you got to work that way." Happy looked at him in awe. "They probably ain't another man in the county could do what you're doin'."

Jim was embarrassed. He didn't say anything, but started carrying things to the stack.

McGee climbed down off the rudder and came over to the stack.

"Been chewin' too much tobacco," he said. "Ain't got much of an appetite."

Happy knew the old man was sore, and she knew Bud must have been pretty bad to make him sore.

"Well now, that's a darned good thing for the rest of us," the scratcher said. "Now if you had a good appetite I reckon we wouldn't have no chance." The scratcher laughed real loud. "We might have to haul the eats out in one of the barges." He laughed some more.

Bud was sulky at first, but after he got cooled off he perked up a bit. "You gonna sell your wheat in town, Mr. McGee?" he asked.

"Oh, no," Mack replied. "I'm gonna feed it to the chickens. Them thirty old hens need a lot of grain to carry 'em over the winter."

Happy turned red, but she couldn't think of anything to say.

"What you gonna do with the straw?"

"Why, I sell it to these people that make shredded wheat. You've seen these here shredded wheat biscuits. Well, they take this here straw and wash it and wrap it up thataway."

Everybody was quiet. Jim was rolling a cigarette, and the corners of his mouth were turned down. Happy was impatient with the old man. He had no right to do this.

Nothing was said for a while, then Bud looked at his wrist watch and asked Mr. McGee what time he had.

Mack pulled out an old silver watch. "Ten after four," he said.

"You must be fast," Bud said. "I got seven minutes after."

"Naw, this here watch is right," Mack said. "It don't look like so much, but I don't dare to take it out in the sun."

"Why not?" Bud asked, very much interested. "It won't hurt a watch to be in the sun."

"Oh, no, it won't hurt the *watch*. You see, I found out about it when I was a kid up in Kansas. This watch belonged to my dad, and it was famous up in that country. One day dad and me was standin' around with a bunch of fellers in front of Ike Marlow's general store, and somebody asked dad what time it was and he told him. Well, they was a feller there named Steve Stevenson, and Steve took out his watch and he said dad was wrong. Well, there was an argument, and finally Steve said that his watch was right oftener than this here watch of dad's, and he said he could prove it, and he offered to bet five dollars that he could prove it. Well, Steve's watch was an old tin turnip, and dad took him up, and the other fellers was to be the judge.

"So Steve started out to prove it. He said his watch lost ten minutes every day, and every morning he set it up ten minutes, that is, he set it about five minutes fast every morning. And he said that his watch was exactly right twice a day. It was right sometime while he was settin' it ahead. It had to be right, he said, at the instant when the minute hand crossed the right time. Then it was right once again when the time caught up to it and passed it. It had to be right twice a day.

"And Steve said that dad's watch was a better watch and dad didn't have to set it so often, so that it trailed along maybe for a month just a leetle bit behind the right time or just a leetle bit ahead of the time and it wasn't hardly ever exactly right. So Steve's watch was right oftener than dad's watch, which was what he said he would prove.

"Well, the other fellers standin' around said they thought Steve had proved his point and they was goin' to give him the five dollars, but my dad says, 'Wait a minute,' he says. 'If I can prove that this here watch don't trail along just a leetle bit behind the time or just a leetle bit ahead of the time, but it stays right exactly on the time always, I reckon I win the bet.'

"The fellers said that if he could prove that he would win the bet. So he says, 'Now, boys, I don't want you boys to git scared and run. The last time I done this everybody took out and run. But it won't hurt nobody,' he says. 'Now I want you boys,' he says, 'to line up here and look at your shadders, and look at 'em right careful.'

"So the boys lined up and looked at their shadders, and then dad took out his watch and held it in the sun and every shadder jumped about half an inch. Well, it scared everybody, but dad told 'em that they wasn't no harm done. He said that the sun gets a leetle bit behind sometimes, but as soon as it sees this here watch it jumps up where it ought to be and that's why everybody's shadder jumped. Well, the fellers said that proved it, and they give dad the money. And so I don't never take this here watch out in the sunlight."

A sickly grin spread over Bud's face, but it died when he looked around and saw that everyone else was solemn. He knew then that he was an outcast, pitied by Happy but despised by the rest.

One of the barge horses started and looked up suddenly. A new automobile was coming toward them across the stubble. Bud's mamma was sitting in the front seat beside the driver.

The car stopped fifty yards from the stack, and Bud hurried over to it. He talked for a while and then returned. "Mr. McGee," he said, "Mamma wants me to help her decide on a new car, so I guess I won't have time to work any more."

"Well," McGee said, "I guess we'll have to worry along. Le's see. You worked a quarter of a day. That would be a dollar." He took a bill out of his pocket and handed it to Bud. "Come out and see us some time."

"Yes," Bud said. "You come over."

When the automobile had started back toward town the crew started laughing and laughed for five minutes without a break. Mack grinned and picked his teeth, very much pleased with himself.

"Oh," the stacker said. "Them thirty old hens can eat a thousand bushels of wheat over the winter, can they! My God, Mack, you shore got *some* hens! And *some* watch. By God! I thought I wouldn't live through it."

Happy got in the buggy and drove away silently.

ELEVEN

JEANNIE WAS ALL SWELLED UP with a baby that summer but she kept on working fifteen or sixteen hours a day. Happy helped her, and they did all the cooking for the harvest hands. Jim wanted to hire a girl but Jeannie wouldn't listen to it. "We're not getting a cent ahead," she said, "even as it is; and I simply won't go any more in debt."

She had red splotches on her face, and sometimes her ankles got puffy. When Jim worried about her she said she was strong and nothing ever hurt her.

One day in the late summer when Jim came in he saw that her face was pale and he was scared for a minute for fear the baby was going to come too soon. He asked her what was wrong, and she didn't answer right away. Then she said, "I want to talk to you." Then he knew that something else was wrong.

"Jim," she said, "you wouldn't fool around with my sister, would you?" Her voice was tight so that he couldn't hardly tell what she said, but when he understood he was scared and didn't say anything.

"Because I saw you today," she said, "down at the barn, scuffling around with her—and I couldn't tell—but from here it looked like, from up here, that you kissed her, on the mouth. That's what it looked like, from here."

"My God, Jeannie," he said, "you don't think—"

She started to cry, and he went over and put his arms around her. "I knew I was mistaken, Jim, but you know what people would think. You be careful. You hadn't ought to scuffle with her, now. She's grown up. I was so scared it made me sick all afternoon. You and Gladys are just alike. You never think about what other people will think. You're always wrestling around, and I know it don't mean anything, but if other people see it—if dad had seen you today, I don't know, he might have killed you."

Jim broke out in a cold sweat and his throat hurt. He had kissed Happy real hard, and anybody that happened to be around could have seen. "I know I been a damn fool," he said, "and I promise you it won't happen any more." He wanted to change the subject. "God, when I first come in," he said, "I thought you was sick. I wish you wouldn't work like you do, till after the kid comes. You're just riskin' your life for nothin', just so a bunch of bankers and wheat speculators can make a little more money."

"People like us has *got* to risk their life," she said, "if they're ever gonna get ahead. We can't help it if other people make money off of us. The reason they do is they've got money ahead and we ain't, and they ain't any way that I know to get money ahead except by workin' like a nigger dog."

"Well, what's the use of livin'," he said, "if you got to work like a dog all the time, and never have a bit of fun?—"

Jeannie got up and put some cobs in the stove. "Havin' fun?" she said. "You're just like dad. He always likes to have his fun, and where has it got him? He'll end up in the poor farm."

"Yeah," Jim said, "and so will a lot of fellers that worked like dogs always. The whole damned system is rotten and people that work themselves to death ain't got time to find it out, and they don't do a damned thing about it."

"Well, what can you do about it?"

"I guess I can vote, can't I?"

"Well, suppose you do vote, and a lot of other fellers vote and elect a bunch of Socialists. What'll happen? The grafters will come around and buy off your Socialists."

Jim was pretty mad by this time. "Well, if they do, by God, we'll git out our shotguns and go to Washington and blow hell out of them, Socialists and all."

"All right, they'll have to be a lot of people shot before there's any justice in the world. But that won't come in our time."

"Well, if you could hear some of the farmers around talkin' you might think it would happen sooner."

Jeannie shook her head. "What I want," she said, "is a decent house and some decent clothes, and some money to educate this baby of ours when he grows up so he won't have to slave."

When Jim went out to milk he thought about their poverty and wondered whether Jeannie was right or not. He thought about what a damned fool he'd been with Happy, and he decided that from now on he would work like a horse and never touch Happy again as long as he lived.

And for a couple of months he stuck to his resolution. He worked all the time and got the farm in good shape. He didn't even stop to read the *Appeal* for fear he would get mad and quit working. Then, about a month before the baby was due, Jeannie had to have help, and Happy came over every afternoon after school and stayed all night.

With Happy around so much Jim was miserable. He couldn't touch Jeannie any more, of course, and Happy left a trail of perfume in the air all the time. Happy sometimes didn't wear any stockings around the house and Jim could see the bright little hairs on her shins. Sometimes she sat around with her dress up to her knees. He thought he would go crazy.

Once after dark when Happy and Jim were rinsing the milk buckets down at the pump he brushed against her and she pulled his nose. He grabbed her and started kissing her. He was shaking all over. She broke away finally and ran, and he sat down on the curb to get his breath and cuss himself. He knew then that he didn't have any self-control.

But the worst thing happened one afternoon. Jim was harrowing, and a dirt storm came up so that he could hardly see his horses. He unhitched and went to the house. He stopped at the water tank and washed the dirt off of his face because he knew that Happy would be there by that time.

The wind was pretty strong. Jim saw a half-grown chicken go end over end. Everything was banging. Jim blundered into the kitchen and there stood Happy, stark naked, taking a bath in the wash tub. Jeannie was in the other room some place. Jim couldn't do a thing for a minute but stand and stare, then he backed out and went down to the barn and worked for a while. He was afraid Happy couldn't look him in the face again.

She didn't hardly look at him at supper, but she went down with him after dark to feed the calves.

He thought he ought to say something. "I'm sorry about this afternoon," he said.

"I guess you saw plenty," she said.

He couldn't tell by that what she thought about it, so he kept silent.

"It's a good thing they wasn't any flies around," she said.

"What d' you mean?"

"I mean you would of swallowed half of them and I would of swallowed the rest."

"I guess we both looked pretty funny," he said.

She took hold of his arm. "Listen, Jim," she said, "will you tell me somep'n? Did you ever see Jeannie that way?"

"God, no. She would die, I guess, if a man saw her without any clothes on. The worst thing she dreads about havin' the kid is havin' the doctor see her."

"It's funny the way people are," Happy said. "I don't see what difference it makes, much, whether a person has on clothes or not."

"You mean you don't care if I saw you naked?"

"No, I don't care. Not *you*. I guess I would run around naked all the time in front of you if people didn't make so much of it."

"God," he said. "I guess I'd go crazy if I couldn't—do anything." He grabbed her and wrapped his arms around her.

She wouldn't let him kiss her. "You're pretty awful to talk that way," she said, "but I don't care. Anyway, it's my fault. I'm a damned fool. Turn me loose, Jim."

She pulled away from him but on the way back to the house she held to his arm and put her face against his shoulder.

After that he couldn't think of much else but Happy.

 TWELVE

NED WELLHOF never could get ahead unless he sold whiskey. He tried to farm and worked hard, but nothing much came of his working. People said he worked from the neck down or said he didn't have any head, that his neck just grew up and haired over.

He got into trouble with his whiskey-making, of course. Didn't know enough to fix things with Sam Gladson, the sheriff. He was arrested and sentenced to the pen. Birdie, his wife, and their four kids moved to town, and Birdie took in washing for about a year and a half. They had a hard time. People couldn't understand how they kept alive.

Then Ned got out of the pen in the fall of 1916, a little before his term was up, on good behavior, and came home without letting Birdie know he was out, to surprise the family.

He asked around and found out where they were living. It was a two-room shack at the edge of town, with boards nailed over the windows, such a miserable place that Birdie could rent it for little or nothing.

Ned was full of ambition when he got off the train, although he was not very well from eating the prison grub. He had decided to let liquor-making alone in the future and stick to farming, even though he could make only a bare living at it. Farming paid better in the long run. He had found that out.

His head was full of plans for farming. He would lease a quarter out in the sticks, borrow money from the bank, and put in a spring crop. He thought he could borrow money because he never had voted the Socialist ticket and never talked socialism much.

When he got to the door he didn't knock but just stuck his head in and yelled, "Hey!"

Birdie was so surprised that she screamed. The oldest kid was the first one to recognize him, and yelled out, "Dad!"

Birdie just stood there for a minute over the wash tub with soap suds dripping off of her puffy blue hands. Birdie was not like her name, but big and fat and blue. She was not very healthy because she stayed fat even when she was weak with hunger.

When she saw who it was she was more scared than ever because she thought he had broke out of the pen and the officers would be after him. "What did you come here for?" she asked. "And don't stand there in the door where people can see you. What did you break out for, when you just had a little longer to serve?"

This was a big joke. Ned laughed and laughed. "Sure I broke out," he said, "right past the warden, and he was so darned surprised he give me five dollars and shook hands with me."

"Ned," she said, not understanding him. She started to cry. "This ain't no laughing matter."

Ned got serious when he saw how she was taking it. "Aw, Birdie. You take things so damned serious. Can't I have a little joke? I'm a free man. Turned loose for good behavior. Ain't nobody after me."

Ned looked around the room. It was cold in there, even with the little laundry stove going, because of the wind that came in through cracks in the floor that you could stick a pencil through. Ned rubbed his hands together and held them around the stovepipe. "Why ain't these kids in school?" as asked.

"It's too cold today," Birdie said. "They ain't got any shoes, and the frost was too thick for them to go barefooted when they ain't any too well anyway. Besides, they're ashamed to go barefooted on a day like this because of what the other kids say, and I don't blame them any."

"Well, they ain't gonna grow up in ignorance like we had to," Ned growled, "and never have a cent to their name."

In the room there was a stove, old and rusty, and on it a boiler that leaked; a bucket on the floor; the wash tub on a box; a pile of dirty clothes and a pile of clean clothes; irons and an ironing board; a few dishes and pans; and nothing else. Not even a chair. The four kids were huddled together on a ragged overcoat near the stove.

The oldest girl, eight, had on a sleeveless dress that looked as if it had been made out of a piece of worn-out carpet. Her feet were folded under her and you could see she had nothing on under the dress. The six-year-old boy was completely wrapped up, except for his head, in one of Ned's ragged coats. The four-year-old boy was likewise wrapped up in a sweater. The two-year-old girl had a piece of quilt around her.

"That there is Ory," Ned said as if he didn't quite believe it. "I been wonderin' about her a lot. She ain't growed a bit in the last year, has she?"

"Ory's slow," Birdie said. "She can't walk a step. Seems like her legs won't hold her up. They bend. Sissie's teacher come to visit us, and she said the kids ain't got the right victuals. But I been spendin' every cent on groceries that I didn't have to spend on rent and wood. I don't know what a body can do."

"God," Ned said, "these kids has been havin' it harder than me, and it ain't their fault if I git into trouble. But listen, from now on things is gonna be better in this family. We're gonna stick to farmin', an' no more corn whiskey."

Ned got happy and picked up the baby and tossed her to the

ceiling. The baby began to cry. Ned put her on his shoulder and patted her. "Scared of your dad, eh? Scared of your old dad. Well, from now on you don't need to be."

Birdie came around from the tub and wiped Ora's nose. Ora was still screaming. Birdie took her and hushed her and put her back on the overcoat.

Ned was feeling good now. "We're gonna move out to the country now," he said. "Maybe next week. We're gonna put in a crop. What about Sissie and Jimmie? They big enough to help?"

He grinned and grabbed up Sissie, nearly jerking her naked out of her rags, and threw her over his shoulder and spanked her.

"Daddie," Birdie said, "you got her dress up. Look at you!"

Ned put Sissie down and grabbed up each of the boys. Then he hugged Birdie. The kids huddled on the overcoat again. It was too cold to stand around, and there was no room to play.

"Where you all sleep?" Ned asked.

"In there," Birdie said. She went to work again over the tub.

"Where?" Ned asked slyly. He didn't even look where she pointed.

Birdie wrinkled her forehead. "In there," she said again.

"You show me," Ned said. "I can't see very well. Just come in outa the sun."

Birdie looked at him in astonishment. She went to the door, opened it, and pointed to a pile of rags in the corner. "There," she said.

Ned was looking over her shoulder. He pushed her into the room. "You kids stay where you are for a while," he said.

"Ned," Birdie said. "It's cold as ice in here. And I got to get that wash out."

When they came out five minutes later Ned gave each of the kids another hug. "I'm goin' down town, now," he said, "and see about getting a place and some cash, and we'll be movin' out to the country pretty quick. Maybe next week."

# THIRTEEN

JIM WAS PLOWING one warm morning in the fall when he saw Happy running across the field toward him. He knew that the baby was coming at last and he started unhitching before she got to him.

She was so excited and panting so hard that she could hardly get it out. "Jeannie's having the pains, and when you get the horses tended to you go over to our place, Jeannie said, and phone the doctor and tell dad." Happy stood there for a moment as if she felt something more should be said upon such an occasion. "I'm glad it is happening at last," she said, then she ran back.

Jim headed the team toward the barn and when the brown mare lagged to grab at a weed he popped her with the end of a line to impress her with the seriousness of it all.

This was a damned funny time to have a baby, with them so poor and maybe war coming and Jim would have to go and fight, but if people didn't have babies except when they could afford it there wouldn't be any human race.

Having a kid of your own would be a funny experience. Imagine a little cotton-top snot calling you dad. Jim would get him one of these cheap little 22's and teach him to shoot sparrows, and teach him a lot of things, and see that he got an education. But maybe it would be a girl.

When Jim got over to McGee's place and told him, the old man was more excited than Jim was. "By God, I'll be over right after the milkin' tonight. Reckon it won't happen much before that. I mean if everything goes all right. If things don't go right you tie a gunny sack on the windmill fan and I'll be right over. I can't leave here very easy because that horny cow is gonna have a calf and she's pretty old and I'm afraid it won't come easy or she won't clean herself out. I've got cow-cleaner to give her if I have to."

When Jim got back home he went into the bedroom. Jeannie was pale except for a red splotch here and there. Her belly stuck up like a haystack under the sheet.

"Hurt much?" he asked.

"No," she answered. "I'm gonna have an easy time of it. Did you tell dad?"

"Yeah, and he got so excited he like to jumped up and down, but he can't come over right away on account the horny cow is gettin' ready, and he wants to be there to see she gets cleaned out and all."

"Well, if he comes tearin' over here you send him back to tend to her. They ain't nothin' he can do here, and he's likely to let that cow die if you don't watch him."

Jeannie breathed hard and looked at the window shade where the sun came through in little points. "Glacys can do everything till the doctor comes," she said. "You didn't need to leave your work if you don't want to."

"Reckon I couldn't do any good at anything," he said. "We don't have a kid every day, and it makes me nervous. Maybe I'll go out to the barn and tinker around a little bit."

He knew Jeannie would feel better if he was at work so he went down to the barn. But there was not much use. He sat down on a half-bushel and took a chew. He was excited, but he wasn't very scared. He felt like he ought to be more scared than he was. Maybe Jeannie would die. But every time he thought of that he thought about Happy. He was so God-damned low down that something inside of him wanted her to die. Whenever he let himself think about marrying Happy he felt kind of wild, and felt like nothing else made a damn bit of difference. But you can't think things like that without kicking yourself all over the place. Jeannie was a good woman, and they'd had so much fun before they were married. She worked for him like a horse, and there wasn't any other man that she would ever look at. She pushed in the collar when he was loafing. He was God-damned low down not to be scared to death that she would die.

It was a good thing that people couldn't tell what he was thinking. He would commit suicide if anybody knew what went on inside him. But you can't help what goes on inside your brain.

Maybe you can't blame anybody for anything, because they do what they have to. You can't blame a rattlesnake for being a rattlesnake, but you got to hate him and kill him before he kills you. You can't blame a capitalist for making money. Anybody would do the same thing. But still if there is going to be any happiness in the world you've got to destroy the capitalists, just like rattlesnakes, and change the rules so there can't be any more capitalists. But then he quit thinking about it because everything seemed all balled up and he couldn't make head or tail of it.

The doctor came in the afternoon and Jim sat around in the kitchen and marked on the oilcloth with his thumb nail. The doctor was cheerful and said everything was going fine. He said he would use a little chloroform and Mrs. Tetley wouldn't suffer scarcely at all. Happy hurried in and out very excited but not saying much. Jim didn't look at her very often.

Jeannie cried out once in a while and Jim knew it was hurting. Then there was a scream that made the cold sweat come out on Jim. Jeannie was not one to take on, and when she yelled like that it was pretty bad.

Then for a while everything was quiet and Jim thought everything was over. The doctor came through the kitchen once to get something in his car and Jim asked him how it was going.

"Everything is all right," the doctor said, "only when she gets sleepy she quits working and I'll have to go easy on the chloroform. She's gonna have some pain. Lots of women are that way, and it don't mean anything."

The screaming started again and Jim got kind of sick listening. He couldn't imagine any such pain. Jeannie was completely licked, he could tell by her voice. It went on a long time.

"Oh, doctor! Quit! Help me! Let me die!" She was begging for anything in the world to stop the pain. Jim thought she would be awfully embarrassed at having a baby, and not make much of a fuss, but he knew that the pain was so awful she couldn't think of anything else.

Happy ran into the kitchen for something. "It's red-headed," she said.

"Is Jeannie—gonna pull through?"

"Sure—I guess so. The doctor ain't said anything, but he ain't scared—"

"Is it a boy or a girl?"

"It ain't born yet!"

Jim felt like he would go crazy. Red-headed, not born yet. Will she die? Why does anybody have to suffer like that? Jeannie had worked like a horse and been good to him. God, he didn't want her to die! He wanted her to live so he could do things for her and try to make up to her for all she had suffered.

Then after what seemed a long time the screaming stopped and Happy came out smiling. "It's a boy," she said. "God, Jim, what's the matter with you?"

Jim was sick. There was a splash of blood on Happy's apron. "I'm all right."

"The doctor's dousing it in hot and cold water to bring it alive." Happy returned to the room.

Jim got up and walked around the room. He was ashamed to be such a weakling. Then Happy came out of the bedroom with something wrapped up. She showed him a shriveled, red monkey-face—a horrible little animal with eyes tight shut. Its hair looked golden against the beet-red skin.

Jim was shocked at the sight. He had expected something kind of angelic, but this maybe was an idiot baby.

"Look at him!" Happy was saying. "Ain't he sweet! He's wonderful!"

Jim looked at her to see if she was serious. Maybe she was just trying to save his feelings. He didn't know what to say.

"Look at his little hand. Look how cute it is!" Happy fished a little possum hand out of the blanket. 'He's a perfect baby."

"How's Jeannie?"

"She's all right. The doctor said she come through it fine. Didn't have much trouble."

Jim didn't quite believe anything she said, but maybe she was right. He had heard that new babies looked funny.

At twilight old man McGee came in. He went straight to the basket where the kid was sleeping. "I be damned!" he said. "That's the finest lookin' kid I ever seen. Why, look at him! Jeannie and Gladys looked like the missing link when they was born, but look at this one! He's a dandy!"

"Jim says he looks awful," Happy said, pouting.

The old man snorted. "You don't know a damned thing about kids," he said to him. "You don't know a good-lookin' kid when you see one."

Jeannie was calling rather weakly from the bed.

"Dad," she said, "how's that cow?"

"How you feelin', sister?" he asked. "You got by fine, didn't you? I knew you would."

"How's the cow?"

"The cow? Oh, you mean the horny cow. All right. Fine. By God, Jim, you're ignorant—"

"Dad," Jeannie said desperately, "is it a heifer?"

"Oh, sure. Fine. You mean the calf? Yes, it's a bull. By God, you're lucky. Jim, you come out here a minute. Want to talk to you. You don't know how lucky you are."

When they were outside the old man pulled out a bottle of white corn. "That's the best lookin' baby I ever seen at his age. Here, take a drink, but don't let the wimmen folks know about it. It's a strain on a feller, bein' a father. I been through it."

Jim took a couple of swallows and shuddered, but he felt warm.

A thin, weak little "wa-a-a" sounded from in the house. "Listen, he's yellin'. Ain't that a fine pair of lungs? Le's go in and lissen at him."

They went in. Jim looked at the wrinkled little face, wide toothless mouth, red hands jerking impotently. "By God, he is kind of cute," he admitted. "I reckon I'll get used to him and claim him finally, like that yellow bitch with her first litter."

"You gonna call him *Jim*, ain't you?" the old man asked. "Jim, junior."

"Well, I guess we'll name him that, but on account of his hair we're gonna call him Sandy. That's what everybody will call him anyway when he grows up, and we might as well start now."

"His name is James," Jeannie said.

"I'm gonna call him Jimmie," Happy said.

"Naw, sir," the old man decided. "His name is just naturally Sandy, and they really ain't nothin' you can do about it. Jim is right. He's Sandy from now on."

FOURTEEN

THE WELLHOFS had moved to a lease not far from Tetley's place, and Mrs. Wellhof was the first neighbor woman to show up after the baby was born. A little after dark she came in and said that she was going to stay all night to "set up" with the mother and baby.

"I pitched in and fixed up my house work," Birdie said, "so's Ned could get along fine without me tonight and tomorrow. I says to him that he might as well make up his mind to it that wherever the's a teensie in the neighborhood there I'm gonna be, because they ain't no better hand with little babies than I am, anywhere. Now, the rest of you folks just go to bed like nothin' happened, because I know how tired everybody is with the strain and all. Well, look at him! Well I never! He raised up his little head! One of my cousins had a little baby that done that and the doctor said they ain't one baby in five hundred that can do that. That was the cutest baby you ever seen, and, you know, they lost him before he was six months old. My cousin was all broke up. Over where I come from they always wash a baby's head with stump water to make his hair grow, but you got to be careful not to get it too far down on his neck so he won't have too much hair on his neck. But I reckon that ain't really necessary because—I mean it ain't necessary to wash his head with stump water—because I bet they ain't a stump in this county with water in it right now, and in a dry country you can't get stump water if you looked you head off for it, and still the babies out here grow up with good hair. I guess if babies really had to have stump water the good Lord would have stumps everywhere with water in 'em. And, Jeannie, honey, if your hemrage ain't stopped like it ought to we'll burn chicken feathers under the bed. And Jim really ought to bury the afterbirth in the right-hand chimney corner, or is it the left-hand? I swear I can't remember. I think it's the right-hand. But you know when they ain't anybody got chimneys in this country how can you, I'd like to know? They ain't a one of my babies was born in a house with a chimney, and the pain always stopped anyway. I guess if you just had to bury the afterbirth in the right-hand chimney corner, or maybe it's the left-hand—I can't remember for the life of me, it's been so long—but I guess the good Lord would provide chimney corners for everybody if they had to have 'em."

Birdie was waddling around all of the time, trying to find something to pick up or straighten out, but when she finally decided that there was nothing to do she picked out a chair that she knew would hold her up and sat down on it.

"I declare, when Mack come over this evenin' and wanted some whiskey I knew right then that the baby was here, because that's just the way a man is, especially a grandfather. As soon as a baby comes he wants to get tanked up, and I can't blame him one bit, but that's the last drop of corn you'll ever git at our house, Mack, because Ned ain't makin' any more. That there is some he had buried when they caught him, and the bank just wouldn't let us have enough money to git started on, and so I let him go and dig it up and sell it to a few fellers that he knew was all right, and it ought to be the best corn you ever drunk because it's so old. Most of this stuff you git ain't a month old. But, anyway, that's the last you'll ever git at our house, because Ned ain't makin' any more. I don't care how poor folks is, they can't afford to make that stuff, because it don't pay in the long run."

Birdie was still talking when Mack, full of the ancient corn liquor, rolled off his chair sound asleep. Jim got him up and half dragged him to a bed in the other room and took the bottle of liquor out of his pocket.

When Jim came in from the milking the next morning at daybreak, Happy was ready to start home. "I've got to do our chores," she said, "because you couldn't wake dad up if you tried."

"Jim," Jeannie said, "you go with her, because there's too much for her to do. She's awful slow at milkin'."

"No, honest, I can do it."

"Naw, I'll go along," Jim said. His fingernails were kind of cutting into his hands. He knew he hadn't ought to go, but at the same time he wanted to.

They didn't say much at first as they walked along in the cool of dawn. Jim kept looking at the side of her face in the dim light. When they got into the blackjacks he put his arm around her and tried to say something, but his throat was too dry. He had what was left of Mack's liquor in his pocket, and he stopped and swallowed a good drink.

Happy watched him. "Is that stuff as good as Birdie claims?" she asked.

"It's smooth," Jim said. "Don't make you shudder much."

"Let me taste it."

"Happy, have you ever took a drink?"

"Sure, but don't you tell the old man."

"I didn't think you ever had."

"I ain't no angel, Jim, and I don't care if *you* know it, but I don't want dad or Jeannie to know it." She took the bottle from him and drank what was left.

"By God, you took a lot on an empty stomach!"

She held her hand over her face while the stuff burned down. "It'll wear off," she said, breathing with difficulty, "before we get the chores done and have to go back, but I'll be happy till then—like my name." She threw the bottle down.

Jim took her by the shoulders. "What you mean," he asked, "when you say you ain't no angel?"

"You know what I mean, or you ought to."

"You mean you—stepped out with some fellow?"

She nodded her head. He stood gripping her shoulders, and she held her head back with her eyes closed, feeling the liquor.

"Who was it, by God?"

"Maybe it was more than one, Jim. It ain't their fault. I didn't tell you this so you could go around raisin' hell with somebody. You're the only friend I got, and that's why I told you."

"Well, was it my fault maybe, because I loved you up and got you excited?"

"Of course it ain't your fault. You suppose you could love me up if I didn't want you to? It's *me*. It's the way I'm made—well, I suppose it's because I just couldn't stand not bein' popular. You know how it is. I don't have any decent clothes, and I got it into my head that the boys wouldn't look at me unless I was fast."

Jim suddenly felt very happy because of the liquor, "Hell," he said, "what difference does it make? A lot of girls step out before they are married. And they get by as good as the good ones. Maybe better. They have some fun. A person don't have but one life to live, and these people that don't ever have any fun they might as well be dead. You're a good kid, I don't care what you do, and I'd rather kiss you than anything on God's earth."

He started kissing her, and there was nothing to stop him. After a while they were down on the leaves beside the empty bottle. Jim was careful.

"I love you, Happy, by God, more than anything in the world, and I'm glad this happened. If I die right now my life was worth the trouble, and if this hadn't happened why it wouldn't be worth it if I got to be a millionaire and lived to be eighty."

"Well, I'm glad it happened, too," she said. "And you promise me that you won't ever be sorry, and I won't be sorry."

They got up and brushed the dead leaves from their clothing and went on to the house. Happy kept laughing at the way they couldn't walk straight.

"Life is worth it," Jim kept saying. "A fellow can get a hell of a lot out of life if just once in a while he does what he wants to. And I'm not sorry for a damned thing, and I won't ever be sorry."

When he had milked and fed the calves Happy had breakfast ready. "I been thinkin'," Jim said, "while I was milkin', that we're married this morning. Really married. Me milkin' and you in the house gettin' breakfast. Just this morning. But three hours of bein' married like this is more than most folks have in their whole life, because most folks get married so they can settle down and start gettin' ahead. That's the worst reason in the world for gettin' married. Just to get ahead. By God, I hate it! I hate the whole God damned system that makes geldings out of everybody except the capitalists."

As he finished eating she put her arms about him and her cheek on his. "You ain't gonna be sorry, are you?"

He picked her up and carried her into the other room.

He went home alone, and on the way the liquor wore off. He was scared, but not sorry. He thought about Jeannie and the little red baby and old Mack, but still he wasn't sorry.

The barnyard nagged at him like it always did. The bare cracked ground was littered with bent nails that horses might pick up. The henhouse door was off its hinges. The barn roof was sway-backed.

An old hen was out with three miserable chickens that she had managed to hatch out secretly somewhere because he hadn't gathered the eggs very carefully since Jeannie had been staying inside so much.

Manure was two feet thick on the barn floor and was hanging in little dobs to the ceiling where the horses had splashed it, fighting flies.

A bucket calf, shut in a little pen, was bawling. It had never been out of this pen since the hour of its birth. Jim went to the pen and yanked a couple of boards off and then stood back to watch the calf.

It looked at the gap for a while, then very cautiously stepped out. It leapt with fright at this new freedom, stuck its tail in the air, and started running straight toward the old hen and her miserable chicks. The hen stood her ground, swelling with indignation, and the calf swerved into a rickety wheelbarrow. But it was off again in a new direction the next instant, through the potato patch and into the fence. The wire squeaked in its staples and the calf was thrown hark on its haunches.

"You gotta learn," Jim said. "But after you learn you won't be so damned frisky."

Two bony horses came up to the tank and started drinking the blue-green water. Their throats squeaked as they drank, and air sucked in at the corners of their mouths where the bit had made round calluses. When they had finished drinking they hung their heads over the gate, wanting to be let into the barn, but Jim threw a cob at them.

"Get the hell back out to the pasture," he said. "You ain't workin' today."

He went to the house to look at the new baby. He felt good. "I'm a shiftless, no-account bastard," he thought, "but I don't give a damn."

 FIFTEEN

TED HAD A HABIT of coming out to Jim's place once in a while of an evening and talking about things, but it wasn't very pleasant now because Ted was getting very patriotic. He was in favor of going over to France and whipping the Kaiser to a stand-still.

"Damned Huns," he said, "hadn't ought to be allowed to live on the face of the earth, and this country ought to go over to Europe and end that war in short order."

Jim argued with him, and Jeannie just listened. Jim thought the war was just a rich man's war and a poor man's fight. "The capitalists," he said, "just drive us poor fools to war and get us killed off so they can make profits."

That made Ted mad. "You been readin' that damned *Appeal to Treason*," he said. "The Kaiser ain't got a better friend in this country than that sheet."

Then, one night in April, Ted came out with a newspaper. "We're in it now," he said, "and, by God, I wish I could go. There's nothin' I'd rather do than enlist and go over and fight them Huns. I wish I was—strong and all."

Jim was surprised at this. He couldn't remember ever hearing Ted talk about being crippled. All at once Ted looked like he was going to cry, and he got up and walked out without saying a word, and got in his car and left.

But Jim wasn't surprised about America's getting into the war. He read the newspaper out loud to Jeannie, and they talked a little. Jim couldn't say what he thought to Jeannie because she got scared and cried, and said Jim and her father and all Socialists would be shot or sent to jail.

"If you'd keep your mouths shut," she said, "both of you would be all right. Dad is too old to go to war, and you got a wife and baby."

That sounded sensible. Jeannie always had good common sense. Jim decided to take her advice and not talk about the war to anybody.

For the next two weeks he worked hard and didn't see anybody except Jeannie and the baby, and Mack once for a few minutes.

The old man was busy in some kind of Socialist activity. He even went out of the county once in a while. When he talked to Jim all he said was "By God, there's a lot stirrin' around here. I want to tell you all about it some of these days, but don't say anything to Jeannie. You just keep still, and don't say anything about it to anybody. We're tellin' all the fellers around here to keep still, and not talk war, till things shape up. Then we'll say a hell of a lot. And don't argue with that brother of yours any more."

Jim kept still, but all day long as he worked in the field he thought about it. And the longer he thought about it the madder he got.

Ted came out one night, weeks after war was declared, and left a bunch of magazines. "Here's some *decent* stuff," he said. "Not like your *Appeal to Treason*. Some of these are a month old, but they're good stuff. I want you to read 'em."

Jim was eating bread and milk. "Much obliged," he said.

Ted was standing in the door. "They tell me that a lot of these Socialists out here are pro-German."

"I ain't talked to any of 'em," Jim said.

Ted looked at him for a little while and then turned and left.

After Jeannie went to bed Jim read for quite a while in these magazines. He read an editorial that said it was a fine thing what had happened in Russia, the Czar being kicked out and so forth. It said that the Czar was a prisoner in a palace and had fits of crying.

There was a lot of fancy writing about Russia. "The revolution in Russia and the establishment of constitutional government in that great country have naturally aroused much enthusiasm among lovers of liberty in the United States. To celebrate this great event in the progress of democracy meetings have already been held in various places throughout the country. . . . Sympathetic meetings in this country are especially appropriate. They can be made the occasion not merely of expressing friendship for free Russia, but for reaffirming American faith in and loyalty to the great fundamental doctrine of the Declaration of Independence."

This sort of stuff made Jim tired. A lot of high muckey-mucks slingin' bull. Faith in and loyalty to the great fundamental doctrine—hell! Ted, the damned fool, swallowed that sort of stuff and thought it was great. And Ted was educated.

The magazine said that "The new Russia is preparing to fight to the end in unison with her allies and for the perpetuation of the self-government gained by the Revolution."

But what made Jim real sick was when the high muckey-mucks started to talking about God. One paragraph made him so mad that he wanted to slam the damn paper across the room. It was written by a fellow named Hoover. It said: "The world cannot stand by and witness the starvation of the Belgian people and the Belgian children; God still reigns, and other people must carry on the work. The obligation of the American people toward Belgium continues. It is an obligation toward humanity, and is far greater than the obligation of the rich toward the poor."

The rich sons-of-bitches start a war and make things so that a lot of poor people are starving to death—let alone the millions that get shot—and then talk about God still reigning and about the obligation of the rich toward the poor. The stinkin' bastards!

The magazine told what Wilson said to Congress: "Property can be paid for; the lives of peaceful and innocent people cannot be."

Jim had read enough about the war to see through that kind of bull. A bunch of capitalists had started it to settle their own argument as to who was to get the most profit. And now the lives of millions of peaceful and innocent people had to be sacrificed because of property. Woodrow Wilson knew it, too. He wasn't that much of a fool.

Wilson said: "The right is more precious than peace, and we shall fight for the things which we have always carried nearest to our hearts—for democracy, for the right of those who submit to authority to have a voice in their own governments, for the rights and liberties of small nations, for a universal dominion of right by such a concert of free peoples as shall bring peace and safety to all nations and make the world itself at last free."

Jim wished, by God, that he had an education so that he could write up some of the things he thought. He would like to write to this magazine and say what was in his mind. Of course, it wouldn't do a damned bit of good.

 SIXTEEN

ONE HOT MORNING when Jim stopped his team at the end of a row he found Mack there waiting for him. The old man didn't say anything at first but fixed a piece of gunny sack close over the throat of one of the mares so the flies couldn't sting her there. Then he walked around, looking at the harness and picking and sucking at his teeth. "I ain't told you much about what's goin' on," he said finally, "because it's kind of dangerous business, and if nothin's gonna come of it, why, I want you to be able to swear that you don't know nothin'. But it looks like hell's gonna break loose over this war business, and I'll know for sure about Wednesday. I'm goin' to Oklahoma City Wednesday with a fellow from the next county by the name of James— Bill James—that more or less heads things up over there. He's got his own car, and I wondered if you couldn't git off to go along. It won't cost you nothin', and you'd have a chance to see the country. We won't say nothin' about this business on the way down, and if nothin' comes of it we won't talk about it on the way back, so you'll be in the clear."

"Well, now, I ain't afraid of a little risk," Jim said. "And I'm gettin' hotter under the collar all the time at this God damned war, and just because you're my daddy-in-law you hadn't ought to protect me from everything."

"Well, on account of Jeannie and the kid you ought to keep out of it, if they ain't nothin' gonna come of it, but I'll let you know, by God, soon as there's anything you can do, and we'll know Wednesday. You think you can git off to go to the city?"

"Yeah, I can get off."

"We'll be around about sun-up," Mack said. He walked around the horses once more, arranging the fly nets, and then left.

Jim had felt mighty lazy that morning before he talked to Mack, but now he was excited and didn't mind working. He pushed the horses and got in an extra round before dinner. He decided to work hard all day Sunday so he wouldn't get behind on account of going to the city. The automobile ride to the city was something to think about. He had never ridden that far in an automobile. Maybe he would have a chance to see a show. Then he got to wondering again what the Socialists had up their sleeve. It seemed like life was going to get pretty exciting all at once, and he hoped it would. He was damned tired of being a work horse.

The next few days he worked hard and felt better than he had felt in a long time. He didn't sleep very much and didn't seem to need sleep. It was easy to work when he felt this way, and maybe people with ambition felt this way all the time.

One night, while he was milking, he decided that if the Socialists got into power and fixed things so that a man would have some chance in the world of getting what he wanted—if there was a big shake-up—he might get to be the most ambitious fellow in the country and work day and night.

You can't blame anybody for being lazy, he decided, if things are fixed so there's nothing worth doing.

Jeannie washed his white shirt and two collars, his necktie and handkerchiefs. She also cleaned his suit, and Tuesday night she worked late getting everything ironed. He went to bed early so as to get a good night's sleep, but he was so excited that it must have been after midnight before he dropped off. He dreamed about a horse that got tangled up in the harness and kept whirling around and around. Jim was so slow that he couldn't move. Finally it seemed that Jeannie was there, and the horse whirled over her and maybe killed her. Jim woke up scared. It was daylight and time to get up. Jeannie wasn't there. By the time he got the dream out of his mind he remembered that he was going to Oklahoma City and jumped out of bed in a hurry. He got dressed, and on the way out to milk he met Jeannie carrying a chicken that she had killed.

He finished the chores as fast as he could, and washed his hands in soap a couple of times to get the smell of the cow off of them. "I don't want nobody in the city to come up to me and say 'hist,' " he said. He shaved the best he could considering the light, and only cut himself once. Jeannie told him that he had left a patch of whiskers under his ear, and she stopped her work to shave him around the corners of his jaws.

He got into his clean clothes and walked around stiff-legged so he wouldn't hurt the crease in his pants. When he looked in the mirror he decided he must look funny with his face as red as a beet and a white collar on that was a little tight.

Jeannie set breakfast on the table, and he ate as much as he could although he wasn't very hungry. The sun was already up, but the car wasn't in sight. Jim kept looking down the road. He was afraid there had been a breakdown. Jeannie had his lunch packed—fried chicken, bread and butter and pickles, and a jar of preserves—enough for all three in case the others didn't bring any lunches. "I know dad won't have a thing," she said, "unless Gladys makes him take something, and she's about as careless as he is. He would rather spend a quarter at some expensive restaurant for a meal not half as good. Now, you make 'em eat every scrap of this," she said. "It will be bad enough to stop in some place for supper, but I can't very well fix up your supper too for fear it would spoil in this hot weather."

Jim rolled a cigarette and walked up and down stiff-legged, looking out of the window. He felt sure that something had gone wrong. He offered to cook Jeannie some pancakes, but she knew he would spill batter on his clean suit.

Finally there was a cloud of dust and a car appeared sure enough. It looked like a big car and not a Ford. Jim picked up his coat and lunch, but waited on the porch until he was sure that it was the right car. Cars passed sometimes, and people would think he was crazy if he went running out at them. So he waited until he saw Mack in the front seat, then he ran out to the road forgetting all about his creases.

It was a big car sure enough, with six cylinders. An Oakland, almost as good as a Buick six.

"Jim, this here is Bill James I told you about," Mack said.

"Proud to meet you," Bill said.

Jim got in the back seat and pulled up his trousers legs as far as he could.

"I guess you fellers won't mind if we make a little time," Bill said. He was a small man and had a red face like a farmer, but you could tell he had money because of the car and his clothes.

"I'm plenty safe," Bill said, "but I tell you what I done the other day. I beat the train into Shawnee. I started when it pulled out of the station and I was a half of a quarter ahead of it when I got to Shawnee. Of course I had to throw considerable sand when I turned corners. On a road like this I didn't get under twenty-five, and on good stretches I had it up to fifty or sixty."

Jim leaned forward and rested his hands on the back of the front seat. "Is it hard to learn to drive a gear-shift car?" he asked.

"It's easier," Bill answered, "to drive a car like this than a Ford, as soon as you get used to it. I can drive any kind of car except a White Steamer, and this kind is the easiest kind to drive."

He pulled out of the ruts so that one wheel was in the center of the road and one in the sandburs. "One thing you got to watch, and that is high center. These big cars ain't got the clearance that a Ford has got. First thing you know you're hung up if you don't watch."

They rode along at a good clip, and going down a long hill Jim felt a funny feeling inside. Bill kept talking about automobiles, tires, and self-starters.

Once they were plowing along through deep sand when they met another car, and neither car could get out of the ruts. Jim watched the car ahead coming slowly toward them, its wheels cramped, and tightened up all his muscles trying to help. Bill stopped and backed a ways, and the other car stopped and two men got out. They started pulling weeds and placing them in the ruts. Bill, Jim and Mack got out and helped them, then the driver of the other car started it, and everybody else pushed. This way they got both cars out of the ruts, and with a good deal of pushing got them past each other. Jim's clean shirt was sweaty by this time, but he cooled off when they got started again.

Once they passed a scary team which reared up and jerked the wagon out into a ditch. The farmer driving them looked pretty mad, but Jim looked back and saw that they got back into the road all right.

"You know," Mark said, "it's old horses that raise the most hell about automobiles, and not young colts. The old ones can't get used to 'em. I got an old horse, he must be twenty, and he's worked around a threshing machine all his life so he ain't a bit scared of a machine and will stand there and go to sleep with the big belt an inch from his ear. And a threshing machine makes a hundred times more racket than a car. But when that old fool sees a car, by God, he turns himself wrong side out. It just don't look right to him to see a buggy runnin' around without no horses hitched to it. And I don't blame him none. There's a lot of things I can't git used to, like the way these young girls run around nowadays. It just don't look right to me, although I reckon I'm like that old horse. All the kind of hell-raisin' I got used to when I was a kid seems all right to me, but when they git out in these damned automobiles and start huggin' each other at thirty miles an hour it makes my hair stand on end."

There was a pig in the road and Bill slowed up and passed it cautiously. "By God, a fat hog is the worst thing in the world to run over," Bill said, "because they're so low and solid. They'll turn the damned car over before you know what happened. A bunch of yearlin's is bad to get through. A young heifer is just as likely as not to jump right in front of you. Colts is got a lot more sense, although they do jump in front of you sometimes. The silliest damned thing is a chicken. An old hen will get clear out of the road on one side, then all at once she'll change her mind and sail right under the wheels. You'll see up here when we get to the good roads where there is lots of cars, you'll see chickens mashed flat on the road just like the picture of a chicken on the road. But nobody ever run over a guinea. They're too damned quick and smart. You couldn't run over one if you tried."

When they got to the main road Bill speeded up, and Jim from the back seat watched the speedometer. Thirty, forty, fifty, sixty, and finally, down a long hill, sixty-five miles an hour. More than a mile a minute. About twice as fast as a Ford would go. He kept thinking about what if a wheel would break or the steering gear break. He felt easier when Bill eased up to about forty. Forty miles an hour was damned fast, but it seemed safe after sixty-five. He leaned back in the seat and took it easy. He felt tired like he had been at work.

The wind was whistling past and he stuck out his hand to feel it. The wind pushing against the palm of his hand was cool and soft and felt like it was alive. It felt like Happy's arm. He closed his fist and the sensation was gone. The wind whipped the hairs on the back of his hand and gave him a funny feeling.

He leaned his head back and closed his eyes and opened his hand to feel the arm in the wind. He thought about Happy and wished to hell she was along to ride sixty-five miles an hour and have all these experiences. He wondered what he wanted more than anything else in the world, and he decided that the best thing in the world would be to be married to Happy and have a car like this and be going off somewhere on a honeymoon to God knows where, maybe to the Grand Canyon that his dad used to tell about. He imagined Happy there beside him, smelling the wind with her little round nose and smiling with her big mouth. But thoughts like these made him feel empty and hopeless because he knew damned well that nothing like that could ever happen to him in God's world and he might as well not make himself miserable thinking about it.

The car hit a rut and tossed him up and he came out of his thoughts. He leaned forward and yelled to the other two: "Say, fellers, when you think it's time to eat dinner let's stop some place where we can get water and eat this lunch I got. There's a lot of it, and it'll just spoil if it ain't et up today."

"Well, now," Bill said, "I just figgered we would stop somewheres and buy us something."

"They ain't no use of buying anything," Jim argued. "Because this stuff won't last."

After some debate they pulled up at a farm house and asked the woman if they could eat their lunch there and get a drink afterwards. She said "Sure, jist help yourself. There's a dipper at the pump."

Eating chicken and bread and butter Jim got philosophical. "You know, by God, a feller sticks around home so much, workin' all the time, that when he *does* git out once in a while on a trip like this he just don't know how to act. A feller ought to arrange to get away oftener or he just kind of dries up and dies workin', forgets that there's anything but work in the world."

"Well, by God," Mack said, "there'll be a time when it will be so a feller won't have to work fourteen hours a day, and will have money to do *with*. I used to think I'd never see it, but maybe I will, and maybe I won't."

"Well," Bill said "my dad left me a little money, and I got things a little easier than lots of fellers, but still I know that things ain't like they ought to be, or like they could be, and I'm ready to organize and get together with everybody else that's poor as I am or poorer, and as soon as us fellers git organized they ain't nothin' we can't do."

This was all that was said about socialism on the way to the city.

They finished eating, and each took a big drink. Bill poured a dipper of water into the radiator and looked at each one of the tires. Then they got into the car, waved at the ragged little kids who were watching them from the doorway of the farm house, and drove off. Jim thought that those little kids must look upon them as very rich and important fellows, riding in a car like this.

It was hot and dry here, and the roads were dusty so that a layer of dust settled over everything. It was still early, not yet noon, when Bill pointed out the state capitol. It was a huge building standing on a hill 'way off from everything else. Off to the southwest you could see the Colcord building, twelve stories high, towering over the other buildings. "Have you ever been up in the Colcord building?" Bill asked. "You ought to go up in it to ride on the elevator and to look down at the streets from up there. It's quite a sight."

Soon they were on pavement and the car rode as smooth as a train. They passed many horses who were not at all afraid of cars. The horses' hooves clattered as they trotted along. There were many other cars. Jim counted twenty lined up along the curb on one block.

Jim couldn't imagine how it would be to drive a team of horses along a street like this, with cars honking, people rushing around, and street cars grinding past. There were fellows on the streets selling newspapers who yelled all the time like carnival barkers and it made you feel like you were at a carnival all the time.

It was surprising how the horses and mules got used to it. Jim saw a team of mules standing dozing in the midst of all this clamor while their driver was delivering ice, and a street car came past, clanging its gong, so close to one of the mules that the mule's collar scraped along the side of the car, and the mule didn't pay any attention. Any horse Jim owned would go hog-wild in a place like this.

Bill pulled up to the curb and pointed to a large building. "That there is the Huckins Hotel," he said, "and if you fellers want to make water or anything we can go there in the basement. It's a swell place, all marble. Ain't much like a farmer's privy. Seems like a shame to use a place like that, but that's what it's for."

"Well now, we better make some arrangements," Mack said. "Bill, do you know this place we're goin' to?"

"Yeah, I know where it is."

"Well now, me and you'll go over there and see how things is, then we can meet Jim somewheres around here about four o'clock, and in the meanwhile Jim can run around and see the sights."

"Yeah, we'll meet right here at the Huckins. There's seats in there where you can set down and nobody will bother you, and stay as long as you please."

Jim got out of the car and stretched his legs and wiped the dust off his face with one of his clean handkerchiefs. He walked along the street slowly after Mack and Bill had driven off, and took his bearings carefully so he would be able to find the hotel again later.

 SEVENTEEN

Jim decided to go into the hotel and look around. There wasn't any law against it. He had always heard that it was an expensive place and very swell. Nobody would know but what he had business there.

Carrying his coat over his arm, he walked in. There were lots of people hurrying in and out but some were standing around, and on the lounges here and there fellows were sitting and smoking, talking or reading newspapers. The ceiling was two stories high and very fancy. The place was fixed like a big barn with a driveway where you brought in a load of hay and on each side a loft. Only it was very high and you couldn't pitch hay into the loft from the top of the biggest load, let alone clean out the wagon. He had a funny feeling, supposing himself to be driving his old mares in here with manure on their legs, and starting to pitch crab-grass hay into the lap of the swell ladies sitting 'way up there looking down.

There was a big flag hanging down out of one loft. A couple of pigeon-breasted army officers came strutting past and looked at Jim, as if from habit, wondering why he hadn't enlisted maybe.

A young fellow in a hotel uniform was walking around fast and yelling out something that sounded like, "Calling Mistah Feenah, please. Calling Mistah Feenga, please. Calling Mistah Peanut, please," over and over again.

It took quite a while for Jim to figure out why the fellow was doing this, then he wondered what he would do if the fellow started yelling, "Calling Mistah Tetley, please." It scared him some. He wouldn't know what to do. He couldn't yell out, "Hey, I'm Mister Tetley," and have everybody stop talking and look at him and say to themselves, "*He's* Mister Tetley." He decided he would sneak out and pretend he didn't hear.

He saw a stairway going down, and over it was a sign, "Barber Shop. Men's Toilet." He knew he had to go some place, but for a while he couldn't get up enough nerve to go down. He knew where there was a bathroom in the cheap little hotel where he stayed the other time he was in Oklahoma City, but if he didn't have a room there they wouldn't let him use it. Then he decided that, by God, he was as good as anybody else, and a lot better man than anybody standing around here, and why the hell should he be nervous in a place like this?

He walked down the stairs and saw that in each corner of a step there was a white place painted there. He couldn't figure it out until he saw a spittoon at the bottom of the steps. The corners were painted white to keep fellows from spitting in them. He felt more at home to think that fellows in a place like this would chew tobacco and spit.

The men's toilet was swell, like Bill had said. He saw where to go after looking around a little. A Negro with a white coat on was standing near with a whiskbroom, and the Negro looked Jim up and down but didn't say anything.

Jim looked at himself in a big mirror and wondered why it was that when he got dressed up he didn't look like much, but when he had on his old greasy overalls he looked pretty good.

He realized all at once that he was tireder than if he had done a day's work, but he forgot about it the next minute.

He went back up to the main floor. The whole thing still

seemed like a carnival, with the newsboys outside yelling at the tops of their voices, and it seemed like all hell had broke loose suddenly, but he saw a Negro walking around sleepy-like, sweeping the floor with a big push broom, and he realized that all this was just an ordinary every-day affair and nobody thought anything of it.

Jim went outside and walked along. Most of the people were in a hurry. He saw a policeman, and he walked faster because he knew it was against the law to block the sidewalk. Jim didn't know much about officers, except Sam Gladson, the old sheriff back home, but he didn't want to get mixed up with them.

It would be swell to live in the city. If he had it to do over again he would manage to get an education somehow and live here in the city, until he began to get old, maybe, then he would move back to the farm.

He stopped in front of a picture show and looked at the pictures outside to see what was on that night. But he saw that there was a pretty girl in the ticket booth and a sign over it saying, "Now Playing. Lower Floor 35. Balcony 25. Vaudeville." He got to thinking about it and decided that he might go, right then. He looked at his shadow and saw he had plenty of time. He made up his mind and got a quarter out of his pocketbook. Balcony was good enough. Without wasting any more time he walked up to the booth, paid his quarter, and got a green ticket. The girl was chewing gum and didn't even look at him.

He walked along a brass fence to a fellow in uniform who took his ticket, also without looking at him, and pointed to a stairway and said, "That way, please." The stairway was dark, with little green lights here and there and thick carpets. A pretty girl with perfume all over her almost bumped into him. He turned a corner and everything was black as pitch, except that way down below him was the screen and on it a soldier blowing a trumpet, then a flag was waving, then smoke and a line of soldiers running into the smoke, then a title saying, "Ready to Give Their All."

Jim couldn't see a thing in the balcony except a row of little lights along the aisle. He went down as far as he could, to a brass fence, and felt for a seat to be sure he wouldn't sit in anybody's lap, like he had done once.

It was a war picture, with smoke and airplanes, and an old mother back home on the porch, and so on. At first he was sorry he had paid a quarter for this kind of junk, but the picture was exciting, and pretty soon he forgot all about not being patriotic and was tickled when he saw a bunch of Huns captured.

When the feature show was over he looked around in the theater and was surprised that now he could see quite well, and was amused when people came down the aisle and felt of him.

The comedy was good. It was about a girl who went bathing, and once for an instant you saw her naked so far away that you couldn't really see anything. A goat ate up her clothes and then started after her, and every minute you thought you would see something, but you never did. There was always a bush or something in the way. She must have been naked, though, and Jim wondered how they made a picture like that. There must have been a camera man and a lot of other men around when the picture was being taken, and they would have to see her stark naked for hours and hours. He wondered how a fellow could stand anything like that, or how the girl could stand it. He wondered if Happy could do anything like that if she got paid enough for it. The girl in the picture had a sort of sweet innocent face. Did she have to stop once in a while and give herself to the moving picture men in order to keep her job?

In the vaudeville a bunch of girls with almost nothing on danced around. There was a good orchestra. Jim wondered if fellows in the audience with lots of money went around to the stage after the show and picked out one of the good-looking girls, and how much it cost. He would like to get acquainted with a girl like that and just talk to her and find out all about her. If she was a sport, how did she get to be one?

Did girls like that ever get married and have children, or what became of them? How would it feel to discover that a woman you had married had been a show girl? A man who had an education and lived in the city and made money might have an experience like that and not be a damned bit happier than a country jake in the long run.

Or maybe you would get used to things like that so that it wouldn't make a damned bit of difference how many men your wife had slept with.

He saw the first part of the feature picture and it made him mad. A lot of patriotic bunk about a young fellow enlisting and leaving his sweetheart and his old mother. And the dog followed him and, he sent the dog back saying, "Not this trip, old pal." It made you sick at the stomach. Jim was sorry he had forgot himself and enjoyed the last part of the picture.

He got up and left and went outside and was surprised at the sunlight. It was so bright he couldn't see very well for a while. He knew it was afternoon, of course, but he had got to thinking it was night without realizing it, and he was surprised to see that it was broad daylight.

He walked fast to the hotel, wondering if it was past time to meet the other fellows, but when he got there it was not quite time yet. This time he felt at home in the place. He went down the stairs with the white corners, then came back up and sat down in one of the lounges. There was a spittoon there but he didn't like to chew because he didn't see anyone else around there chewing, so he went to the cigar counter and bought a couple of cigars, two for a nickel. That made thirty cents he had spent that day on foolishness, but this was the first time he had spent any money that way for a long time. He went back and sat down. The hotel fellow was running around yelling, "Calling Mistah Bandeh, please. Calling Mistah Bendah, please. Calling Mistah Bandow, please."

Jim was tired as hell. In spite of all the heat and noise he got drowsy and nodded, and his cigar dropped out of his hand on to the thick carpet and he grabbed it up in a hurry.

 EIGHTEEN

HE WAS LOOKING at a swell-dressed woman when something hit him on the shoulder. He jumped and looked around, and there stood Bill and Mack smoking cigars. "By God, he was sound asleep," Mack said.

"Naw, I wasn't either," Jim said. He stood up and scratched under his sleeve holders.

"Well now, I think we might go somewheres for grub," Bill said. "This here hotel is expensive."

"Yeah, it's too expensive," Mack agreed. Jim was scared just to think about eating at a place like this.

"I know where there's a cafeteria," Bill said, "where you wait on yourself and save money that way."

Jim didn't have any idea how to wait on himself, and he felt like he would pull a bonehead and everybody would laugh at him. "I guess I wouldn't know how to act at a place like that," he said.

"You won't have no trouble," Bill said. "You just watch me and you won't have no trouble." He started off, and Mack and Jim followed, but before they got out somebody was yanking at Jim's sleeve. He looked around and was scared to see one of the hotel fellows pulling at him. It came to him that he was supposed to pay for sitting in the chair and he turned red, but the fellow told him that he had left his coat in the chair.

"Oh!" Jim said. "Yeah." He started trotting back to the chair but remembered that he hadn't ought to run in a place like this because he hadn't seen anybody else running. He cussed himself. Just when he was getting kind of used to the place he pulled a damn fool stunt like this.

When he got back to Bill and Mack he felt like everybody there must be looking at him. "I hadn't ought to brought this damned coat," he said.

"Yeah, you'll need it on the way back," Bill said, and then started talking about something else like it wasn't at all important that he had forgot the coat. As they walked along Jim got to feeling better. Anyway, he didn't have to pay for using the chair, and that was something.

They had to stop and wait in one place for a freight train to go past, and quite a crowd collected. It was surprising how many automobiles and teams lined up on each side of the track while the train was passing. Finally the caboose went past and everybody rushed forward.

Then, a block farther, they had to cross the street and this wasn't easy because of the street cars and automobiles, but they got safe across and Bill took them into a rather large building. Jim didn't see anything that looked like an eating place, but Bill led them into an elevator and said "cafeteria" to the man who was running it. A fat woman followed them in and they took their hats off. More people came in until the thing was full, then the operator closed the door. There was a buzzing noise and the elevator started up. You felt like your feet would push through the floor. When it stopped your heels went up. The door opened, and people walked out.

They went into a big room full of rattle and talk and hung up their hats and coats. "You take one of them trays," Bill said, "and a knife and fork and napkin, and then you slide the tray along the rail and pick out what you want. It's easy. You follow me."

Jim watched Bill and whenever Bill made up his mind and pointed to something Jim said, "I'll take the same." Women in white dresses behind the counter put the stuff on your plate. They walked past a woman at a cash register and Bill said, "All on one." Mack started arguing and the two argued while the woman was punching keys, but finally Bill got a slip of paper and they went to a table.

It was damned good stuff, and Jim felt like he could eat more, but when he was through he felt full. Mack and Bill argued all through the meal about who would pay for it, and Bill finally won.

Jim looked around and saw that there wasn't a single fly in the place. The water was ice cold with pieces of ice floating in it, too cold to drink. Jim wished for a dipperful of cool well water. He couldn't seem to drink enough ice water to satisfy his thirst. It hurt his throat.

When they had finished they walked out past another woman and Bill handed her two dollars and twelve cents. That was the price of the three meals. Jim figured up how much each meal was and he couldn't believe it. He had never in his life paid more than a quarter for a meal.

They got in the elevator, and going down was a lot worse than going up. Your feet seemed to leave the floor almost until you didn't weigh a thing, and a horrible ticklish stabbing feeling started between your legs and went up into your belly. It seemed like your hair stood up. Jim caught his breath and held onto a hand-rail. He was glad when the thing stopped.

"By God, that's a funny feelin'," Mack said when they got off.

"In some skyscrapers," Bill said, "they drop like that ten stories, and when you get to the bottom you've got to stop and swallow all your guts because they've lodged in the top of your head."

"Looks like a fellow would go crazy runnin' one of them things," Jim said.

"Aw, he don't notice it at all," Bill explained. "In the city you get used to so darned many things, and you don't think nothin' of 'em."

Mack and Bill told Jim that some mighty big things had been arranged that afternoon and that he was going with them to a meeting that night and would hear all about it, but they had orders not to speak about it outside of meetings. The three of them walked around the streets for a while, and sometimes Bill would point out a woman to them and say, "She's a chippy. How'd you like some of that, eh?" Jim usually didn't believe him because how in the hell could he tell at first sight?

Jim didn't think much about this socialist business until quite a while after dark when they got in the car and started some place to the meeting. Mack and Bill quit talking then, as men do just before a funeral service starts. They rode quite a ways along the city streets, and Jim wondered how Bill could remember the way. Sometimes they passed a street car. When they met another automobile the lights were so bright that it was hard to see the road.

The wind had come up and it was almost hot. It waved the branches of the trees around the street lights so that the whole street seemed to be alive. Finally they pulled up by the sidewalk and got out and walked up to a two-story house. Bill knocked on the door and a man looked out, and Bill said something to him and he said, "Come in." They went into a hallway and then into a big living room. The plaster was off of the ceiling in one place. An electric light hung down from the ceiling and swung back and forth a little bit because the wind was shaking the house. About a dozen fellows sat around and talked in low tones.

Mack went up to one fellow and said something to him, then motioned to Jim to come over. "This here is Comrade Stevenson, the state secretary," Mack said. "This here is my son-in-law, Jim Tetley. He's with us."

"How da do," Comrade Stevenson said. He was kind of lean, with a big Adams apple and a long mustache. They shook hands.

Then Mack took Jim around and introduced him to the other fellows, but Jim didn't remember any of the names.

The next fellow to come in was Fred Niek, the famous Socialist speaker. "How da do," he said, and went around shaking hands with the comrades. Then Stevenson pounded on the table, and everybody sat down and got quiet. "This here is a special meeting," Stevenson said, "and most of you comrades know what it was called for. We decided to get Comrade Niek here to find out whether he was a red Socialist or a yellow Socialist."

Jim looked at Niek. The room was still and all you could hear was the wind outside. Niek had just filled his pipe and now he was lighting it. Every time he sucked on the stem the flame of the match turned down and stuck its nose into the tobacco.

"All right, poys, go ahead and shoot," Niek said. He shook the match and looked around for some place to put it, then he threw it into a corner.

"Well, Comrade Niek," Stevenson said, "here's how things are stacked up. We're gonna stop this God damned war."

Niek puffed a while then he asked, "How you poys gonna stop this Got damned war?"

"The Working Class Union has got a hundred thousand members with guns and ammunition all ready to march to Washington. We're gonna take over the gover'ment. We're gonna start a march to Washington pretty damned quick, and we want to know if you're with us. Comrade Carson here is head of the Oklahoma army." Stevenson pointed to a big, rather fat man in the corner of the room.

"Well, poys," Comrade Niek said after he had puffed two or three times. "I want to give you some advice, and you won't like it. You poys petter scatter, right now, in ten minutes, and get out of town, and get out of the state as soon as you can." He raised his voice. "I'm talkin' loud now so the dictaphone can get it. Eferything you're saying here tonight will pe on file in Washington tomorrow morning. If you got a hundred thousand members you got two, three hundred government spies, some of 'em paid detectifes and some of 'em folunteers. For one mont' now wherever I go, if I leave my suitcase in my room or anywhere else, somepody goes t'ru it as soon as my pack is turned. Whenefer I set down to eat a meal a trafeling salesman comes along and talks to me.

"Now you poys forgit all about stoppin' this war and scatter out very thin. You petter hide your guns and ammunition where you can't never find 'em. It's a goot thing the light is bad in here and I didn't wear my glasses tonight so I couldn't see none of you fellers plain, and if the dicks pick me up and peat hell out of me I still couldn't remember what none of you looked like. And now you found out I'm a yellow Socialist, and the reason is, I guess, that even though I'm a Dutchman I know more about this country than you fellers. Well, goot luck."

He stood up and put on his hat and walked out.

"Well," Comrade Stevenson said as soon as Niek was gone, "I guess you fellers was right when you said he was yellow. It's too bad, but that ain't gonna stop us. Comrade Carson, have you got something to say?"

Comrade Carson stood up and walked to the table and pulled up his trousers. "I know you comrades are not going to be discouraged by what this fellow Niek just said." Carson talked smooth and easy, like he knew just what he wanted to say. Jim knew that he was an orator. There was something peculiar about Carson's appearance and at first you couldn't tell what it was, but Jim saw after a while that Carson didn't have any eye teeth, but just a narrow space between his other teeth where the eye teeth were supposed to be.

Jim was pretty scared by what Niek had said because he hadn't heard the other side of the story, but after Carson talked a while he wasn't afraid to go into this thing. "A fellow has to take risks," Carson said, "and I guess if you fellows have to be shot you'd rather be shot at Washington, fighting the capitalists, than be shot in France fighting the working people of Germany. If every Socialist and I.W.W. and W.C.U. member was as timid as Niek, of course, what he said would be true, but they are not, and more than a hundred thousand of us will prove it.

"You all got your orders. This new man—," Carson pointed at Jim. "What's your name?"

Jim was so taken aback that he couldn't answer, but Mack answered for him.

"He's Jim Tetley," Mack said. "My son-in-law."

"He comes from your part of the country?"

"Yeah, lives close to me."

"All right, Comrade Tetley. You're under Comrade McGee's orders, and you do what he tells you to until you get other orders."

Jim nodded.

There was some more talk, but the meeting broke up early. Jim, Mack and Bill got in the car and started home. They talked some about the rebellion that would start that July. There would be an army in western Oklahoma, one in central Oklahoma, and one in the eastern part of the state. On a certain day all three armies would meet and would join up with other armies from other states, and the whole crowd would march to Washington. When the American working class heard about what was happening, men would join by the millions, and there would be no stopping them.

It was hard to believe what was happening. You worked along for years and nothing happened any more exciting than a coyote stealing chickens, then all at once you were riding along at forty miles an hour late at night talking about the revolution that was going to start in a few weeks, right here and now. When things happened they happened so fast that it made your head spin.

"Say, Jim," Mack said. "Didn't Ted give you a Springfield rifle, 45-70, that was made for the army in the Spanish-American War?"

"Yeah, he picked it up for a few dollars somewhere and thought I could kill coyotes with it."

"Well, you order a batch of ammunition for it from Montgomery and Ward."

NINETEEN

JIM DREADED to tell Jeannie about this thing that the Socialists planned to do. On the morning after his trip to Oklahoma City he thought about it while he was milking. He had a habit of thinking things over while he milked and it slowed him up so that sometimes it seemed to take hours to finish the milking.

He wondered why it was that he dreaded to tell Jeannie things, or that he lied to her or didn't tell her everything, which was the same thing. He knew that if he was married to Happy he could tell her everything and not dread it. The reason Jeannie was not like him or Happy or the old man was that she wanted to make good. That's all she thought about.

It wasn't always your own fault if you told a lie. Sometimes it was the fault of the person you lied to, or sometimes it was the fault of conditions. The big capitalists were the worst liars and thieves in the world. That's the way they got ahead. If people tried to get ahead and stay honest, like Jeannie, they didn't get ahead, but they turned into drudges, and other people lied to them and stole from them. Any way you looked at it, it was this damned competitive system that made people liars and thieves.

Now Jim was ready to risk his life to help change the damned system, and he dreaded to tell Jeannie about it.

But there was no way of putting it off, so during breakfast he told her everything that had happened. She was working on a batch of bread and kept her back to him, but he could hear her sniffle. When he had finished he waved his hand over the butter dish to scare away a swarm of flies, and two of the flies got bogged down. He fished them out with a spoon and threw them on the floor. Jeannie blew her nose on her apron, and said, "Well, if you and dad are willing to risk your lives, and mine and the baby's, on a wild goose chase to Washington, I guess there's nothing for me to do but stay to home and do all the farm work by myself. I ain't got enough to do as it is."

She always tried to make it seem like everything he wanted to do, whether it was taking a cow to the bull or fighting against the capitalist system, was just to get out of work. It made him mad. "Yeah," he said, "you stay at home and work your fingers to the bone, and me and Mack will go on a nice vacation to Washington and have a big dance in the White House and fool around with the pretty girls." He got up and went out without saying anything else.

A few days later when Jim had to quit work and go around the neighborhood talking to farmers Jeannie didn't say a word. She was real good about it. She felt like her first duty was to her men folks.

Jim's job was to go around and talk to farmers that he knew and find out what they thought about the war. And if he could get them to admit that this was a rich man's war and a poor man's fight he told them about a meeting that was going to be held at Center Point, a country school house in the neighborhood. That way he got a couple of dozen of them to promise to come. Most of them were the poorest farmers in the neighborhood, tenant farmers who could not borrow money at the banks because they had voted the Socialist ticket. Some of them were Negroes, and a few were half-breed Indians, half white or freedmen.

On the night of the meeting Carson was there. The school

house was crowded. There was not much oil in the lamp, and the wick was so short that one of the farmers had to shake the lamp every few minutes to keep it burning.

By God, Carson was a real orator. He talked about the horrors of war, about men with their faces shot off, still alive and eating through a tube, about fellows with their guts shot out crying what would become of their babies back home. Then he told about the rich devils who didn't have to go to war but made millions selling ammunition not only to their own country but to the enemy country, and laughing about how they could make working men shoot each other to pieces.

Then he told about the Working Class Union, which had nine million members all over the world and more than a hundred thousand in America. The W.C.U. was going to start a march to Washington in July and put an end to this slaughter, and kick the capitalists out of power forever.

He asked how many wanted to join the W.C.U., and every hand in the room went up. Jim wished to hell that Jeannie could have been there and heard the speech. She would have changed her mind, maybe.

It gave you a lot of confidence to see all these fellows excited about what was happening. If the people in this part of the country felt this way it was likely that people in other communities felt the same way, and it was just a matter of organizing.

He had always thought of socialism as something a long ways off, something to argue about, like an after-life, but not anything which might happen right away, say the middle of next month. You'd be working around the barn on one of these ordinary hot days and the revolution would come due, like a debt at the bank, before you knew it. A line of men marching through the fields, cutting fences and turning cattle loose, burning bridges and cutting telephone lines. Taking over towns and dragging bankers out of their chairs and printing the truth in newspapers, and telling the poor to come in and be issued what they needed from the local stores, and marching on and meeting the enemy, fighting at crossroads and bridges and in the timber. He knew what marching through the country would be like from hearing his grandfather tell of marching through Georgia.

But Sherman's army was never welcomed by the people, and the revolutionary army would be. After thinking about these things, as in a dream maybe, it made the back of your neck get cold and the roots of your hair wiggle to realize that it was all starting three weeks from yesterday. You went nuts all at once and yelled with the other fellows and stamped your feet.

Carson had to warn them not to get too excited and not to talk about it except among themselves. "Wait for the word, and don't go off half-cocked," he said.

Carson told them that Mack was their local commander and that they should order guns and ammunition right away from a mail order house. "If you got a good shotgun," he said, "order buckshot, but if you ain't got a gun order a high-power rifle and plenty of cartridges."

After the meeting the men stood around and talked. They were rarin' to go, as they said. The sooner the better.

The next day Jim's 45-70 cartridges came. He cleaned the rifle carefully, stuck a few shells in his pocket, and went out into the timber.

He walked a long time, trying to imagine how it would be to fight a capitalist army, and how he would feel shooting a man.

He saw a big jackrabbit with his ears up about a hundred yards away, and took careful aim. He knew enough to press the rifle against his shoulder, just like he did a shotgun, because it kicked. He took a fine sight, because a gun like that would not have a drop to amount to anything at a hundred yards.

He pulled the trigger. There was a crash louder than a shotgun and a hard chug against his shoulder. It was a good shot. The rabbit was almost blown in two. A man at two hundred yards would be an easy mark unless a fellow got the buck ague.

TWENTY

JIM HAD GOT REAL FOND of the baby. He really started to be fond of the kid when a skinny red little finger got an infection and had to be tied up with a rag. It was a funny sight to see such a small hand with a sore finger, and it was a ticklish job getting the rag on just right so it wasn't too tight and still wouldn't come off.

The baby was real cute when he smiled in his sleep. Mrs. Wellhof told them that if the baby smiled and jerked in his sleep he was hivy and ought to have onion juice and be held up for a few minutes in the sunlight that came through a window pane.

The first two months were not easy. Jeannie was sick part of the time. When the baby cried he got very tense and seemed like he was about to explode. His belly-button stuck way out, and they found out that this was a rupture. They had to keep a band around him with a collar button sewed into it to hold the rupture in, but even with the band on when the kid cried the rupture stuck out.

Jim wished to hell the kid wouldn't get so excited. It seemed like he was determined to pop himself open in spite of anything they could do. When he dirtied his pants he got the same way, red and swollen.

Before they put him on the bottle he was a hard one to take

care of. He would scream for his dinner an hour before time, then when he got it he would suck about a minute and go sound asleep. It didn't do any good to shake him. You had to bathe his head in cold water or slap his legs real hard. Then he would wake up and scream, start sucking again, and after a minute go to sleep. What he wanted, evidently, was to hold the nipple in his mouth twenty-four hours of the day and just take a swig now and then.

Sometimes they had to work with him an hour this way in the middle of the night, and Jim would start to sneeze and wake up the next day with a cold, feeling rotten.

After they put him on the bottle things were not much better so far as sleep was concerned. Jim had to get up at midnight or one o'clock, and stir up the fire or build a new one, and heat a little water to warm the milk. Often the kid would be screaming himself into spasms all the time this was going on. No use trying to explain to him that you were doing all in God's earth you could to get him something to eat.

Once Jim got so damned mad that he pulled up the covers and gave the skinny little legs a couple of hard slaps. Sandy yelled all the louder, with a note of terror now in his voice.

"Ain't you ashamed of yourself," Jeannie said, "spanking that little baby?"

Jim sat down on the edge of the bed and rubbed his frozen feet together. He was ashamed of himself. He picked up the kid and bounced it on his shoulder and felt a toothless mouth against his cheek trying to suck.

"Well, it ain't his fault," Jim said, "that I have to get up and risk my life every night in this kind of weather, but, by God, nobody ought to have to take care of a kid with no more than we've got to do *with*. Kids ought to be taken care of by the state, with everything fixed convenient. What are we doing but shortening our lives so that the bosses twenty years from now will have another work horse?"

"You know very well," Jeannie said, "that the only way that baby can escape being a nigger dog like we are is for us to get something ahead so he will have a chance in life."

Bottle-feeding was a lot of work. Bottles, nipples, and, for a while, the milk itself had to be boiled. The kid's temper got better so that he seldom cried, but from an hour after he got his first bottle he smelled different. He was all the time puking up sour milk so that he smelled like a sour cream jar. Jim said he was like a young buzzard. If you handled him he got even with you by puking on you and turning your stomach. His rupture healed up and they took the band off. He got quite fat.

But Jim found out that it is taking care of a kid that makes you like him. The more misery he puts you to the better you like him in the long run. Jim got so he wanted to play with the kid all the time, even if he did stink like sour milk.

When they decided to break him of the habit of eating at two o'clock in the morning they didn't get much sleep for three nights, but after that they could generally sleep from ten o'clock until four in the morning.

In the spring, when there was all the excitement over the trip to Oklahoma City and later over the rebellion, Jim didn't have much time to play with the kid, but all the time he was in the house he sat around and held the kid or talked to him in his basket, and grinned and tapped the kid's chin to make him grin.

"I can't hardly wait," he said, "till he gets big enough to walk and talk and do something besides suck and dirty his pants. I'm gonna get him one of these little cheap 22 rifles with a bronze barrel and some shot cartridges and teach him to kill sparrows. He can kill a lot of sparrows around the barn."

"We've got to arrange to send him to high school and maybe

through college," Jeannie said, "so he'll have some chance of getting ahead in the world. Ted's got an education, and he's not as smart as you are but he gets thirty-five dollars a week without working half hard."

TWENTY-ONE

AFTER THE W.C.U. MEETING at the school house the whole business seemed to die down. Word came through that July 27 was the date and then further word that another date would be set. Working by himself in the field Jim thought it all over and became skeptical. It was just one of the things that couldn't happen, and he would go on year after year plodding behind a plow. Nothing ever did happen to him and nothing ever could.

But Mack didn't lose his enthusiasm. He made trips now and then to talk to other commanders. He didn't say much to Jim, but once he told of carrying ammunition into a cellar and seeing there a couple of sticks of dynamite and a dozen rifles. "It ain't just in this here little spot," he said, "but all over the country. We're gonna start out strong, destroyin' the crops that belong to the bankers, burnin' bridges that belong to the big railroads, but not any highway bridges that belong to everybody, and blowin' up pipelines of Standard Oil. We'll put the fear of God into these capitalists the first jump out of the box, and after that the movement will spread like wildfire."

Mack had decided to have a dance at his house. "The folks need a sort of last get-together," he said. "The next time we have a dance we'll have it in the White House—or else," he added thoughtfully, "the capitalists will be dancin' on our graves."

All the W.C.U. farmers and their families were invited, but since other fellows always came to a dance it was understood that the rebellion would not be talked about.

Jim went alone. The baby was not feeling well, and, besides, Jeannie never enjoyed herself at dances. The people who went to them were generally the most shiftless in the neighborhood, and there was likely to be drinking.

After milking Jim walked over to the McGee place. Mack was dressed up and had a fresh cut on his face from shaving. He was standing around talking to some of the old-timers and already they had him going on his horse story.

". . . then one of the boys got a bright idea and we put a wheelbarrow under him to carry his belly, with the wheel between his front feet and a rope tied to the handles goin' over his rump, and this worked swell on smooth ground, except that right at first, before we greased the wheelbarrow, it made so much noise that the old fool got scared and run away, wheelin' his belly out over the prairie.

"But we caught him and brought him back and greased the wheelbarrow and then took him out to plow, and the first rut that the wheel dropped into, there it stuck. Well, when he tried to go forward naturally his hind feet was lifted off the ground and he kept pullin' with his front feet until his rear was pointed straight up. He got excited and wouldn't stop until finally he was bent into a hoop with his rump on the back of his neck and his hind feet pointin' up and his tail hangin' over his eyes. The wheelbarrow was upside-down, and there he stood like a circus acrobat. Well, some of the fellows run out to help me, but we couldn't think of no way to get his hind feet down. We talked about lassooin' them and pullin' them down, but while we was arguin' all at once he broke wind in his own face, and it scared him because he didn't recognize the smell and thought there was another horse in front of him. So he started backin' and unbent himself.

"Now some of the boys wanted to try it the other way, that is, with the wheelbarrow backwards and the wheel between his hind feet, but we'd have had to cut a hole in the wheelbarrow for him to make water through, and the boss allowed it wasn't worth it to ruin a good wheelbarrow. If he'd been a mare we would of tried it."

While the crowd was laughing Mack took Jim into the shed room and gave him a drink and showed him where to find the bottle when he wanted another one.

The front room was the only one large enough for a set. It had been cleared except for a couple of chairs in the corner where the floor sloped worst. These chairs were for the fiddler and his second.

Uncle Billy Turner was the fiddler. He reminded Jim of a turkey gobbler, with his long neck and red face. His lower eyelids hung down and you could see their red lining.

Uncle Billy was telling the boys how he learned to fiddle. His folks thought that music belonged to the devil, he said, and when he was born his mother prayed that he would be a preacher, and she prayed that if he wasn't a preacher he wouldn't be a fiddler, and she prayed that if he *was* a fiddler he wouldn't be a left-handed fiddler.

When Uncle Billy was in his teens he made him a gourd fiddle and kept it hid in a hollow tree, and he learned to play on it. "But I never could do no good fiddlin' left-handed," he said, "and that thar proves thar's somepin' to this prayer business."

Jim stood around listening and saying something once in a while, but mostly he just watched the people and thought about what happened to them and how they took it.

Here was Johnny Fane, the second. Johnny was not to say

handsome. His front teeth stuck out. He'd fallen in love once with Violet Tatum, but Violet just led him on to make her steady, Jewel Brown, pay more attention to her.

Jewel was a big fellow and ready to fight at the drop of a hat. At a dance one night Violet paid a lot of attention to Johnny, until Jewel got tired of it. Jewel liked to tell about it. "I tuk him out," Jewel would say, "and I whupped him. Then I went back and danced a while and went out and whupped him some more."

When Jewel said "whupped" he meant that he had knocked Johnny down and sat on him and pounded him in the face. Every whack had sounded like thumping a green watermelon.

Johnny never fooled with girls after that but learned to second real well on the guitar. The end of the story was that Jewel left the country when he found out that Violet was going to have what the Arkansawyers called a "woods colt."

Jim stood around a while and listened to the tuning up. It sounded good; sounded like there was going to be a lot of fun in a few minutes.

He decided that he had wasted a lot of time feeling sorry for himself. He was better off than old Uncle Billy, who didn't have long to live; or Johnny, who wanted a woman and didn't know how to get one; or Claude Waters, who had asthma so bad that he had to sit up every night during the harvest and threshing season.

The liquor made him feel good. He went back and took another drink. He didn't dance because too many fellows were waiting for a turn. Happy danced the first set because there hadn't enough women got there yet, but after that she got busy with the coffee for the lunch. He watched Happy dance, and he wanted her so bad that it hurt.

He felt reckless. A lot of things had happened lately, and it seemed like a lot more things would happen in the next few weeks or months. It was just a toss-up whether he would be alive a year from that time, but it didn't make much difference. Might as well be dead as go back to the old work-horse way of living.

He felt like he was going to get a lot out of life from now on, and maybe that was because he was ready to die. Seems like you're not ready to live until you're ready to die. That was the smartest thing he'd ever thought of. You're not ready to live until you're ready to die. War times made you feel that way.

Maybe in a few weeks he would be telling Happy good-bye forever. There was a lot of things he wanted to tell her, or maybe only one thing. Right over there in the corner where Uncle Billy was playing the fiddle Jim had taken off Happy's dress one morning in the sunlight. Before that he had never had any more than just a glimpse of a woman naked. It was the morning after the kid was born, when Mack was dead drunk over at Jim's place.

Jim felt like that morning was better than all the rest of his life put together. One part of the tune Uncle Billy was playing was very pretty when he went up to a high note on the E string.

Happy brushed past Jim and stepped on his toe and acted like she didn't aim to. She smiled, and he knew he would remember it as long as he lived. She had a lower front tooth that was a little out of line and cattycornered, and she put her tongue on it sometimes when she smiled. Her lower lip was bigger than the upper one, and she pushed it out a little bit because she was teasing him.

She was being smart with him and playing a game that she didn't play with anybody else. That morning in the sunlight, over there in the corner where the bed usually was, she had teased him. Chances were he wouldn't be alive a year from tonight.

She emptied the water bucket into the teakettle and started out the door. "Hey," he said, "I'll help you get that water."

It was so dark outside that they couldn't see a thing. He put his arm around her as they went down the hill to the pump.

There were automobiles in the yards, and teams were hitched to the trees.

They went to the pump and felt around and hung the bucket on the spout, but before Jim started pumping he grabbed Happy and kissed her a long time. He was so excited he could hardly breathe. All at once he decided that he wouldn't be alive anyway a year from now. He told her that. He started toward the barn with her and she didn't hold back. They went up into the haymow.

When they came out they could see a lot better. Their eyes had got used to the dark. They brushed each other off to be sure there wasn't any hay sticking to them. Jim felt contented and good all over. Happy said she thought Jim was a swell guy. "But, Jim, honey, we're a couple of damn fools," she said. Jim had the same feeling he used to have when he was a little kid after he had bawled a while and got it all out of his system. He felt like the morning after a good rain.

He didn't stay at the dance very long after that. He couldn't be alone with Happy, and he would rather think about what had happened than stand around and watch her dance with other fellows.

TWENTY-TWO

AFTER JIM LEFT Happy danced for a while, but it wasn't any fun. The boys would grab her and hug her sometimes and grin, but there wasn't one that she liked. But just as she was finishing a set she saw Bud Filmore and another high school boy standing in the doorway. Her face got red. She was kind of ashamed to have him see her there with all these country people.

He smiled at her, and she got a feeling suddenly that he had come back to her. Then she knew she had been a damned fool to let Jim do anything. She liked Jim, and she might have fallen in love with him if he wasn't already married. But Jim wasn't educated and didn't look near as good when he was dressed up as when he had on overalls.

Bud inclined his head, meaning for her to come to the door, and she went over to him.

"Hello, kid," he said.

"Hello yourself." And then, because it was hard to breathe, she said, "Whew, it's hot!"

"Come out and cool off," he said.

She went out.

"I got a car here. Let's go out and set down a little while."

"Aw, I can't run off from the dance."

"Aw, come on. Jist a minute. I wanta talk to you."

"Well, just a minute while I cool off."

"Gee, Happy, you're beautiful tonight. The best lookin' gal I ever seen."

"Aw, cut it out!"

"Naw, I mean it."

The car was parked beside the road. Bud opened the back door and they got in. He threw his arms around her and kissed her and began to breathe real hard.

"Bud, you been drinkin'," she said.

"Jist a little bit. Here, have a drink."

"No! They'd smell it on my breath."

"I got some cloves you can chew." He was pressing the bottle to her lips, and she took several large swallows.

"I jist wanted to tell you I'm still crazy about you, honey," he said.

"You're not. You don't have anything to do with me any more."

"Well, lately. But that's because of my old lady. But I got my diploma now, and I ain't tied to her apron strings no more. If she gits funny I jist leave home."

"But you don't care anything for *me*—"

"I *do,* and you'll find out—"

He was struggling with her. "God, honey, be *careful,*" she said.

He was so excited he could hardly talk. "You want it—just like I do—I can tell."

"Not here—I gotta go back to the dance—somebody'll come by with a lantern."

"We can see a light comin'—please, Happy, I love you—"

An hour later, as Bud and Weenie were driving back to town, Weenie asked, "Well, what kinda luck did you have?"

"Boy, I got my meat."

"Aw, the hell you did! Not in that short time."

"Yes I did, by God!"

"Honest to God! Well, that's what I call fast work. Suppose she gits knocked up or somepin'?"

"Say, listen. After what we found out tonight about her and her brother-in-law, she can't hold me to *nothin*."

"Well, that's what I call fast work," Weenie sighed.

"It never does take me very long," Bud admitted.

# TWENTY-THREE

Sɪssɪe Wᴇʟʟʜᴏꜰ died not long after the Wellhofs had moved out to the Indian lease near McGee's. Birdie always thought she was the strongest one of the children, but she took sick one afternoon and the first thing they knew she was dead.

Ned was working on the roads, and Birdie was busy trying to get a batch of chickens started and taking care of the place and of the younger children. Sissie wasn't going to school. She didn't like to go to school because of the way the other children acted about her clothes. And when they moved out to the farm it was a long ways to school, so they let her stay home. She seemed to like to stay home.

One afternoon when it was still pretty cold Birdie sent Sissie out to drive up the cow. Sissie had to go clear across the pasture to find the cow, and when she got back she had pains in her chest. Birdie put her to bed with a hot iron, and the pains seemed to get better, but she got a high fever. Birdie could tell when she put her face against Sissie's.

As soon as Ned got home he got on a horse and went to town to get the doctor, but the doctor didn't want to come out. He said he thought Sissie just had a little cold and would be up and about in a day or two. The doctor gave Ned a prescription, but the drug store wouldn't let Ned have anything on credit.

The next day Sissie died. Seemed like she didn't have any constitution or any strength to throw off the cold on her lungs. The neighbors came over to help with the funeral. Jeannie Tetley gave Birdie a dress that had belonged to Jeannie's mother, and old man McGee loaned Ned his Sunday suit. Birdie thought Ned looked nicer than he'd ever looked in his life when he got dressed up for the funeral.

They had a nice funeral, with the Holiness preacher. He told them that God had given them Sissie, and now God had taken Sissie away. The whole thing liked to kill Ned and Birdie. The two boys were not old enough to realize

They buried Sissie in the cemetery in Young's pasture. Jim Tetley and McGee and some others dug the grave. It was easy digging because it was so sandy, but the grave kept caving in so they had to dig twice as big a hole as was necessary. Birdie kind of went out of her head. She kept saying they ought to wrap Sissie up more because she would be cold.

The Wellhofs started going to the Holy Roller church after Sissie died. Birdie wore the dress that used to belong to Mrs. McGee, and Ned got him some new overalls. Every Sunday they would hitch up to the wagon and go to church. They got converted. Birdie felt like she would see Sissie again, and Ned prayed that God would help him so he wouldn't make whiskey any more. Ned got real religious and quit chewing and swearing for a while.

Ora, the baby, learned to walk, but just when it seemed like she was getting strong she caught the whooping cough from another child at church. The two boys caught it from her, and for a while it looked like all three of them would die. But Birdie and Ned prayed a lot and the Lord helped them pull through.

Before these kids were through coughing Birdie found out that she was going to have another baby. Ned was scared. He said it would come in hot weather and wouldn't live through the heat, but Birdie was sure that the Lord had sent the baby and would take care of it.

Birdie wasn't very well to begin with, and she had morning sickness that lasted all day. She was dizzy, and had headaches and spots before her eyes. Sometimes she had pains in the pit of her stomach. Her ankles and hands and face got puffy. It was not natural fat. You could press it with your finger and leave a dent there.

The symptoms got so bad that Birdie and Ned hitched up and went into town and talked to the doctor. The doctor said that she had poison in her blood that came from the baby. He told her not to eat very much meat, if any, and not to eat any salt. They said that they just about lived on salt pork, and he said that was bad. He told them to get plenty of fresh fruit and some breakfast food, and things like that, and he told Birdie to drink lots of milk. They told him they didn't see how they could get milk because the cow was dry now. She wasn't a good cow anyway, and the pasture was no good.

The doctor told Birdie to keep off her feet and rest lots during the day, to wear warm clothing, to go to the dentist and have her teeth looked after, and to drink lots of water.

Of course, Birdie could drink plenty of water and put on all the clothes she had, but they couldn't possibly get a crop in if Birdie rested, and of course they couldn't afford to go to a dentist or to buy fresh fruit and breakfast food. Maybe Ned could borrow some money to buy some bananas, but he didn't think he could; besides, if they bought something like that and took it home the kids would set up a howl for it, and it just wasn't in Birdie's nature to sit around and eat a lot of good things when the children were just starved for something besides salt pork and biscuits.

The doctor looked mad, and he told them that they would have to get this stuff and Birdie would have to do like he said if she expected to live through childbirth. He gave them a prescription.

They went to the wagon and talked it over. Ned was scared. He thought Birdie was going to die, sure. Birdie wasn't afraid. She said the Lord would provide. She prayed, there in the wagon.

Ned said he would try to borrow a little more money but didn't think he could. He said he knew where he could go in with some boys and make up a batch of whiskey and get the money that way.

Birdie started crying and taking on, and the people on the street looked at them and wondered what was wrong. Ned told her to shut up and he'd go and try to borrow some money.

He went into the bank and sat down on the seat in front of the president's office to wait his turn. He was scared. He started sweating and took off his coat. He kept fooling with a nail that he used to pin his overall bib to the suspender.

A well-dressed fellow came in. Ned knew he was one of the teachers in the town high school. He wore good clothes. He was lucky. Ned wished he had an education so he could do something besides farm. Then Birdie wouldn't die.

It was his turn to go in and talk to the banker. The banker looked real mean. Ned would be glad when this was over. He sat down in a real expensive-looking chair and played with his suspender nail. He knew there was no use. He knew he would just get a lecture from the banker.

"Well, now, what's your trouble?" the banker asked. He rubbed his nose and a blackhead popped out and hung there like a little white worm. The banker leaned forward and dropped a ball of tobacco juice into the spittoon.

Ned told him what his trouble was.

"Special grub for your old woman, eh? I don't know what you

farmers think a bank is for. Looks to me like she's been eatin' too much rather than too little. Tell her to diet a little bit, like my wife does, and not make a hog of herself. You farmers get a lot of newfangled ideas. My mother had seven children, and she didn't have any fresh fruit and special grub. Take a day like this when you ought to be in the field doin' a little work like the rest of us, and instead of that you're in here loafing around, wastin' your time and mine tryin' to borrow more money; that's the trouble with you farmers, you'd rather sit around on your behinds than get out and do some work. It ain't the bank's fault if your wife's gonna have another baby. We can't do anything more for you until you get out and show that you are willing to do something for yourself. Go on back home now and get out in the field this afternoon and do something."

Ned walked out of the bank and stood outside for a little while around the corner where the banker couldn't see him. He didn't want to go back to Birdie and tell her what had happened.

Some town loafers were standing there in the shade talking. Ned listened for a while. They were talking about a seventh-grade teacher who had just left town. She had given some of the high school boys, Bud Filmore and some others, a dose.

Denny Payne, who had pie-a-rear and had to chew tobacco all the time to keep his teeth from falling out, thought that something ought to be done about a woman like that. He told how they did a woman like that down in Texas where he used to live.

"Everybody thought she was a respectable woman, but they found out that she give the syph to a bunch of boys around town, and they tuk her out and they tuk off her clothes and they laid her on her back on a log, and they tuk a buggy whip and, by God, they wore that old gal out. They whipped the hairs off of her, by God, and when they let her up you ought to seen that log." The fellows laughed, and Denny grinned, and you could see how bad his pie-a-rear was.

The high school teacher, Mr. Hardman, came out of the bank. "That son-of-a-bitch ain't any too pure himself," said Denny. "Pete Taylor, who used to be janitor up to the high school, said he seen him with one of the high school girls in the building one day after school was out."

Ned walked on, trying to decide about making up a batch of whiskey.

TWENTY-FOUR

IT CAME TIME for Happy to be sick, and nothing happened. Washing up the milk things after breakfast, feeding the chickens, cleaning a fry for dinner, washing clothes, she began to worry. She had neither seen nor heard anything of Bud since the night of the dance, and knew now that he was fooling with her or had been too drunk to know what he was doing that night. If there was a kid it was Bud's. Jim was careful.

Her flat little breasts started growing and got sore. She could see blue veins and red veins under the skin, and little bumps appeared. If her mother had been alive she would have noticed it.

Then one morning she was very sick at the stomach and that scared her almost into a faint. She remembered how Jeannie had been sick every morning the first six weeks. She couldn't eat any breakfast, and Mack worried a little about her appetite. But it was easy to fool him. He was always thinking about the Socialists and the war.

She was sure now that something was wrong and she wrote Bud a note. "I want to see you just a minute. It's important. H." She didn't get any answer but decided he might be out of town.

One afternoon when she was in the blackjacks looking for the cows she decided to try strenuous exercise and ran and jumped until she was so tired she was sick at the stomach again, but it didn't do any good.

As she drove the cows into the corral Mack looked at her with surprise and asked her, "What makes you so red-faced? Looks like a spanked baby's rear."

"Aw, I seen a young rabbit," she said, "but he was too old for me."

Mack laughed. "You ain't much like your dad," he said. "Now, when I was your age I could run fast. One day I was workin' in the field and I seen a deer not far off. Well, I didn't have a gun or anything so I started after the deer, and I got just clost enough to get the end of my finger in the deer's behind, and you know I had to run three-quarters of a mile before I could gain enough to crook my finger."

Happy grinned. She didn't feel like joking.

She had to stay in bed the next two days and couldn't hold anything on her stomach. Jeannie and Jim came over in the evenings and she joked with them, but she couldn't stand the smell of tobacco smoke and wouldn't let the men smoke in the room where she was.

The third day she was up and feeling a little better. It was hard to breathe. The air was still. It was beastly hot, and she could always smell horse manure.

She wandered about the house doing a little work. Sometimes for hours she couldn't remember what she had been doing. She decided that maybe Bud really loved her but his old woman was giving him trouble.

She made up her mind to write him and tell him more. If he understood he would marry her and then everything would be all right. She wrote two letters and tore them up. Every day she went out to the mail box expecting a letter, but no letter came.

Then she wrote a third letter. "Dear Bud. I guess there is going to be a baby and I thought you ought to know. Now if you don't love me just forget about it and everything will be all right, but if you do love me now is the time to let me know, because I'm in a bad fix. H."

When she finished the letter it was time for the mail man and she put the letter in the box and hurried back to the house for fear she would grab it out and destroy it. When the mail man had taken the letter she felt relieved. At least she would know.

The next day at the same time she was trembling. The mail man came along over the hill, taking his time. His horses looked like they had never been in a hurry. He stopped and put something in the box, and Happy waited until he was out of sight before she went to see what he had left. She didn't mind waiting because she felt that so long as she didn't know what was in the box she would have some hopes.

The only thing in the box was a seed catalogue.

But she got to hoping again. Maybe Bud's mother destroyed her letters. The old bitch would know all about it, of course, but Happy didn't care now.

The next day was Saturday. She decided to go to town and see if she could run into Bud on the streets. Right after dinner she put on her school dress and told her father she was going to town. "Well, it'll do you good to get away from this hole for a while," he said, "but them town folks is pretty worked up, I guess, over the Socialists. I guess they won't arrest you or anything, but they might arrest me. I don't know just how much they know, but they know quite a lot."

Happy walked to town along the sandy road. There was a hole in the bottom of one of her shoes and the hot sand kept getting in. She got a streak of axle grease on her dress from a weed along the road and wondered if it would come out. But it didn't seem to make any difference. It was so hot that the hills in the distance danced up and down.

When she got to town there was the usual crowd, but not so many farmers. The loafers on the shady side of the bank stared at her, and one of them, Denny Payne, smiled at her. The fat squaws on the sidewalk rolled cigarettes. She wished she were one of them, with nothing to worry about. They kept their blankets on, even in such weather.

Happy passed Sam Gladson. The sheriff looked pretty old. Happy was afraid he would arrest her, but he didn't even look at her.

She didn't want to run around alone, but if she met any of the high school kids they said "howdy" and walked on. She was afraid they giggled after she passed. Then she saw Effie Graham and grabbed onto her. Effie was a short, fat country girl with a red face and funny clothes, but Effie was friendly and Happy was glad to see her.

"What you doin', kid?" Effie asked. "Le's walk down by the racket store and look at the windows." That would be past the drug store where some of the country boys were loafing, and Effie liked to go past them and maybe cod a little.

The boys grinned at Effie, and one of them asked, "Is this hot enough for you?"

"Say, what'd you make it so hot for?" Effie countered, and giggled. Bud wasn't on the streets that day.

Happy saw Ted Tetley coming toward them and dragged Effie across the street so they wouldn't have to meet him, then she got to feeling pretty weak and said she guessed she would have to be getting back home. She told Effie so long and started out.

There was just one more hope. She could walk past Bud's house and she might possibly see him. When she got to the block she didn't know whether to walk on the sidewalk or in the road and finally decided on the road. She looked at the house out of the corner of her eye but didn't see anyone. She walked past looking down.

But when she was nearly past she heard the door slam and got very excited. She didn't look around, but she heard someone coming across the porch and then down the walk, and it didn't sound like Bud's walk.

"Say, wait a minute!" It was Bud's mamma. Happy's heart jumped. She stopped and looked around.

Bud's mamma, fat and sweaty, with a lock of hair hanging in her eyes, was coming toward Happy as fast as she could. Mamma was trying to say something, but seemed so excited that she couldn't talk. When the old lady was a few yards away she stopped and wiped her hair back, and then Happy made out what she was saying.

"Huzzy! You shameless wretch! You leave my boy alone. You understand? I know all about it. You and your brother-in-law. He told me all about it. If you ever look at him again I'll have you arrested for adultery." She was screaming now. "You slut!"

Happy walked on and left the old lady yelling. It didn't make any difference.

She had to stop for a while on the way home. Although it was past the middle of the afternoon it was as hot as ever. She scratched at the streak on her dress and wondered if it would come out.

When she got home she automatically put on her ragged apron and started out to get the cows. She walked along the lane in a daze, pulling up a weed now and then and waving it around. She walked through the blackjacks but didn't find the cows immediately. From long practice she knew that on a day like this they would be at the far corner of the pasture. When you get to know a pasture you get to know where the cows are likely to be.

The herd was standing in the fence corner, but two of them had crawled through the fence and were grazing along the road. She found where the fence was loose and crawled through. It was not hard to drive the two to the loose place, but they didn't seem to know how to push through again into the pasture. She took the oldest and laziest first and by jumping around and waving her arms finally induced the cow to crawl back. The other was a heifer. Happy had to run up the road and head her off, chase her back, then run and head her off again. Her apron got full of sandburs and her bare legs all scratched. She was so angry by this time that her strength came back for a little while. The heifer dodged and jumped and ran. Happy would have given it up and herded the rest toward the barn but she was just mad enough to be stubborn and wanted to show the heifer who was boss.

Then she heard a motor, and a car came around the corner throwing sand. It was Bud's car, and he was at the wheel. Happy's feet were far apart and her dress was above her knees. She straightened up and dropped her scratchy apron and stared at them. The car was full of high school kids she knew, and hanging to the doors were wet bathing suits. They had been out to the river on a swimming party.

They looked surprised, then laughed, and waved at her as they passed. Bud kept his eyes on the road and didn't look up. A cloud of sand and gas swirled around her, and she heard a shriek of laughter from one of the girls.

She forgot all about the heifer and crawled back through the fence, but before she had taken the rest of the herd a hundred yards the heifer came trotting after them bawling with worry at being left alone.

✹ TWENTY-FIVE

BILL JOHNSON, Negro farmer and veteran of the Spanish-American War, had always depended upon making a hundred dollars in the summer working on the threshing crew, but this year the doctor had told him that if he worked heavy it would be the end of him. Something was wrong with his lungs and he would have to do light work. The dust was bad too, the doctor said.

But keeping alive through the winter was the problem. Without cash how could he get sowbelly and flour? Bill worried so much that the worry was as bad as heavy work.

When threshing started he was restless and hung around a machine once in a while watching the boys on the bundle wagons and wishing he could climb up and start pitching in. Sometimes he picked up a fork and scratched up around the feeder just to get the feel of it. Fellows asked him was he rich nowadays and had he retired, and when he told them doctor's orders they laughed and said they guessed they ought to go to a good doctor.

Nancy, his wife, didn't say very much, but she was worried and short-tempered. She held her hand over her mouth when she talked because she had lost most of her front teeth and they couldn't afford a set of false teeth for her. If she hadn't been young and pretty it wouldn't have made so much difference to her. Bill said she ought to leave him and go back to her folks in

Tennessee and get a job, and when she had made enough to buy some teeth she could get another man who'd be a better provider. She told him to shut his mouth and not talk so much, but she must have thought about it quite a lot.

When he thought about her with another man it made him half crazy, but he wasn't much of a man where heavy work was concerned, and hadn't been since he'd had yellow fever in the army. Felt like he would be all right if he could crawl off and sleep for a year.

When he worked hard for a long time he got nervous and goosy. Fellows working with him would punch him to see him jump. He told them not to do it, but he couldn't explain that it made him so tired and weak that he could hardly lift a bundle.

This year when he smelled the coal smoke and wheat dust of a machine he felt like he ought to be there working and earning money.

He heard that Glen Rehlin, a white man who owned a lot of land, needed men to drive wheat wagons. That was light work and didn't pay very well, but it was better than nothing. Bill went to Rehlin and took off his hat and asked for a job. Rehlin treated colored people like dogs, but Bill thought he could stand it for a few days. Rehlin was pretty sharp and called him no-account but gave him the job.

Bill had his wagon in place long before sun-up, and when the machine started he felt good. He caught a handful of wheat and threw it in his mouth. He hadn't had much breakfast that morning and it tasted good, like bread and milk. He kept tossing wheat into his mouth until he had a good-sized wad. When the wind shifted a little and the sharp dust drifted over his wagon he went up to the horses and stood there until he had to start leveling.

He enjoyed the trips to town. He was using a heavy team of Rehlin's and they didn't have to stop and rest even after a soft stretch in the stubble. On the road they walked along without any strain. Always as soon as he got out of sight of the machine he stretched out in the sun on top of the wheat. He felt good and didn't let himself worry about what was going to happen to him and Nancy that winter. If he didn't do heavy work this summer maybe his trouble would clear up over the winter and he would be like he was before he went into the army.

The job lasted for a couple of days and Bill felt good until he was leveling up the last load of Rehlin's wheat. Then he got to thinking that he was out of a job again and mighty little cash for the winter. The crew cleaned up the setting and the machine shut down. Bill was watching the layer of dust that showered from the inside of the belt wheels as they lost speed. Something soft struck him in the face and he whooped and threw his arms up. It was a dead mouse and Rehlin himself had thrown it in his face. Men standing around laughed because Bill was so goosy.

Rehlin was drunk. He was not a dirt farmer and he had on white pants like a merchant or banker in town. Bill grinned and tried to quit shaking. "Shaw stawtled me," he said.

"Lissen," Rehlin said. The machine had shut down now and everything was quiet, and the men on the crew were rolling cigarettes. "Lissen, nigger. If you'll eat that there mouse, tail and all, I'll give you that load of wheat."

"Ah reckon Ah likes 'em bettah fried," Bill said with a chuckle. He had to keep on good terms with Rehlin until he got paid.

"Lissen," Rehlin went on. "You think I'm coddin', but I ain't. A load of wheat more or less don't mean nothin' to me. I'd ruther see a nigger eat a raw mouse any time." Rehlin laughed and slapped his white pants. "An' what's more, of you don't eat that there mouse it's gonna take me a long time to git around to payin' you what I owe you."

This was something to think about, because Rehlin had a

reputation for beating Negroes out of what he owed them. Bill looked down at the mouse on the ground. It had a big belly and you could see it was a she-mouse full of little ones.

Rehlin picked it up by the tail and looked at it. "By God, it's in the family way, but you won't mind a few extra little mice thrown in because they're nice and tender."

He tossed the mouse at Bill again and Bill jumped back. "Guess Ah bettah get stawted with this heah load," he said.

"Naw you don't," Rehlin said. "When you drive that there load off it's gonna be yours because you'll be digestin' this here little mamma mouse by that time."

Rehlin was looking serious. The other fellows stood around waiting, some of them grinning. Bill felt himself getting trembly again. The load of wheat was worth a lot of money. It would be as much as he could earn and save, probably, in a season working on the machine. The idea came to him that he might actually eat the mouse. It was very small. He remembered hearing that Chinamen ate mice, and if he could get it down somehow his troubles would be over for a while.

"Shaw enough," he asked, "you mean if I eat that mouse I get this load of wheat?"

" 'At's what I mean. And if you don't eat it you'll be in trouble about your pay."

Everybody got quiet. Even the engineer and the machine tender had come up and were watching. Bill stared at the mouse on the ground. It wouldn't hurt him any to swallow it. He had done a lot of things in his life that were really dangerous. It would just take some extra nerve, and he certainly needed the money if anybody did.

"Naw. Ah couldn't eat no raw mouse."

"Yes you can, by God! An' you're gonna do that very thing."

Bill stood staring at the mouse for a long time, then he picked it up by the tail. It didn't look very big.

He held it up and opened his mouth. "Hey," one of the fellows yelled, "it's got fleas on it."

Bill whooped and threw it down. He backed off. "Naw sah. Ah can't eat no raw mouse."

"Yes you can, fleas and all. My grandpap's niggers eat horse turds when he told 'em to, and liked 'em, by God! And you ain't no better than they was."

Bill had time to wonder if he would get the wheat after he swallowed the mouse. He knew most of the men on the crew. They didn't like Rehlin. There would be a fight if Rehlin didn't let him have the wheat. He could count on that.

He tried again. After all, it was just something that took a couple of seconds and wasn't dangerous. He picked up the mouse and brushed the grains of sand off it. He crammed it in his mouth. It was too big to swallow at a gulp and he crunched down on it two or three times and swallowed hard. It was down then, and the wheat was his. He felt sick. The men stared at him with expressions of horror. Suddenly he doubled up and retched and the whole mess in his stomach flooded out through his mouth and nose.

Rehlin jumped back, but the puke spattered on his pants. Bill settled down with a groan. Somebody laughed and said to Rehlin, "You got nigger puke on your white pants."

"Well, that black bastard didn't eat it after all," Rehlin said. "That there's too bad for him."

"Well now, wait a minute," the engineer said. "He eat it all right."

"The hell he did. There it is on the ground."

"But he eat it all right. You didn't say nothin' about pukin' it later."

Rehlin was brushing his pants leg with a wad of straw. He looked at the members of the crew and saw that they didn't like him any too well. He grunted and walked to his automobile and drove off.

Bill felt better in a little while. He got up and climbed onto his load of wheat. It just took a little extra nerve. He wasn't sorry.

On the way to town he got to feeling good. He thought how he would surprise Nancy when he showed her the money. They could get her some teeth. He popped one of Rehlin's horses with the end of a line. "Step lively there, boy," he called out.

He drove onto the elevator scales as he had with all the other loads and waited while he was weighed in. He wished he could make himself heavy now and light when he weighed out. The elevator man would be surprised when he found out whose wheat it was.

He guided the team carefully onto the dump and climbed down. There was a swish when the end-gate came out and another one when the wagon tilted. A brown cloud of dust formed as the wheat rolled out.

When he weighed out the elevator man yelled to him, "Rehlin's wheat?"

"Naw. This here is my wheat. Johnson's wheat."

The elevator man came out to the wagon. "What you mean, your wheat? Ain't you haulin' for Rehlin?"

"Yeah. I was haulin' for Rehlin. But this last load belongs to me. He turned it over to me."

"Well, that's damned funny. He's right inside now, and I'll ask him. Hey, Rehlin! Come out here."

Rehlin walked out of the office and Sam Gladson followed him. Bill was amazed.

"Whut you mean, nigger, tryin' to steal my wheat?" Rehlin asked.

"Mistah Rehlin, you give me this here load of wheat."

Rehlin looked at the sheriff and nodded his head. "Ain't no damned nigger can take a joke," he said. Then to Bill, "What the hell you think I'd be givin' you a load of wheat for? Ain't no damned nigger can get anything through his head. They're all alike. Git down outa that wagon now and beat it before I tell the sheriff here to pinch you for stealin' wheat."

Bill lost his temper. "Mistah Rehlin, you're the lowest down skunk I ever seen in my life. They ain't nothin' dirtier—"

Rehlin turned white. "Git down outa there before we come up and git you, you sassy black bastard."

The sheriff climbed in the wagon and Rehlin followed him. Bill swung out blindly with his fist, but they grabbed him and dragged him out of the wagon. While Sam was beating him over the head with his pistol butt Rehlin was kicking him in the groin. The horses, startled by the commotion, started off, ran across the road and smashed a wagon wheel against a culvert.

They loaded Bill, unconscious, into the sheriff's car and took him to jail, and a crowd gathered to look at the blood on the bed of the scales and to hear from the elevator man how a nigger got sassy with white men and got put in his place.

The next morning the sheriff told Bill that he would release him from the charge of stealing wheat if he agreed to pay for the wagon wheel that had been broken. What Rehlin owed him for hauling would about pay for the busted harness. And he could get out of the charge of resisting an officer if he'd promise to behave himself after this and keep his place. "If you don't," Sam said, "we'll send you up for five years to a place where they'll learn you to keep your place."

Bill didn't say anything at the time, but that afternoon when Nancy came to see him and cried a while he agreed to pay for the wheel as soon as he could get the money. He was released on good behavior.

TWENTY-SIX

THE LAST MORNING that Jim worked on the farm before hell broke loose was a quiet morning and very hot. He was turning over a little patch of wheat stubble with the walking plow, and he took off his shoes because the bottom of the furrow was smooth and cool.

He turned up lots of fat white grub worms, especially when he went around an old straw stack. There was a big melon on one of the vines there where he had planted a few seeds in the rich soil. Later in the morning, when he was getting thirsty, maybe he would stop and eat it. But he couldn't leave the team close to the stack because the flies were bad there. They bred in the rotten straw. He hated to go by the straw stack for that reason. The horses danced around and fought the flies. He would have to leave the team at the end of the field and walk back here. That would waste time, but he was not in any hurry. He didn't expect to get the field plowed anyway.

The grub worms were white, except their heads were tan and their hind ends were kind of dark blue as if they were full of dirt. They must live on dirt, and probably their hind ends were full of it. They rolled up in circles, shaped like a piece of chicken manure. Sometimes the plow shaved right over the top of one and left him there exposed in a little hollow. Sometimes the plow cut one in two.

A couple of crows came along and followed the plow, coming so close to Jim that he could see their feathers shine blue-black in the sun. They were not a damned bit afraid of him because they knew he didn't have a gun. Sometimes he would stop and point his whip-stalk at them and they would go right on picking up grub worms, but let him go to the house and get the shotgun and they would get out of range mighty quick.

He wished he had a pistol so he could blaze away at them when they didn't expect it. He would probably miss because a pistol was harder to hold steady than a rifle, but at least he could give them the scare of their life. Sometimes crows were pretty mean carrying off little chickens, but most of Jeannie's chickens were starting to feather out now and a little too big for a crow to tackle.

Jim got to thinking about all that had happened the last few weeks. The early morning is a good time to think, especially when you have some job like plowing that you can do without watching very close. A fellow is cheerful in the morning and feels like everything is going to turn out right. Later, when he gets tired and thirsty and hot, he quits thinking and just watches for his shadow to get around to north so he can unhitch and go to dinner.

It was hard to imagine what would happen in the next few months. If the farmers all over the country were just like the farmers in his neighborhood, there wouldn't be American soldiers going to France to be killed, and America would be the first country in the world to have a Socialist government.

Over here in town they would kick out the damned banker the first thing. Jim hoped he would be on the committee that kicked out the banker. Drag him out and beat hell out of him for the way he had been treating the farmers. Charging them sometimes forty per cent interest because they were helpless.

No, they wouldn't beat him up unless he got smarty and tried to resist. Just tell him to get out, and maybe send him to the poor farm and put him to picking cotton. Make him do an honest day's work.

Put some Socialists in as teachers in the town schools and tell the kids the truth once. There was plenty of brainy men in the Socialist party that had more sense in a minute than these damned teachers had all their lives.

What would happen in Oklahoma City and other big places? When you thought about the cities you wondered how anything could happen that would change things. So damned many people, and you felt like most of them never even heard of socialism. Patriotic, and ready to go to war and fight for the capitalists. How could you ever knock anything into their heads?

When you thought about the cities you felt like the whole damned thing would blow up and not amount to anything except some excitement. Maybe this country wasn't ready for socialism for twenty or fifty years yet.

Jim stopped at the end of the row to let his horses blow a little, because it was getting pretty hot and he was not in any hurry. He was looking at the fly nets when he noticed Mack coming down the road walking fast. Jim knew that something was up by the way he walked.

Probably it was time to get into action and the word had come to start the rebellion. Cut the fences, turn all the stock loose in the crops, cut the telephone and telegraph wires, burn the railroad bridges and start for Washington. Jim hoped so. He was rarin' to go.

But when Mack got a little closer Jim saw that something was wrong. Maybe it was the way Mack walked or something. Some kind of trouble. Jim was scared and just stood looking at Mack, wondering.

He tried to guess. Maybe Fred Niek was right and the government knew all about it and had smashed the whole thing up over night—had arrested the big leaders and would now be grabbing the little fellows. That meant, maybe, that Jim and Mack would have to grab their guns and take to the sticks and hide out, like the members of the "Jones Family."

The Jones Family was an organization of fellows who didn't want to go to war, and they were hiding out in the timber and in caves in the hills, and they came at night to houses of people they knew to get grub.

But if Mack was on the run he would have his gun along. Jim tried to think of what could happen, but he knew that whatever it was he couldn't guess it.

Mack came up and he was white as a sheet. Seemed like he couldn't say anything for a minute, but kept opening his mouth and shutting it. He went up to one of the horses, as if from habit, but he got hold of the top of a hame and held to it to keep from falling and put his head on his arm and groaned, trying to say something.

Then Jim saw a big blood stain on Mack's overalls and ran over to him. "You been hurt?" he said.

Mack shook his head. "I'm—I'm all right."

"You got blood on you—!"

Mack looked down at his overalls and then said "Oh, yes! It ain't mine—." He didn't seem able to go on from there.

Jim grabbed his shoulder and shook it. "Well, whose is it? What happened?"

"It's Happy's," Mack said. "She killed herself."

Mack stood leaning against the horse and breathing hard, and Jim stood and stared at him, not moving. He tried to talk, and his voice stuck at first. "What the hell you mean, Mack?" he asked finally.

"She got knocked up, and she shot herself with my gun. You tell Jeannie it was accidental."

Mack turned loose of the hame and sat down in the dirt. "I'll tell you how it was,' he said. "But you ain't to tell Jeannie a damned word." He put his face in his hands.

"She's been sick every mornin' for some time now, but I didn't think nothin' of it," he said. "But she acted so damned worried. An', you know, she was real sick a while back. This mornin' I told her that, by God, we was goin' to the doctor. Well, she didn't want to go, but I made her. We hitched up to the wagon and went in. The doctor he looked at her and made an examination, and she was in the family way, he said. But it was worse than that, by God. He told her she would have to be awful careful not to have a miscarriage because she had a dose too, and if she had a miscarriage before the dose was healed up, why the germs would get up inside her where you couldn't get at 'em with medicine, and she couldn't ever get well. And he give her a treatment and told her to come back.

"Well, it just made me plumb sick. And I blamed myself for not lookin' after her better. If her mother had a been alive it wouldn't of happened, Jim. I'm a God damned failure at everything, Jim—"

Jim couldn't say anything. He stood there, just as if Mack had been talking about wheat going up, and didn't say anything, remembering what had happened the night of the dance—and Happy couldn't have got a dose from him—it all sounded crazy.

"Well," Mack went on, we got in the wagon and come home, and I asked her who the feller was and she wouldn't say anything. She just set there and looked at the road. And I said, 'Now you got to tell me, and I'll see, by God, that he marries you or I'll shoot the son-of-a-bitch,' and she said she wouldn't marry him. She would rather die. I asked her if there had been more than one, and she nodded her head like there had been but wouldn't say anything. Well, I asked her what made her do it, and she started bawlin', and the rest of the way home she didn't hardly say a word. I told her to tell me who the fellers was and I'd shoot every last son-of-a-bitch and she said, 'What good would that do?' and then she shut up again. When we got home she jumped out of the wagon and went in the house, and I didn't have no idea what she had in mind, and I went on down to the barn to unhitch, tryin' to think what the hell to do. And I heard the gun go off and I run up there, and she was on the kitchen floor with a big hole in her side and the gun layin' there in the blood. Well, I grabbed her up and run to the bed with her, and she opened her eyes once and looked at me and she said, 'Tell Jim so-long,' and then she was dead."

Jim got sick and had to flop down on the ground for a while, then he pulled himself up and started to, unhitch.

"We're gonna tell Jeannie and everybody it was accidental," Mack said, "and don't you let out a damned word of what I told you."

TWENTY-SEVEN

As Jim drove the team toward the barn he was trying to plan what he would say to Jeannie, but all sorts of things went through his mind. He even had to excuse himself for quitting work before dinner and remind himself that Jeannie wouldn't blame him this time.

He even wondered if he felt as bad as another person would over a tragedy like this, or was he so, damned selfish that nothing really made any difference to him except his own little troubles?

He didn't want to tell Jeannie about it. He felt sorrier for her than he did for Happy. Then he had cold shivers when he remembered once hearing Jeannie tell Mack that he shouldn't leave a loaded gun around the place for fear Gladys would kill herself. But Gladys—Happy—was a little kid then, and nobody could blame Mack for that now.

When Jim walked into the house Jeannie looked at him kind of surprised, but probably she could tell by his face that he had a good reason for quitting work, and she didn't ask him about it but kept on scraping a greasy skillet. He sat down by the window and couldn't say anything for a little while, until Jeannie turned and said, "What's happened now?"

"Happy shot herself—accidentally—with Mack's gun."

"Oh, my God!" Jeannie said in a quiet voice, and stood there staring at him.

Jim wished he hadn't said "accidentally" because that might give it all away.

"Mack come and told me just now. He was out to the barn and heard the gun go off, and she must have been putting the gun in the closet when it went off. She died right away."

"This'll kill dad," Jeannie said. "I got to go over there right now and you watch the baby."

Jeannie always had to be doing something. That was the way she kept alive and met all her troubles. Maybe if she stopped for a moment she would suffer more than anyone else, and if she took time to try to be happy her misery would kill her. She couldn't be selfish like Jim or Mack, so she had to be a slave.

Jim thought about it as he wandered about the house after she had gone. In his place now, she would be working very hard straightening up the front room because neighbors would probably be coming in. But he just mooned around and excused himself and amused the baby.

He knew now that Jeannie wouldn't blame anyone for this tragedy, and maybe if she knew the whole story—knew more than Mack knew—she still wouldn't blame anyone. Because it was too late. She blamed people when she thought there was still time to change things, but she never said, "I told you so."

Jeannie kept going through all the miserable business of the funeral and acted about like she had at Birdie Wellhof's funeral a week before. She took care of Mack and the baby, and even of Jim, and talked very little. Jim never saw a look of anger or resentment on her face, but sometimes he thought he saw the young girl he had married—scared and perplexed and ready to break down completely if she stopped doing things for an instant.

Then after the funeral Jeannie went about her work, crying all the time though never stopping work. But she never cried when

Mack was around, and Jim was always grateful to her for that.

Mack went around in a daze, white-faced, and looked as if he might drop dead any minute. Only the excitement of the coming rebellion kept him going. Jim felt hopeless and reckless. It didn't matter what happened to him. When he got word that the rebellion was to start August 3rd it didn't seem real as it once had.

"I suppose you'd rather I didn't go on this march to Washington," he said to Jeannie.

"You got to go," she replied. "You know you can't go back on your word now to dad and the others. It's a crazy wild-goose chase, and you'll get killed probably, but you can't go back on your word."

"I know it," Jim said.

 TWENTY-EIGHT

ON THE AFTERNOON of August 2nd Mack drove his milk cows over to Jim's place so Jeannie could take care of them and have them if everything went wrong. "We'll come past for you after dark," he told Jim.

Jeannie fixed up a lot of fried chicken and bread and butter and cake, so much that Jim objected. "I can't carry so much," he said. She put it in a flour sack and rolled the sack up in the blanket he was going to take.

Jim cleaned his rifle again and stuffed so much ammunition in his pockets that he felt like he was loaded down. "Jesus, I won't be able to walk," he complained. He fixed the blanket roll with a rope so he could throw it over his shoulder, and when he put it on he felt like a Civil War soldier. He got the milking done early and tried to eat supper but he was too excited. "God," he said, "it just don't seem possible that this here is really happening."

He sat beside the supper table and yawned, though he wasn't sleepy. The blanket roll was at his feet and the rifle beside him. He got to thinking about what he would wear on his head and decided that his old straw hat would be too floppy. "It blows down over my eyes in the wind," he said. But he didn't want to wear his good hat because that would look funny as hell.

"You got that old cap you used to wear before we was married," Jeannie said. "It won't git in your way, but it'll be pretty hot."

She went into the closet and rummaged for a long time and let the trunk lid bang down and woke the baby. The kid didn't like to be disturbed and felt real sorry for himself and cried desperately for a while. "You'd almost think he knew what was goin' on," Jim said. "If he don't shut up I won't be able to hear the signal."

But the baby soon forgot his worries and the house was silent again. Jeannie came out of the closet with the cap and Jim tried it on. It was a little small. "That's because you've let your hair get so long," Jeannie said. "Maybe I'd ought to cut it for you right now while you're waiting. Oh say, you forgot your razor."

"Never mind the razor. I'll just let my whiskers grow. And you ain't got time to no more than get started on my hair."

They sat quietly for a long time. "I would have had plenty of time to cut your hair if I'd started then," Jeannie complained.

Outside there was a shrill whistle as if a man were calling a dog and Jim jumped to his feet. He grabbed up his blanket roll and then put it down again and tiptoed into the bedroom and kissed the baby on the forehead. Then he threw the roll over his shoulder and grabbed up his rifle. "Now don't you worry none," he said, "because things will be all right." He was on the porch when he heard her calling in a low, strained voice.

"Jim, Jim! Wait a minute." She sounded scared. She was coming out to him. "You forgot your tobacco," she said, handing him a big sack of dry tobacco.

"Oh, yeah, sure," he said, relieved. "Now don't worry!" He trotted out into the night.

The other men were waiting for him in the road. It was dark and he couldn't see who they were at first, but he recognized Ned Wellhof's voice and then Mack's, and he got that swollen feeling in his throat again that he had had most of the time since Happy killed herself. He wondered if Mack had enough strength to stand up on a long march.

There were about a dozen men in the party. They walked along not saying much for a half mile. "Let's take across the field to McSlarrow's place," Mack ordered. They came to the railroad right-of-way fence and Jim started to crawl through but Mack stopped him and cut the wires.

Mack stopped beside a telegraph pole and felt of it. "It's kind of smooth to climb," he said.

"Here's an ax," one of the men said. He stepped forward, waving a hand to get the others out of the road, and began to chop. "It's hard as iron," he said.

Jim dropped the roll from his shoulder, and when the man stopped to pant Jim took the ax from him and started to work. He could see fairly well by this time. This was the first thing he had done to help out the revolution.

One other fellow took a turn with the ax, and then they got around the pole and pulled and pushed. It cracked and tilted, and they pulled it to the ground and cut the wires.

"Let's leave it on the track," someone suggested.

"Naw," Mack said. "Might cause a wreck and some innocent person would be killed. We got better ways of stoppin' the trains without riskin' nobody's life."

They cut the other right-of-way fence and walked on. This reminded Jim of the times when he went around on hallowe'en with a bunch of boys and upset privies, only this was damned serious business.

McSlarrow was ready for them and came out immediately, but the next house they came to was deserted. "The bastard run to town this afternoon, I guess," McSlarrow said. "I thought maybe he would. He's yaller." They cut his fences and marched on.

The man who lived at the next place was at home but didn't want to come. They yanked him out protesting, but after someone kicked him in the pants he walked along quietly.

They came to the river bank and walked along in the sand, still warm from the sun. There was a big glow up ahead. "Is that our camp?" Jim asked.

Mack answered in his queer strained voice. "No. That's the Indian camp, but we're goin' by there because some of the bucks are with us. John Medicine and Dick Cottontail and some others. They been tryin' to farm and know what it's like. The rest of the tribe lives off of the government, and they're so damned lazy that they won't turn over a finger to win back the whole state. Ain't much like their daddies and granddads, but I reckon it's the white man's fault, not theirs."

When they got to the Indian camp Jim saw the Indians were having their Green Corn Dance which was supposed to make the crops good, although most of them didn't care whether the crops were good or not.

They had put up a pole about forty feet high, and on top of the pole was a horse's skull. A big fire lighted up the scene. The only music they had that night was made by rattles which the squaws had tied around their legs under their skirts. The rattles were hollow gourds with pebbles in them.

When the dance started a few men, women and kids began hopping around the pole in a circle, singing and keeping time. Others crowded into the ring until it was full, then another circle formed just outside this one but going in the opposite direction, then another, and so on, until finally eight or ten circles were packed tight and swinging around the pole.

They all kept good time, and the rattles and the singing made good music. It was quite a sight. Jim thought how they must have danced this way before there was any such a thing as a capitalist system and maybe would dance this way after it was destroyed.

At these dances the Indians ate barbecued beef and what they called tomfuller. Tomfuller was made by cutting green corn off the cob and boiling it in a big kettle.

Two or three of the whites in Jim's crowd got into the circle and danced with the Indians, but Jim didn't feel like he ever wanted to dance again as long as he lived. All he wanted to do was to get into the big fight.

After a while they walked on. Jim's blanket roll had been hot early in the evening, but now the air began to get cool and he was more comfortable. They tramped for a couple of hours, adding a few new men to the group. Jim knew that some of the older ones must be getting tired, and he wondered how Mack was holding out.

But at last they saw a gleam in the distance and Mack announced that they were nearly there. They got out into the middle of the river bed. There was hardly any water in the river that time of year and the current was a half mile away against the other bank. A little later they came up to the fire and found about two hundred men milling around or sitting in the sand. The little fire, made of driftwood, was the main source of light, although a lantern gleamed here and there.

There were no sentries, but a man named Daniels, who seemed to be in command, held up a lantern and looked them over as they came up. He recognized Mack. "These fellers all right?" he asked.

"They're our crowd," Mack answered.

"Well, make yourselves comfortable," Daniels said, "and pretty soon there'll be some orders."

Daniels had a big red sash around his middle. After a little while he ordered everyone to sit down and he made a speech.

"Comrades," he said, "we're here to see that the big slick in Washington don't send us over to France, us and a million other fellers that don't want to go, to kill German working people who don't want the war no more than we do."

The crowd yelled and applauded.

"The whole damned country is up in arms tonight. We got word already from Holdenville, Konawa, Wewoka, Lone Dove, and Friendship, and other towns, and at every one of these places the farmers is raisin' hell. There's been eight or nine of our boys arrested in Pottawatomie County. The waterworks at Dewar was blown all to hell and they got nine of our men in jail. But it don't make no difference if they got a few fellers in jail. We got 'em whupped."

The crowd yelled. Men jumped up and threw their hats in the air. Everybody went crazy with excitement, and it was a long time before they got quiet again. Jim and Mack forgot their troubles and joined in as much as anybody. It made them feel good to know that things had really started to happen.

Old man Daniels went on with his speech. "We been hearin' what the town people thinks of this here rebellion. They're so scared that the ones who've got outdoor privies is afraid to go to 'em for fear the farmers'll git 'em. We got all the wires cut, so they can't send out no messages or git no news, and tonight we're gonna stop the trains. The bankers is goin' crazy about all the crops bein' destroyed, and they're tryin' to git the officers of the law to go out in the country and arrest us, but they ain't no officer got guts enough to git outside the city limits. Even old Sam Gladson ain't in no hurry."

More yelling.

"Now tonight, we're all gonna march to that big hill in my pasture. You fellers that's got gunny sacks, when you go through a field of corn you pick a sackful of roastin' ears. And tomorrow mornin' we'll rustle around and find a few nice fat calves. All this here is ours. It ain't the banker's in town. We raised it. He didn't. We're gonna take what we need to eat on the march. Tomorrow, when we've got a lot of beef and corn ready, we'll get word to start marchin' to Washington, and we'll be joinin' up with about a million other fellers like us, and they ain't nothin' can stop us."

More cheers.

"Now I want a few volunteers to do a little job or two, and then the rest of you can organize to march to the hill."

Most of the men jumped up to volunteer, but Jim crowded to the front and was chosen for one of the crews. They had to wait about a half hour for orders because there was a lot of confusion, but Daniels finally got around to them, took them to one side, and told them in a low voice that their job was to burn the railroad bridge over the South Canadian.

There were five of them, all young. Daniels looked them over by the light of his lantern and poked his finger in Jim's direction. "You take command and don't come back till that there bridge is burnin' good. If they got guards there you find out a way to burn the bridge anyway. Go up on it easy and take 'em by surprise." He handed one of them a fruit jar. "That there is full of kerosene," he explained. "You know where my pasture is. You report there when you git the job done."

Jim and the four others started silently down the river. When they were out of sight of the encampment one of the fellows pulled out a bottle and suggested a drink. "I don't think we ought to git stewed," Jim said, "till we git this bridge burned."

The others agreed and they walked on. It was several miles to the bridge and Jim was afraid that daylight would come before they got the job done. He had no idea what time it was. "We better walk kinda fast," he said.

It was hard to see where they were going and once they stumbled into an oozy place where they sank in to their ankles. "We're too far to the left," Jim said, "gittin' over close to the current."

They veered to the right but soon found that the current was directly ahead of them. "It crosses the bed here," one of the boys decided.

They followed the edge of the stream to the bank and crawled up through the cattails. They found a cowpath along the bank and kept it for a mile. They were stopped by the right-of-way fence. By stooping they could see the bridge outlined against the sky. Jim gripped his rifle and whispered to the others, "We hadn't ought to come at it along the track because the guards would be there, and besides, we gotta set it afire at the bottom. Le's go back a ways and get into the bed again."

They sneaked along the path for a hundred yards, and then Jim pushed cautiously through the weeds to the bank. He slid down and his feet splashed into water, making a big noise. They stopped and listened for a while but heard nothing alarming. "Even if they heard it they'd think it was just a piece of bank cavin' in," Jim explained. "We gotta wade, but go mighty slow so you won't splash."

The damp and froggy smell of the river reminded him of fishing trips and the fun he and Jeannie used to have on the river. He waded through an oozy little pond, and when he found a dry sandbar he dropped to his hands and knees and crawled along, as he used to do when he was hunting ducks, careful not to get sand in his gun.

When they were within fifty yards of the bridge they huddled up to talk it over. "I don't think there's anybody there," Jim said.

A popping noise came from the bridge and they started. "Hell they ain't!" one of the boys whispered. They listened for a long time but heard nothing else.

"Well, if they got guards they're all asleep," Jim said.

"I know what we can do," said the boy with the jar of kerosene. "You and me'll sneak up there, and you get two or three matches ready and I'll bust the fruit jar on the poles, and you strike a match and we'll beat it."

"Yeah," another agreed, "and if anybody cracks down on you we'll start shootin' at the flashes of their guns."

"All right," Jim said. "You fellers keep our rifles and git down here on your bellies, and if trouble starts keep shootin' until we git back."

"Here, take this pistol," one of the boys said, handing Jim a large revolver. "It's single action, you know."

Jim and the boy with the kerosene crawled forward on their bellies. The bridge looked enormous as they got close to it. Jim realized that five hundred men could be perched out of sight on its timbers.

Inch by inch they got to it until Jim felt one of the big poles. He took hold of the sleeve of the other fellow and pulled him around the pole and to one of the big cross timbers. Jim got a couple of matches ready. "All right," he whispered.

The fruit jar crashed and Jim felt a drop of kerosene splatter on his cheek. The other was running. Jim struck his matches and held them under the beam but couldn't get the flame to take hold of the flat surface. The matches burnt his fingers and he dropped them. Immediately a flame leaped up from the sand where the kerosene had spilled, and began to lick around the beam. Jim sprinted after the other fellow. He looked back and saw flames dancing.

The others were ready to run when Jim reached them, and the five trotted along in the soft sand. They splashed through the little pool and crawled up into the weeds. They were safe here so they slowed to a walk. They kept looking back, expecting to see the sky lit up by great flames, but they could see only a flicker now and then through the jungle on the river bank.

"Le's climb that knoll," Jim suggested, "and see what we can see."

They scrambled up a dune and looked back. There was no flame, but the eastern sky was gray.

Jim was worried. "I don't think it's burnin' like it ought to," he said. "I'm gonna take this pistol again and go back and be sure. You boys wait for me on the path."

After a little hesitation he started back. It was easier to see where he was going now and he avoided the slimy little pool that they had crossed twice.

He walked fast. He was fairly sure there were no guards, but he kept the pistol cocked. The blaze had gone out and the bridge was as good as ever.

Daylight was coming rapidly. He let the hammer of the pistol down and thrust the gun, handle down, into a hip pocket. Against one of the poles of the bridge was a pile of dry driftwood. Methodically he went about breaking off twigs and building a camp fire under the big beam. He dragged up larger sticks and piled them carefully until the space under the beam was filled with good fuel. The job took a long time, but when he left man-sized flames were jumping up about the beam.

It was broad daylight now, and he walked along carelessly, sure that there were no guards. "It was all right," he told the others. "Just a little slow." They could see smoke rolling up now.

A mile farther on they stopped, and Jim unrolled his blanket roll. There was enough chicken and bread and butter for the five of them. When they finished eating they drank the sandy water of the river current and took a few swallows of corn whiskey.

As they were crossing a cornfield a little later they came upon a cow lying on her side. She was badly bloated from eating too many roasting ears. One of the boys whetted his pocket knife on his gun barrel, measured off a span from the left hip bone, and plunged the knife into her belly. Gas hissed out of the wound. "She'll git all right," the boy said, "but maybe it'll learn her a lesson."

# TWENTY-NINE

JIM AND THE OTHERS were dead tired when they got to the hill about eight o'clock. On the horizon they could still see a column of smoke.

As Jim unslung his blanket roll he estimated that there were about a hundred men on the hill. They were all busy. Some were building a stone fence around the edge of the hill top. Others were carrying wood and water, butchering, digging trenches for barbecuing, shucking roasting ears, or cutting corn of the cob. A big pole was just going up with a red flag nailed to it. As the pole settled into the hole and the dirt was tamped about it the men stopped work for a while to cheer.

Jim wondered if other red flags were going up all over the nation, or was this the only one? Maybe this was the first flag of the new workers' and farmers' republic, or the first red flag in the world to be put up by a farmers' army. Or something important. Jim felt drunk from lack of sleep. Most of the men acted like they were having a picnic.

Daniels walked up to them and said in a low voice: "Well, I seen a lot of smoke down the river, and I guess you boys done a good job. Now, don't talk about it to nobody. If you ain't too tired you can shuck roastin' ears for a little while."

Barbecuing was already under way. A pit had been dug as

large as a wagon box, and in the pit was a heavy bed of coals. The fire was kept up by the addition of fresh sticks constantly, but never enough new wood to make a big blaze. Over the top of the pit a piece of chicken wire was stretched, and hunks of beef lay on it browning and oozing molten fat into the fire. It looked and smelled good, although Jim was full of fried chicken.

Jim joined some men who were shucking the green corn. It felt good to sit down. He pulled off green shucks and shook fat white worms out of the wet silk. "Maybe we otta leave a few worms in, to kinda flavor the tomfuller," he said.

Mack, not far away, was cutting corn from the cob. "You know," he said, "if that there flag was a horse's skull we could have us a Green Corn Dance."

Jim saw that the old man was looking quite natural, even though he had been up all night.

"You know, them Indians get quite a lot of fun out of life," the fellow next to Jim observed. "They do something like this every year."

"We ought to overthrow the government once a year," Mack said. "I don't see why we put it off so long."

Jim smelled coffee and remembered he hadn't had any that morning. He wondered if going without coffee would give him a headache, and after he thought about it a while his head began to ache, and he quit work long enough to drink a cup of very black coffee. He wasn't used to being tired and sleepy at this time of day, and the sleepiness made the sunlight seem wrong and out of place. It was hard to think of the day before as yesterday because he hadn't slept between the two days.

In spite of the coffee he grew more and more sleepy and he was glad when the work slackened an hour later and he could spread his blanket under a blackjack. He rolled off into sleep and dreamed he was a kid in school and was afraid of the teacher, but the teacher turned out to be a cow he was taking to the bull, and he didn't know where the baby was, and he spent hours, very worried, looking for the baby in Oklahoma City.

He slept so well that he forgot where he was, and when the flies finally bothered him awake he sat up and looked around surprised. It was late afternoon and the sun was on him. The back of his shirt was wringing wet, but the front, where the sun had shone, was hot and dry. He felt tired through and through, but he knew he couldn't sleep any more. He put his back against the shady side of the tree and stretched. Then he rolled himself a cigarette. His head was full of springs and he shook it to feel them buzz. He closed his eyes and dozed a minute and started looking for the baby, and when he woke once more he wondered if he'd ever see the kid again.

He wondered why the army was not on the march to Washington. Some of the men were still asleep, and others were milling around doing this or that little job, but no one seemed to be making preparations for the march. It was probably too late to start that day and they would wait and get an early start the next day. How long would it take to march? Maybe months, with fighting along the way.

Not far away a Negro was sleeping, with flies on his face, and Jim remembered that he was Bill Johnson, the one who had been tricked into eating a raw mouse by Son-of-a-bitch Rehlin, as the poor farmers called him.

Up here on the hill Negroes were treated just like whites. It was always like that among Socialist farmers because Socialists knew that all working men white or black, were in the same boat. Jim got to studying Johnson's face and then remembered the Negro he had seen lynched when he was a boy. It still made him sick to think about it.

He'd been about fifteen years old at the time. He'd heard that a colored man was going to be lynched, and he'd gone with a couple of other young fellows to see what would happen.

In those days he had no idea of what human beings could be at their worst. He had never seen anything more horrible than a herd of pigs pulling the entrails out of a sick horse, and he thought that pigs were the lowest of all animals.

He and the other boys arrived just in time to see the lynching. They crowded up and saw a half dozen town loafers wrestling with the Negro, who was a middle-aged man with a high forehead and streaks of gray in his hair. The Negro, Jim learned later, was a school teacher and an excellent musician, and was not guilty of the crime charged against him.

At first it was hard to realize that anything serious was going on. It looked like friendly scuffling that you might see on the school grounds. The white men were half grinning and half serious. The onlookers were quiet, and you could hear the Negro gasping and hear the thud of a fist against skin wet with blood. They were carrying the Negro to the top of a little knoll so that everyone could see.

It was the sight of blood on the Negro's ashy face that made Jim understand what was happening. He had heard of lynchings but had never before realized what they meant. He couldn't help but put himself in the Negro's place and imagine a dozen hands gripping him while fists crashed against his mouth.

Jim saw one of the whites insert the blade of a pocket knife into the Negro's nose and heard a choking yell. Then they stood the Negro on his feet, and one fellow yanked open his pants and reached in. Jim saw the white man's hairy elbow jerking back and forth as he sawed with a dull knife, heard the Negro screaming and gagging. The crowd closed in.

Jim began to get sick. He saw the dried tobacco juice on the chin of the white man, saw the thing that the man held up and the stream of blood picking its way among the hairs on the man's arm. The crowd surged on, but Jim fell behind. He had had as much as he could take, and he lay down under a tree and tried to keep from vomiting.

All this had been a long time ago, but Jim still remembered it when he thought of the Negro people. Because his folks had been Northerners he was never taught racial prejudice and could not understand it. He saw that Johnson was waking up and decided to strike up a conversation with him.

The Negro groaned and struck at the flies, then sat up and looked about in surprise, as Jim had done.

"Feller sure can't sleep very well with all these damn flies," Jim remarked.

Johnson rubbed his eyes and focused them on Jim with difficulty. "Yeah," he agreed, "but Ah reckon we'll have wuss than flies to put up with on this trip."

"You think we'll be startin' to Washington tomorrow?" Jim asked.

"Well, Ah'm 'fraid we ain't gonna get ve'y faw if we *do* stawt."

"What you mean?"

"Well, we ain't got no discipline; long's everything's quiet and peaceful we get along fine, but when we run up against some soldiers we ain't got a chance. Ah was in the wah in Cuba, and Ah got a bullet in mah neck that glanced off the side of a buildin'. You can feel it."

Johnson guided the tip of Jim's finger to a lump on his neck. "That one hit me and stuck. Well, Ah know what it's like to be in a battle, and Ah know what fellas will do in a battle when they ain't been trained. Now, we ain't had no trainin,' and jest as soon as the fight stawts weah' blowed up."

Jim studied a while. "Well, I guess you're right," he said. "Maybe we ought to get some trainin'."

Johnson shook his head. "We ain't got no *time*. It takes a good many months and mighty hawd wuk to make a soldier, and you cain't do it all at once. Now, Ah wouldn't say this to nobody but you o' Mistah Mack, somebody that undahstands, and Ah ain't aimin' to discourage nobody. Ah'll stay heah long as anybody; but the way Ah look at it we jest as well quit and go home unless jest about every fawmaw and wukin' man in the whole country is on the mahch along with us, then they'd be so many of us that nobody would try to stop us."

"Well, maybe since you been in the war," Jim said, "you ought to line us up here while we're waitin' and give us a little trainin'.'"

"Naw suh," Johnson said with a smile. "A colu'd man cain't be put ovah a bunch of white men to train 'em. Ain't nobody likes to be trained, and some of these boys wouldn't listen to nothin' Ah said, and Ah wouldn't blame 'em. It jest cain't be done."

They talked a while longer, then Jim said he guessed he'd mosey around and see what the other fellows were doing. What Johnson had said sounded like common sense and he wanted to talk to Mack about it.

His whiskers were long enough to make him itch under the chin and he longed for a razor to dig into them. Fingernails didn't do any good. The Indians had a good system. They pulled the hairs out one by one with a pair of tweezers.

Jim saw Mack talking with Daniels, but they didn't seem to be saying very much, so he walked up to them. Mack was looking white and weak again.

"Didn't you sleep none, Mack?" Jim asked.

"Yeah, I had a snooze."

Jim hesitated for a little while before he asked the next question. "You fellers know yet when we're gonna start?"

They were slow in answering. "Ain't no word," Daniels said, "and Carson ain't showed up or sent any word, but don't talk about it among the men that we're down in the mouth or anything, or some of them might git scared and beat it."

"One feller already left," Mack said grinning. "You remember that feller we picked up last night, I forget his name, that we had to argue with? Well, he slipped off somehow, and I reckon he tore his tail into town and told 'em a story that'll make 'em have to go to the privy, even if it is out in the alley."

"Well, Mack," Daniels said, as if he were resuming some talk they had been having. "I think you ought to git up and say somepin' after supper. You're one of the commanders here, and it'll do the fellers good."

Mack squatted and began tossing his knife into the ground. "Well, I don't take much to makin' speeches, but I reckon it won't hurt me none."

Many of the men were up and milling around now, and some of them were fixing to eat. Jim was hungry, and he went over to where the barbecued meat was spread out on a tablecloth. He waved the flies away and picked a piece that looked juicy. He dipped a tin cup into the big kettle of tomfuller and began to eat. It tasted good.

"Perty good, eh?" he remarked to Dick Cottontail, who was standing beside him.

"There's not enough salt," Dick said. Jim knew that Dick was educated but was a little bit surprised to hear him speak so easily. As the Indian said "salt" he made a quick gesture as if he were sprinkling salt into the pot. Indians talked with their hands as well as their mouths, but it was not the same as when a white man got excited and waved his hands around. Jim knew that an old Indian who didn't know a word of English could make himself understood that way and could understand a white man's clumsy gestures in answer.

"It cooked too long," Dick said, making the flames dance under a pot. "White people don't know how to cook outdoors." He turned his palm up and swung his hand around as if he were fingering the sky, and you knew the motion meant "outdoors."

The Indian seemed not much interested in the conversation and Jim went on with his eating.

After supper the men built a smudge and sat around it. Somebody started an argument on religion and Ned Wellhof said he wouldn't be a Socialist if he wasn't a Christian.

Another fellow spoke up and said that you couldn't be both if you understood what Socialism and what Christianity meant. Jim felt sorry for Ned. He didn't have a chance in the argument.

"If there is a God he ought to be horsewhipped," the atheist went on. "He's all-powerful and He's all-wise. He knew before He made me that I would be an atheist, and He could make me any way He pleased, and yet He made me an atheist so He could burn me in hell forever for his own mistake."

The argument went on. Ned said he didn't know whether they ought to take guns or not and kill people on the way to Washington. "It ain't God's way. If God wants us to go to Washington He'll provide a way."

"Well," the atheist said, "if we let Him provide a way He sure don't want us to go, because we wouldn't never get there."

The argument went on until old man Daniels got up to make a speech. The men uncovered the smudge a little to let the flames come through so they could see him.

"Comrades," he said, "we're lookin' for word tonight to start early tomorrow. There's a fellow here from the western part of the state, Comrade Allen, who says there was a gully-washer there yesterday and the farmers didn't get together. But he thinks they'll get together tonight. I ain't heard from the Army of the East, but I heard from a good many places around close and I know of over a thousand men in this section who are out with their guns. They ain't a train runnin' or a wire buzzin'."

The men clapped at this. "Now Comrade McGee is goin' to say a word," Daniels concluded.

Mack stood up and snapped his knife shut and stuck it in his pocket.

"Well, tomorrow mornin'," Mack said, "a bunch of the fellers that live around close will have teams and wagons down in the timber, and when we git word to start we'll load the wagons with tomfuller and meat that's well-cooked so it won't spoil. And you fellers don't need to hold back on the eats because there's plenty more where this come from. It's ours because we raised it, and we're gonna take it, by God, and use it like we're entitled to."

He sat down and there was more applause.

Jim spoke up and was surprised at himself. "There's one feller here that's been in real fights," he said, "and I think we ought to hear a little bit about how to march and fight from—Comrade Bill Johnson."

Everybody clapped at this. Johnson had to be urged by the men around him, but he stood up at last, grinning with embarrassment.

"Ah guess Ah ain't got so much to say, but all of us boys has got to stick togetheh, no matteh if wea'h black owa white owa red. And if we do that and get the otheh wukin' people with us on owa mawch they ain't nothin' can stop us, even if we ain't trained soljaws, all of us."

Speechmaking went on for some time. A couple of sentries came in and said they were tired and wanted to hear the speeches. Daniels called for volunteers and Jim was one of the men chosen. Daniels told him to go down the path toward the river about a quarter mile and to stop anybody that came along, and if anything happened to yell and fire his gun.

Jim got his rifle and sauntered down the path. It was a peaceful night and the stars were shining, and he felt more like he was on a coon hunt than in a revolution. But when he sat down on a stump in the edge of the timber he began to hear all sorts of strange noises. Twigs popped and leaves rustled. It didn't worry him much because he had often been in the woods at night and knew how many noises a fellow could hear, but he cocked his gun to have it ready. It made a couple of loud clicks as the hammer was being pulled back and you might have heard the noise a hundred yards away. If somebody came sneaking up Jim wanted to be ready to fire without making any such noise.

When he got used to the sounds he began to get drowsy, and to keep from going to sleep he got up and walked around. He looked at the stars and wondered about them and felt kind of stuffy and shut in when he thought that he never could find out what was on them.

He got to thinking about Happy and was surprised to find that he was a little bit relieved that she was dead. All the time she was alive she had been a strain on him. He decided he was the most selfish bastard in the world. When Happy was alive he couldn't help but wish Jeannie was dead—but he didn't really wish it, and wouldn't have harmed a hair on her head. He might even have given his own life to save hers. But part of him wished she would die. Now he would give anything if Happy could be alive and Mack could be like he was, but at the same time part of him was relieved.

Then he got to blaming himself for Happy's death and got pretty low and miserable. He wished now that he hadn't volunteered to stand watch. He hadn't ought to be alone to think about things. He hoped the march would start tomorrow so there would be something to do. If it wasn't for Jeannie and the kid he would want to get killed in some battle to sort of square things with everybody.

He walked around and tortured himself this way; then, when

he was a little tired, he sat down and thought about the same things. It seemed a long time before he heard steps on the path behind him.

"Who's that?" he called out.

"It's me, comin' down to take your place," a man answered, coming up to Jim. Jim recognized him but did not know his name.

"Anything happen?"

"Not a thing," Jim replied, "except a lot of poppin' and rustlin' that you'll get used to. You know how it always is in the woods at night."

THIRTY

JIM'S FIRST THOUGHT the next morning was that he wished he had a razor to dig at the whiskers under his chin. As soon as he got awake he felt very much alive and realized that he had been in a sort of daze the day before from excitement and lack of sleep. He went down the hill a ways and squatted behind a rock. He remembered that he hadn't done anything the day before and that was one reason he felt so stuffy. The sun wasn't up yet, but it was warm. He decided that the day would be a scorcher. The grass was wet and blades of dead grass stuck to his wet shoes.

He went back and drank coffee and ate more barbecued meat. The men all looked pretty discouraged. There hadn't been any word to march. Jim wondered if maybe this was the only bunch of men in the country who had really got together and were ready to go.

There was something wrong with Carson and the Socialists in Oklahoma City or they would have got word through before this. Maybe they had all turned yellow. Jim didn't say anything about it to the others but he knew they were thinking the same thing.

Mack came up to him. "You want to go on a little deer hunt?" he asked, "Only we probably won't find a deer, and a nice fat calf will do just as well."

Jim was glad to get something to do. He and Mack and a couple of others sauntered down the path and through a little patch of timber. They heard a cowbell in the distance and made for it. They didn't talk very much.

A jackrabbit hopped up and leaped off a hundred yards, then stopped and looked at them. He would have been a pretty shot but they couldn't waste ammunition on him. A flock of quail exploded out of the weeds along a fence and startled them, and from habit Jim picked out one over his rifle barrel and gave it the proper lead and imagined himself pulling the trigger. "God," Mack said, "I thought maybe you was crazy enough to shoot at a quail with that rifle."

Jim took a chew of tobacco, then stopped a minute to watch some tumblebugs working. "Looks like the stock around here has all got the scours," he said, "so these bugs has got mighty soft stuff to work with."

"A lot of stock will founder," Mack said, "like some of us old farmers if we go ahead and set up the right sort of government. Before we get used to havin' enough to eat we'll founder."

When they came to the herd they saw a plump young heifer and decided she would do, but there was no use carrying her all that distance, so they rounded up the bunch and drove them toward the hill. Pushing the cattle through the fields they felt they were just out at work on a hot morning. The revolution seemed like a dream.

At the foot of the hill Jim separated the heifer from the rest, and at a moment when she was standing still and staring at him a little worried by all this he raised his rifle and aimed at the middle of her forehead. When the rifle crashed her legs doubled under her and she hit the ground with a grunt. Mack cut her throat so she would bleed well. One of the other men had an ax and with this he cut a light pole in the timber a few rods away.

There was a friendly yell from the top of the hill, and Jim looked up to see the men bunched up behind the wall looking down at them. Evidently the shot had caused a lot of commotion on the hill before the men up there knew who had fired it. They had no sentries during the day, because they could see so far from the top of the hill, but Jim decided they could keep a better watch than they had been keeping. Men should be posted all the time to warn them if a body of men approached.

They lashed the feet of the heifer together and hoisted her on the pole, and the four of them trudged up the hill with her. Jim stood a while, when they got to camp, and watched Cottontail skin the calf. The Indian was much faster than any white man he'd ever watched and every stroke was exactly right.

The day before they had put the guts in tubs and dragged them down to the timber, but now they left them where they dropped because they didn't expect to be there much longer.

There were dozens of dogs around, but the dogs were as full as the men and didn't do much except sleep in the shade or start a little fight now and then.

It was all a queer picnic, but everybody was tired of picnicking by that time. Some of the men were wondering how the women-folks were getting along, and one of them wished he had known it would be so long before they started because he could have gone home last night to see how everything was.

Jim saw Ned off by himself by the wall praying.

The day got hotter and hotter. The men sat around and talked, or worked slowly at the barbecuing. The smell of burnt meat hung heavy over the hill.

Mack seemed just about all in. He told Jim that if they didn't get word mighty soon they would have to scatter and hide out like the Jones Family. "This here little crowd sure can't overthrow no government," he said. "Daniels is gonna tell 'em pretty soon to scatter and lay low if we don't hear mighty quick."

As he was talking there came a yell from someone at the wall. "There's a crowd comin' through the timber."

They grabbed their guns and ran over to the wall. Twenty-five or thirty men carrying guns came out of the timber and marched toward them.

At first they thought it must be some fellows from the Army of the East coming to tell them where to march, but then they saw a little fellow swaying back and forth as he walked and they knew it was Ted Tetley. Then they recognized Sheriff Sam Gladson and other men and boys from town: Denny Payne and Bud Filmore and some more.

No one gave any orders, but all the farmers stood and looked down. Jim cocked his rifle and then wondered what to do. This was not what he had expected.

He realized all at once how much you had to hate a man in order to be able to pull up a rifle and kill him. You had to be insane with hatred to do it.

These damn fools from town, including his own brother, deserved to be killed maybe. They had come out here to force the farmers to join the army and hate the Germans and kill and be killed. They wanted to keep the capitalist system with all its cruelty and misery and insanity, so they ought to be killed. But how are you going to blaze away and kill a man you have known all your life, your own brother, just because he is fool enough to believe the lies the capitalists have told him?

Besides, what was the good of killing anybody when there wasn't going to be any revolution anyway likely? Some of the farmers were swearing at the town boys, but nobody raised a gun to fire.

"Well, all we gotta do," said Bill Johnson, "is to fiah one volley and them fellahs'll run like the bot flies was aftah 'em. You fellahs with rifles shoot real high so it'll ca'y ovah theih haids, and doan shoot inta the groun' because the bullets mot glance and hit somebody. But you fellahs with shotguns and buck shot, you doan shoot high because a buck shot mot ca'y up that fah. You shoot inta the groun'."

"Well now, wait a minute," Mack said. "If old Sam Gladson wasn't in that crowd it would be all right. But you know that old cuss. He's been shot a good many times, and you can't scare him. You gotta kill that old devil." Mack was white. "I ain't wantin' to kill that old fool," he continued.

"We was leavin' anyway," somebody said. "Le's git the hell outa here while we got a chance."

"Well, they's moah'n a hundad of us, and they's 'bout twenty-five of them, an' it doan look right foah a hundad men fo'tafied to run away from twenty-five. Ah was in the ahmy, an' Ah reckon Ah jes cain't run like that. Ah ain't gonna *open* fiah and kill nobody, but—"

Somebody started running and most of the crowd followed, sprinting across the top of the hill. Jim grabbed Mack's shoulder and yelled, "Come on, what's the use." Men were jammed tight in the driveway and some were vaulting over the wall. Mack and Jim trotted after them. About ten men, black and white, remained with Johnson.

Mack and Jim, behind the others, found themselves alone in the timber, and they struck off toward home, taking the shortest route.

"Well, that's the end of the whole mess," Mack said, "except we'll get rounded up one at a time and shot or sent to the pen."

"We'll get home about sundown if we hurry," Jim said.

Mack was weak. He stumbled once in a while. "These damn big Socialists in Oklahoma City," he said, "they went back on us. They talked big, but they went yellow. Talked a lot of us farmers into raisin' hell, but, by God, when they seen things wasn't goin' right they saved their hides, I bet."

"We left some good bedding up there," Jim said.

Mack stopped and looked back toward the hill. The red flag had been pulled down. "They's one thing maybe I otta done," he said. "You seen that Filmore kid in the crowd. If I was sure he was the one that got my girl into trouble I woulda taken your rifle and plugged him. After that I wouldn'ta minded what they done to me."

THIRTY-ONE

TED TETLEY had a great deal of news for the paper that week. The main story was, of course, the defeat of the rebels.

"Victory and tragedy," he wrote, "marked the heroic expedition of a little army of citizens that went out to put an end to the arson and terror that had gripped the countryside."

He described the victory first. "The little band of patriotic citizens, under the command of the fearless old fighter Sam Gladson, went to the hill where the traitors were camped and fortified, and without a moment's hesitation marched up and captured the place without firing a shot.

"The traitorous band did not have the courage to fight, although they had every advantage. They ran like turkeys.

"The Boy Scouts could have routed the bunch, who fight just like they farm. But no one knew how yellow the outfit was and for two days it looked as if a lot of help was really needed."

Ted gave the names of the Members of the heroic little band, putting his own name last.

He told the news from the surrounding counties. There were many wild rumors, but nothing very definite. Rioting and bridges burned. In that locality there seemed to be about three hundred rebels, although there were at least a thousand in the whole area, and on the other side a thousand patriots were known to be armed and on the march rounding up the rebels.

Ted gave his editorial opinion without mincing words. He said: "It is unthinkable that three hundred men should take up arms, raise the red flag, engage in wholesale arson and assassination, terrorize three counties, and then be permitted to continue their campaign of preparation for another day of discord and trial of strength. Every man who followed McGee and Daniels in the recent insurrection should ascend a Federal scaffold or spend the remainder of his days in a Federal prison."

In another column he told of the tragedy that had "marred the day of victory."

"As the little band of citizens was returning with their prisoners, the tragic accident occurred which must in the final analysis be blamed squarely upon the traitors, for otherwise it could not have happened.

"One of the members of the band, Bud Filmore, a well-known local boy, was demonstrating to a companion the safety on a new automatic shotgun when the gun was accidentally discharged, the load of buckshot striking Sam Gladson, veteran officer, in the back, and killing him instantly.

"Young Filmorc explained that when he pulled the trigger he was sure that the safety was on. The safety is not plainly marked and he was mistaken at the moment as to which way was 'on' and which 'off.'

"When the body of the sheriff was brought home, Mrs. Gladson collapsed from shock and grief and is said to be in a serious condition. Funeral arrangements have not yet been made.

"The entire community joins Mrs. Gladson in her grief and extends to her its sympathy."

The rest of the column was devoted to a long obituary on the dead sheriff, telling how he had grown up with the community, fighting always on the side of law and order; how he had joined the church when a young man and had always been deeply religious; how he had never shirked his duty and had faced death on numerous occasions, having been wounded many times.

"And on the last day of his life he displayed the same courage that has marked his every act. As he walked ahead of his band up the hill toward this band of apparently dangerous and desperate traitors he did not once falter, rushing forward at the last moment to capture ten of the traitors who were too sluggish or ignorant to get away as fast as the others.

"His service to the community cannot be overestimated. He and his kind have helped to build up this great country to its position as the strongest and most prosperous nation on earth, and Sam Gladson, dying as he did in the performance of his duty, is just as much a hero as if he had died fighting the Huns on Flanders Field."

In still another article Ted described the ten prisoners captured by the patriotic band.

"They are a shabby and worthless lot," he said. "The most noteworthy of them is a colored man, Bill Johnson, who was arrested only a few days ago for attempting to steal a load of wheat but was released on a promise of good behavior. His 'good behavior' consisted of taking up arms against the government."

THIRTY-TWO

JIM AND MACK didn't talk much on their walk home from Daniels' hill. There was not much to say. But once when they were resting Mack got started and talked for a little while about the whole affair.

"Us fellers went off half-cocked," he said. "We wasn't ready to overthrow the government. You can't get ready overnight or in a month, or even in a year. The American people ain't ready. Them fellers down at Oklahoma City, and this Carson the son-of-a-bitch, they backed down on us. They turned yellow. If we have to be hanged, then I hope every one of them is lynched. Now, Gene Debs ain't that kind. If he started something like this he would be there to finish it.

"But they ain't very many Debs in the Socialist party. He's been fightin' the capitalists for years, and he knows something about it. Us farmers don't. We're farmers and ain't had no trainin' to do anything else. Some of us ain't very good farmers, maybe.

"The Socialist party ain't got enough good leaders. You know how it is with farmin', a feller ought to be born and raised on the farm to know very much about it, and I guess it's like that with revolution: we got to wait till we got thousands of youngsters who don't think or talk about anything but revolution before we can do a damn thing. I won't live to see it. Maybe you will. That kid of yours maybe will help finish up this job that we made such a mess of.

"Take me, for instance. I ain't no fighter. I wasn't brought up that way. I been thinkin' about other things all my life. I'm old. When my girl died it jist about laid me out. I'm ignorant. I ain't fit to command a Socialist army. And you. You got a wife and a kid that means a lot to you. And you don't know nothin' either. There wasn't a one of them fellers up on the hill that had the training to do what we tried to do.

"But in twenty years, or maybe fifty years, there'll be thousands of fellers who are real leaders and revolutionists, and millions of farmers and working men like us ready to follow these leaders. Then it'll happen. It's got to happen. I know that much. Ain't no gettin' around it.

"When we talked about overthrowin' the capitalist system we was like a bunch of roosters in the henhouse crowin' at midnight. To listen to 'em you'd think it was mornin' sure enough. But that don't make it mornin'. But, at the same time, you can be sure they'll start crowin' again in a few hours, and that time they'll be right."

They got to Jim's place about sundown. Jeannie was feeding the chickens. She looked tired, and like she had been crying. Her hair kept falling down into her eyes and she kept pushing it back.

Jim leaned his rifle against the windmill. "Well, it's all blowed up," he said.

"What happened?" Jeannie asked.

The old man saw the baby in his pen beside the house. "Hey, there," he yelled and went over to the pen, glad to get away from the story.

Jeannie went on shelling corn and tossing it to the chickens while Jim told her the story of their retreat. "Well," she said, "we're sure in for it."

Jim and Jeannie walked over to the baby's pen. The baby was very dirty. He pulled himself up and reached for his grandfather's face. The old man chuckled. "Hey, Sandy. How you been gittin' along? You been helpin' with the chores? Yeah, I bet you done a lot while your dad was gone. I bet you helped with the chores. I bet you did." The old man kept poking a finger at the baby's fat little belly, and the baby cackled with delight. "I bet you was a big help. Yes you was."

"Just since you been gone he's learned to say 'Da-da,' " Jeannie said.

"Is that a fact!" Jim exclaimed. For a while they all tried to get the baby to say "Da-da," but he refused.

"Of course he won't, now when you want him to," Jeannie said. "If you men will chase the cows in the lot I'll go in and fix some supper. You must be hungry."

"No, no. I ain't a bit hungry," Mack protested. "I'll run my cows over home and git started with the milkin' as soon as the flies let up."

They argued for a while, but the old man had his way. Jim didn't want any supper either. He felt bad. He tried to eat but couldn't.

As long as there was something to do it wasn't so bad, but when they finally got to bed Jim's troubles began. He couldn't stop thinking about what would happen to him within the next few days.

Probably the town fellows were organizing a lynch mob about now and would come out and lynch the farmers that they could find. White men had been lynched lots of times. He thought of what they had done to the Negro. He sat up in bed and looked out the window. The night was very still.

"What's the matter?" Jeannie asked. She hadn't been asleep either.

"I ain't sleepy," he explained. "Guess I'll set up for a while. You go on to sleep."

He got up and put on his clothes. He looked about for his rifle and remembered that he had left it at the well. He went out and got it and came back and sat down in a rocker beside the window and listened.

He heard all sorts of noises again. Several times he was sure he heard men coming. Once they seemed to be right in the yard and he slipped out the back door and crouched by the steps.

He felt like going out into the woods, but he couldn't leave Jeannie in the house alone. She was wide awake, he knew, and was scared too, because of the way he was acting.

The night got quiet again, and after a while he went back into the house. This was the first time since he was a little kid that he had been really scared.

Once he heard a shot—several shots—coming from the direction of town. Of course the town was excited. Probably everybody was up and armed, expecting a bunch of farmers to come in and raise hell. This idea made Jim feel better. Maybe the town boys were just as scared as he was. He sat in the rocker and dozed off now and then.

It was funny—the things he dreamed. Instead of dreaming of fighting and lynching, as might have been expected, he dreamed of nice things—going swimming and eating a picnic lunch with dill pickles. Then it seemed that he was at the depot and trying to get on the train, but people kept crowding off and wouldn't let him on. The train started, and he saw Happy there on the steps trying to get off, but she couldn't because the train was going too fast. He tried to run beside the train, but he was stiff and could hardly move. He put his hands on the ground and caught hold of grass and twigs and pulled himself along, and that way he went faster.

When he woke up after this dream he knew he couldn't sleep any more and wished it was morning. He felt weak now, and washed out, but he wasn't afraid of the town mob.

The baby rolled around in his bed, woke up, and began to jabber. Jim heard the syllables, "Da-da." He felt that he had never been so grateful for anything as he was for that. He laid his rifle down, tiptoed to the baby, changed his diaper, and picked him up; sat down in the rocker again holding the kid. Jim felt relieved and happy.

The baby was delighted and stood up in Jim's lap, pounded his father's face with a soft hand, pulled his hair, jabbered, and tried to climb to his shoulder.

"You little devil," Jim said. "I wouldn't a missed havin' you for anything in the damned world. Don't talk so loud, you little cuss. You'll wake your mother."

For about a half hour the two scuffled in the dark. Then the kid rubbed his slobbery face on Jim's neck, settled down slowly, and went to sleep. Jim sat there until the sky showed a streak of daylight, holding the baby and thinking about all that had happened.

Then he got up carefully and stowed the baby in bed. The front of his overalls was wet where the kid had been lying. Jim felt dizzy and kind of drunk as he went out to milk. It was early, and the cows' bags would get pretty full again before night, but it wouldn't hurt 'em. Jim was damned glad to get to work at something. He wondered why he had ever hated to do things. If he could get out of all this trouble now he would work twelve hours a day every day in the year, like Jeannie did, and be tickled to death for the chance.

He drank some milk and got so sleepy that he thought he would fall off the stool. When he took the milk to the house Jeannie was up and stirring the ashes out of the kitchen stove.

THIRTY-THREE

WHILE HE WAS ON DANIELS' HILL Mack had learned
something which he did not tell Jim. Pete Taylor, who used to be
janitor up at the high school, had told it around before he died
that he had seen Mr. Hardman, the high school teacher, fooling
with Happy in the high school building after school one night.

Mack didn't tell Jim because he was afraid Jim would take it
on himself to go and kill the school teacher, then Jim would be
in trouble, and he had a family. Jim was in plenty of trouble anyway, of course, but this would get him electrocuted or lynched
sure enough. Maybe Jim would be let off with a prison sentence
for this rebellion. Mack was hoping that some way he could find
a chance to shoot Mr. Hardman as soon as the school teacher
returned to town. That was the only thing Mack had to live for
now. After that he didn't care what happened to him.

Since Happy had killed herself Mack had got old, for the first
time. Always before that he had felt like he was good for a long time
yet. He never thought of himself as an old man. But he was really
old now. He didn't have the spring in him that he used to have. He
had to push himself to head off an old cow that didn't want to go
through the gate. It was all he could do to get around her, although
she was just trotting. Mack, all at once, was old and crippled.

He did the milking and put the milk away. The house looked
like a hog-pen. With the girl gone there was nobody to keep

things straight. For the first time in thirty-some years Mack didn't have a woman around to keep things straight.

He had always known that he was a failure, but up until now he had always felt that he still had time to make good; things would get better. Now he knew that he didn't have time. He was honest-to-God old. His hands were shaky. The veins stood out. The hair on them was silver white against the leather skin. He was old and petered out.

When he was young he had always supposed, without thinking very much about it, that he would have as much time the last thirty years of his life as he had the first thirty. But it wasn't like that. When a fellow got to his 'teens he had already lived half his life, even if he lived to be a hundred. That was the way it seemed, and it didn't make any difference even if years now were really just as long as they had been half a century ago. They seemed only a tenth as long, and that was all that counted. When days went by lickety-split they might as well be minutes.

By God, when a fellow is young he ought to take time once in a while just to stretch himself and realize that he is young and strong and that he can do anything, and hop around and enjoy being young. Mack had hopped around plenty, and had plenty of good times, but he'd scarcely ever stopped to think about being young.

While he was busy with the milk he thought about all this, and kept from thinking about worse things. But when he was through with the work, and it was good and dark, his thoughts got worse. He lit the lamp and thought how much different the house would look if the girl were there.

It was his fault, what happened to her. She'd been just a kid and needed looking-after. He wished he could go over to Jim's and Jeannie's now and play with the kid, but the kid would be asleep, and all he would do going over there would be to make

Jim and Jeannie as miserable as he was. He was so damned old and good-for-nothing that he ought to be knocked in the head. The first thing you knew he would be helpless and have to be spoon-fed. God-damned if he'd be a burden on anybody. Blow his own brains out first.

Tonight would be a good time for that. The gun was loaded. But Jeannie would have to work herself to death cleaning up the place and getting ready for the funeral.

Then there was something else to do, if possible. Kill that school teacher. If the government ever turned him loose alive he would shoot Hardman the first thing. Then there would be time to finish himself off.

That was the reasonable way to look at it, but the gun was right there and no telling what would happen before morning. Mack decided that he would have to get drunk to live through the night. He decided to go over to Ned's and get some corn.

He stumbled out across the fields, remembering what his father had done years before to a man teacher that kind of played with one of Mack's sisters, dead now. The teacher put his hand down in her dress, and she told her father. The old man took action.

Mack couldn't get along very fast because he was so old all at once. It seemed twice as far as he had thought. It was a hot night, but his feet got wet and cold with the dew. They would warm up when he got a drink. Jim would need a drink too. Mack decided to stop there on the way back and give Jim a drink.

He called hello when he got to Ned's house, and Ned answered from inside.

"This here is Mack," Mack called.

Ned came out in a minute, and Mack said he was sorry to wake him up but he felt like he couldn't get through the night without something to help him get up steam.

"Oh, I wasn't sleepin'," Ned said, "and I guess I won't sleep very much tonight. I got a little out here that you can have."

They walked about a hundred yards through the trees and Ned scratched a fruit jar out of a wood-rat's nest. "I ain't got a nickel," Mack said, "but of course I'll pay you soon as I can if they don't hang me."

"Now listen, Mack," Ned said. "I've took my last nickel from you. Whenever you need any liquor and I got any it's yours. I ain't makin' any more. It don't pay. It ain't the Lord's way. And if I git out of this trouble we're all in I'm gonna go straight, and I'm gonna git my kids together again and give them an education so they'll have a chance in the world. That is, if I ain't shot for takin' up arms agin the gov'ment."

They talked for a while, but Mack left finally and walked toward Jim's place. He had had one drink and there was a round hot place in his middle where the liquor had settled. His legs weren't any sprier than before, but they didn't hurt. The muscles in the back of his legs felt kind of weak, but good. That's where you feel the effects first, in the back of your legs.

He had been a failure, but he had got a lot out of life. He wasn't sorry that he hadn't been a very good slave for the capitalists, but he was sorry he hadn't looked after his girl better. But he hadn't known it was necessary. Jeannie was so much different. They didn't have a bit of trouble with Jeannie. She was like her mother. It was too bad Gladys hadn't been a boy.

The old man sat down to rest. It seemed like he had to drink an awful lot to feel the effects. When he was young he could get drunk smelling the cork. He would save plenty for Jim because Jim would need a good drink after all he had been through. Jim was as strong as an ox. There wasn't anything Jim couldn't do if he put himself to it.

All at once he found out that he was too *damned* drunk. Wheels in his head that had been spinning quiet and nice all at once cut loose and went so fast, and nothing to stop them, and he knew he was too *damned* drunk. Like the engine in an automobile, when you take out the clutch it is free all at once and it roars so fast you think it will shake itself to pieces.

The grass was just like a bed. It was wet, but you liked it wet sometimes.

He was sick as hell, but he was a tough old codger and didn't care. He had been through a lot in his life. Being alone out in the woods and sick didn't faze him. He vomited in the grass, and while he was vomiting he discovered that it was broad daylight and the sun was up hours. Time had been grinding by like it always did when all at once it slipped a cog, caught again, and the grinding went on; but hours had passed, and the sun had whirled half around the world, and there it was high in the sky. Even the dew had dried up.

Jim would need a drink. McGee got up on his knees to see how much the world would tilt. He decided that it wasn't tilting so much but what he could walk on it. He remembered what his dad had done to the school teacher, and he laughed.

Trying to get through the barbed-wire fence at Jim's place he slipped and tore his shirt and cut himself pretty bad. But it didn't make any difference. He was tough and you couldn't hurt him.

He walked up to Jim and Jeannie in the yard. They looked at him like he was a ghost. They started asking a lot of questions that didn't make any difference. They got him to sit down on a chopping log, but he wouldn't go in the house. Jeannie started washing the place on his back where he was cut, and he said never mind because he'd been a failure all his life.

Jeannie started bawling then, and there was nothing to bawl about. He'd been hurt ten thousand times worse than this. He told them about what his old dad had done to the little school teacher that put his hand down in the dress of one of Jeannie's aunts, dead now.

The old man, Jeannie's granddad, came to school when he heard about it, and he had a piss-ellum club about twice the size of your finger, and he walked right up to the front of the room and he whipped the britches right off of that little teacher. The teacher wasn't big enough to do anything but yell and wrestle. The old man just whipped him so hard behind and in front and up and down his legs that his britches tore, and he just whipped the britches right off of him. The teacher screamed just like a girl. It was kind of a bloody sight. When it was over the teacher just kind of laid there on the floor, bare and bloody, and cried. It wasn't a nice sight, but it didn't make no difference because all the girls had run out scared when it first happened, and didn't any of them see him.

The boys stood around and looked at him a while, then they all went off fishing; and there wasn't any more school that year because the teacher never did show up again.

Jeannie kept shaking him and asking him if he had milked the cows that morning, and he finally told her that he couldn't because of the way the sun had come up, all at once. She didn't know what he meant and he tried to explain, but she couldn't understand. He gave it up. She decided that he hadn't milked and told Jim to hurry over there because the cows would be suffering. The flies would be terrible, she said, but Jim would just have to milk anyway. Maybe he could rope the cows and tie their legs. She couldn't leave the baby and Mack there alone or she would go along and mind the flies off while he milked.

Mack tried to get Jim to take a drink, but Jim wouldn't. Jeannie and Jim pulled him into the house and put him down on the bed. He tried to tell them again how the school teacher looked with his britches off, but they told him to go to sleep.

"That's what a fellow deserves when he fools around with a young girl," the old man said. They agreed with him but told him to go to sleep.

THIRTY-FOUR

LEM EDWARDS, Ted Tetley's boss, hated Ted thoroughly but was unable to get along without him. He knew Ted's peculiarities, and on occasion would quietly torture the cripple by way of entertaining himself.

On the morning after the incident of Daniels' hill Ted was very important and excited. He was even singing at times in his terrible flat voice. Edwards wanted to reduce him to some degree of humility.

"Hey, Ted," Edwards said, "you was kind of gone on the Mc-Gee girl, wasn't you? The one that shot herself?"

"Huh!" said Ted, suddenly tense.

Edwards knew he had scored. "I kinda figgered you was soft on her, but I jist found out why you didn't git no place with her. You had perty stiff competition."

Edwards bared his long yellow teeth in a grin, took out a package of tobacco, and rolled himself a cigarette.

"What you talkin' about?" Ted demanded.

"Well, now, if you was like that brother of yours you wouldn't have no trouble grabbin' off women. But you ain't so perty as he is."

Not knowing that Ted had been desperately in love with Jeannie years ago, as well as with Happy later, Edwards could not quite account for the pallor that spread over Ted's face, but he was glad to see that he had hit upon a tender spot.

"I mean," Edwards went on, "that even if he is married and lives on the farm he can kinda grab women out from under you."

Ted stood beside the linotype holding a wrench in one hand. He was breathing heavily and staring at Edwards.

The latter waited a long time, absorbed in his cigarette, and then turned to a pile of papers on his desk. Ted swallowed several times and finally asked again, "What you talkin' about?"

Edwards pretended to be surprised. "Why, don't you know it was your brother that knocked her up! Some high school kids caught 'em at it."

Edwards was frightened for an instant at the success of his attempt. Ted began to shake and raised the wrench. "Hey, look out!" Edwards yelled. But Ted did not throw the wrench at him. Instead he slammed it into the linotype and went pounding toward the door.

"Hey," Edwards said, "if you busted anything you'll pay for it." As Ted marched out the door Edwards hurried to the machine and looked at it. "If you busted anything you'll pay for it."

Edwards went to the door in time to see a dog, almost hairless from the mange, frighten a flock of sparrows from a dropping of horse manure in the street. The dog passed Ted, stopped suddenly to scratch and whine, and Ted walking blindly almost fell over him.

Edwards watched the little man, and his alarm gave way to satisfaction and amusement. "Boy, I sure got under his skin that time!" Edwards sighed. "Now as soon as this place has time to air out it'll smell better for a while."

If Ted had been armed and had met Jim at that moment he would have killed him. But before he got to his room and had stowed a gun in his hip pocket his plans had changed somewhat. He knew that a big posse was going to assemble that afternoon to go out and round up the farmers. He would tell this posse about Jim and get him lynched.

He sat down on the bed for a while and thought it over. A better way would be to go out now to McGee's, find the old man, and tell him. McGee would do the killing.

But an hour later Ted had cooled pretty thoroughly and had formed a plan which suited him exactly. He would go to Jim directly, tell him what he knew, and force him to come to town and enlist. That would be the noble thing to do. Maybe the army would make a man out of Jim. Cure him of his socialism and his general cussedness.

Ted lighted a cigar and flapped down stairs. He went out into the blistering heat, cranked his automobile, floundered under the wheel, and drove down the rutted street.

Jim wasn't to be blamed because he could take women away from Ted, but Jim was unpatriotic and immoral and had to be taught a lesson.

Ted was a little bit afraid to drive out into the country, but it was not far to Jim's place. The farmers were licked. Most of them would be arrested that day. It was safe enough to go.

When he drove into the yard Jim was working at the woodpile. Jeannie was not in sight. Ted drove close to the woodpile and stopped, shutting off the engine. Jim looked at him in silent contempt and went on chopping kindling.

"I thought I ought to talk to you," Ted said.

"Go on. I'm listening."

"Well, I don't want to talk too loud."

Jim sighed, put down his ax, and sat on the running board of the car with his back to Ted.

"I think you otta go into town and enlist." Ted said.

Jim stood up, red in the face. "Git the hell out of here before I knock you in the face like I used to."

Ted was white now, but he kept to his purpose. "Well, you either git in this car now and come to town with me and enlist in the army, or this afternoon I'll tell the posse in town what happened between you and Happy McGee, and that you're the guy that knocked her up, and you'll be lynched."

Jim went white and closed his eyes "Let 'em lynch and be damned," he said.

"Or I'll stop at McGee's place and tell him, and he'll kill you before the crowd gets out here."

Jim said nothing for a while, then he looked at Ted squarely and said, "I guess you won't if I kill you right now."

"It won't do you no good to kill me," Ted explained, "because I've got all this written down where it will be discovered mighty quick after I'm dead. Besides, I've got a gun in my hand. Either you straighten up and do your duty or everybody, by God, will find out what kind of a guy you are. And if old man McGee won't kill you there's plenty that will. I reckon Jeannie might do it herself."

Jim stood for several minutes, holding to the side of the car, but the fight was gone out of him. "All right, I'll go to town." He went around to the front of the car and cranked it, came back, and got in. The car started with a jerk and then stopped again when Jeannie came running out of the house. "Where you goin', Jim?" she screamed above the noise of the motor.

"I'm goin' to town and enlist in the army."

She looked at him and at Ted, trying to understand. "You're doin' that—for me and the baby! Why you doin' that, Jim?"

He didn't answer.

"You hadn't ought to do that, Jim, if you don't believe in it—they'll jist send you to jail, maybe, and we can get along, and—"

"Drive on," Jim said to Ted. The car leaped. Jim looked back once at Jeannie. She was standing there with her dirty apron over her face.

THIRTY-FIVE

EDITOR LEM EDWARDS took charge of the eight or nine hundred men who assembled that afternoon to arrest the farmers. Now that the farmers were scattered and could be picked up one at a time every man in town who was able to walk was ready to join the patriotic band. The real danger to the patriots, as Commander Edwards realized, was not the guns of the farmers but their own guns. In an ungrammatical speech before the posse left town he warned them not to load their guns until they came in sight of the enemy. "Because we don't want nobody else shot in the back like Sam Gladson."

Denny Payne and the other bank-side boys were Editor Edwards' lieutenants. They would have preferred a lynching, as less dangerous and more fun, but this expedition was well worth while. They wouldn't have missed it for the world.

When they arrested McGee they surrounded the house and approached from every side, guns ready. The old man was sitting quietly in the front room smoking his pipe. Edwards and Denny were the first ones to enter.

"You're under arrest, you son-of-a-bitch," Edwards told him.

McGee stood up and tapped his pipe on his pants leg. One of the young fellows from town hit him, knocking him backwards over a rickety chair. The blow was entirely unexpected. Mack arose and took a step toward the youth, who took a step backward in alarm, but Edwards shouted, "Don't get smart. If we decide to beat hell out of you, you damned traitor, there's nothing you can do about it."

Mack knew that this was true. He thrust out his hands, and his wrists were bound together with a piece of rope. He was battered and kicked for a while and then taken to the automobile for transportation to the jail.

This arrest was so easy and unexciting that the patriotic band was disappointed. The next house was Ned Wellhof's. Ned was an ex-convict and a desperate character. They took counsel and decided not to take any chances. "We'll slip up quiet-like and smoke him out," they agreed.

Since Birdie's death Ned had been living alone. The children had been temporarily adopted by neighboring families, "until Ned could get on his feet."

On the Sunday afternoon of the arrests Ned and three others were sitting quietly in Ned's shack drinking what was left of his whiskey. There was very little left, and none of them was drunk. They were all expecting arrest and wondering what would happen to them when they were taken.

One of them was a weak-minded lad who had dreamed of being a cowboy and had turned out a cautious bootlegger. He sat, pale and with his mouth hanging open, stabbing a pocket knife into the floor. He wore a large hat, a dirty silk shirt with large red stripes, and high-heeled boots under his overalls.

Another was a nervous middle-aged man with a warped brown face and only two snaggle teeth in front. Like Ned, he had spent his life getting religion, backsliding, and getting religion again, and he prospered only while he backslid.

The third was part Indian. He sometimes farmed a little, sometimes helped at the still, usually hunted and trapped.

These were the men who had been in with Ned in his business of whiskey-making.

The first warning they had of the attack was a ragged volley of shots and flying splinters from the walls. They flattened out on the floor, and because Ned had banked the dirt high all around the house, and because most of the posse members shot at the windows, they were fairly safe for a little while.

There were only two guns in the house: Ned's battered single-barreled shotgun and a cheap thirty-two pistol belonging to the cowboy.

Ned wriggled to the corner where the shotgun stood, poked it out a window and fired without aiming. This was useless, of course, but for the moment he could think of nothing else to do. The cowboy emptied his pistol out another window and then began to cry. The half-breed lay quietly, looking this way and that with the expression of a trapped animal.

A rifle bullet penetrated the dirt embankment around the house, plowed through a floor board, struck Ned in the temple, and slid around his cheek bone to his eyeball and the bridge of his nose. He was knocked senseless. Blood formed in a pool under his face and made a little river along the floor.

It was the half-breed who thought at last of what to do. He tied a dirty white handkerchief to the handle of Ned's broom and waved it out the window. The firing slackened and finally ceased.

Members of the mob crept out of their hiding places and came cautiously toward the house, guns ready.

Ned recovered consciousness suddenly and stood up. He was evidently blinded by blood in his good eye, but he staggered out the door and started running. A member of the posse fired and Ned went down.

When members of the mob reached him they flopped him over on his back, kicked him about the head, and then lifted him to his feet. He was unconscious. They carried him into the house, holding him in front of the first man to enter as a shield against possible treachery.

Inside they seized the three others, threw them down, beat them about the face, kicked them between the legs, then stood them up and bound them with ropes.

Ned was still alive and bleeding a great deal from his wounds. He was breathing heavily, blowing blood bubbles out of his mouth.

Edwards studied him for a while. "No use of taking that bastard with us," he decided. "He'd bloody up the car and die on the way to town."

Beating their three captives happily the town boys left Ned's shack. They had had their excitement and were content. "Did you see that ex-convict shooting at us?" they asked each other. "It's damned lucky that we shot 'em out. They'd got a few of us if we hadn't been mighty careful. They'd just as soon shoot a man as look at him."

The next day Ted wrote up the story for the paper:

"Four traitors, all of them known criminals and one an ex-convict, put up a desperate fight Sunday against the forces of law and order. Caught like rats in a trap, these desperadoes staged the best fight of the rebellion, firing until their ammunition gave out at the citizens who were attempting to put them under arrest. Fortunately no one was hit by their bullets.

"The notorious Ned Wellhof, who recently served a term in the penitentiary at McAlester, was leader of the gang. After the pro-Huns had surrendered Wellhof, although wounded, made a desperate attempt to escape. A well-placed shot stopped his flight."

Ted did not tell what had become of Wellhof because he did not know.

There followed some editorial comment upon the bravery of

the members of the posse, "who ricked their lives to capture these desperate and degenerate men." The articles suggested that the citizens who had thus risked their lives should be honored just as much as if they had been fighting in Flanders Field.

There was another interesting item in Ted's paper that week. It said that "Jim Tetley, a young farmer living near town, yesterday realized the mistake he had been led by older men into making, and came to town and enlisted in the army. It is to be expected that a great many of the younger men will take this way out of their present trouble."

Ted was wrong in this prediction. None of the others enlisted.

Jim was not molested by the posse, of course, since it was known that he had turned patriot. He was at home when the attack occurred at Ned's place, and he and Jeannie heard the firing. Jeannie was almost in hysterics, sure that her father had been killed.

After the firing had ceased Jim walked across the fields to Mack's place, discovering nothing except that Mack was gone. Then he circled through the woods towards Ned's shack.

When he was within two hundred yards of the shack he heard a yell and broke into a run. He saw that the house was bullet-riddled.

Inside he saw, by the last rays of the setting sun, Ned lying in a pool of blood. He found a ragged shirt and tried to bandage Ned's head. Then he placed the wounded man on a mattress and started to get Jeannie.

He did not return to Ned's shack with Jeannie though, but went back to Mack's place and phoned for a doctor. Every doctor in town refused to come.

Calling for Birdie and Sissie, Ned died shortly after Jeannie arrived.

THIRTY-SIX

DEPUTY SHERIFF JACK ALLEN got the job of taking a half dozen of the Socialist farmers to the federal penitentiary at Leavenworth. He was nervous about it right at first. He didn't know the fellows, and there was no telling what they might take it in their heads to do. But when he got them on the train he saw that they wouldn't cause any trouble. They looked all in, and they sat in the smoking car and didn't say much. He had lots of time to think.

The deputy had been with one of the gangs that had rounded some of the farmers up, and there had been some shooting, but nobody got killed except one of the farmers. But it was a bad business.

The deputy got nervous whenever any shooting started. That was the only trouble with his job. Once in a while he got in a place where men were shooting. The deputy always lost his head when guns started going off. He was afraid that some day he would disgrace himself, like a couple of years before when they were trying to round up some bank robbers. But it had been dark then and nobody knew exactly what had happened, so they didn't blame him. But he had been cussing himself ever since for deserting his post and hiding in an alley because he knew that if he had stayed where he was supposed to he could have captured the whole gang and got a reward. But if you get scared you don't have any sense.

Naturally the deputy was nervous about his job of taking the men to the penitentiary until he found out that they wouldn't cause any trouble. After that he had a nice trip.

These farmers had gone out against the government because they didn't want to go to war. That was a mighty serious thing to do, and of course they deserved their punishment. But the deputy didn't want to go to war either, although he didn't want anyone to know it. He worried about it quite a lot. He felt like he would sure get shot; and he didn't want to be any dead hero. In a way these farmers were lucky, because they would go to the pen and serve their terms and come out alive, some of them, while a lot of patriotic fellows would be killed on the battlefield.

Well, anyway, this would be the last war, unless the Huns won. It was a fellow's duty to go and fight the Huns. But the deputy sure hoped he wouldn't be called.

The deputy couldn't understand about one of these farmers, an old white-headed Irishman they called Mack. Mack was too old to go to war, so why did he want to get mixed up in this business? Maybe he was just plain nuts.

The deputy watched him out of the corner of his eye. Mack just sat in his seat and stared out the window like he was half dead. He wouldn't live long in the pen. The others seemed to look up to him.

The deputy was dozing, but he woke up when he heard somebody moving in the aisle. A couple of Negroes coming from the jim crow car. That was a sign they had crossed the state line. Couldn't no damned nigger ride in a white car in Oklahoma. It made the deputy mad to see these black bastards coming into a car with white people, but he couldn't do anything about it.

He knew the Socialist farmers wouldn't mind, because they

were nigger-lovers. They had niggers in their army with them. They deserved everything they got, and more. They ought to be hanged for treating niggers as equals.

But the deputy got to wondering about these farmers again. Just to look at them they seemed like ordinary fellows that you shook hands with before election. And when they talked they didn't say anything that sounded like treason except once when they were looking out at a stubble field one of them said, "Well, Mack, anyway we won't be raisin' wheat for the soldiers to eat while they're killin' Dutchmen." The deputy would have bawled them out for talking that way, but they shut up and didn't say anything else so he let it drop.

On the way back he would ride in the day coach and maybe pick up with a gal who was lonesome. Thinking about it he shifted in his seat and scratched between his legs. He would have a lay-over in the city and he would maybe have a little fun there.

Now that they were in Kansas Mack seemed to come more alive and perk up a little. He looked out of the window and sometimes craned his neck a little and acted pretty natural. One of the others asked him, "You used to live in this state, didn't you, Mack?"

"Yeah, west of here," Mack answered.

So that was why he was interested and was looking out the window.

Then the farmers got pretty cheerful for a while, the only time on the trip that they seemed natural.

"Ain't this close to where you had that sway-back horse, Mack?" one of them asked, and they all laughed. It was some kind of a joke. "Sure," Mack answered. "Not far from here." Then they asked him what ever became of the horse.

"Well, didn't I ever tell you? We had to shoot him, that is part of him." Mack looked real serious, but the deputy knew he was codding because of the way the others took it.

"You see, we straightened his back out so often," Mack went on, "that it got real weak, so it would bend every which way, and one day he tried to kick another horse, and he kicked himself plumb in two he was that weak in the back. Well, I never seen a critter look so surprised when his hind end come off. We shot his front end and buried 'em both in the same hole."

The prisoners laughed quite a lot at that, and a seemed to liven up the trip a whole lot for them.

When the train stopped at Leavenworth the deputy ordered the men to get up and march out. Mack seemed to be pretty sick again, and he wobbled back and forth in the aisle. The deputy spoke to him pretty sharp. There was no danger of any trouble now because there would be guards at the station to meet him.

The deputy saw a couple of guards standing there and he was relieved. These penitentiary guards were hard. You could tell. Old Mack was still wobbling when he got out of the train, and all at once he stumbled and landed on one knee and sort of collapsed. "Boys," he said, "I guess I can't go no further."

The deputy kicked Mack but didn't seem to rouse him. Then the guards stepped in and gave him a pistol-whuppin', but still he didn't get up, so the guards ordered the other prisoners to carry him to the wagon. He bled quite a bit along the platform. The old man wouldn't have long to serve at that rate. Of course, he deserved what he got, for tryin' to overthrow the best government on God's green earth.

One of the guards took the deputy aside for a moment. "I think maybe that old bastard's dead," he said. "He slipped and fell when he was gittin' off the train, see, and busted his head. Understand?"

"Yeah, sure," the deputy replied.

✲ THIRTY-SEVEN

IT WAS AGAINST THE LAW for those farmers who had been released on good behavior to get together now or hold meetings of any sort, so no one could come to Mack's funeral except Jim and Jeannie. The Methodist preacher was there because Jeannie wanted a preacher.

Jim felt weak and low most of the time, but he wouldn't let himself get sick for fear when he was called to the army he would be sent back home. He had thought that Mack's funeral would be the hardest thing he had to go through, but when the time came he was only numb and listless.

The preacher didn't like the job, and when he prayed he seemed sort of apologetic to God for even recommending mercy to this sinner. Mack looked better dead than he had the last time Jim saw him alive except for a place on his face where he must have been bruised by his fall. Jim decided that, everything considered, it was a lucky accident when he fell and was killed getting off the train.

The baby was cross and Jeannie wouldn't put him down for a minute. Jeannie looked older than ever, and Jim was afraid she wouldn't keep going.

The undertaker had brought four fellows out from town to carry the coffin and fill up the grave. Jim knew one of them a little bit, Denny Payne. They sat outside during the services and talked and chewed tobacco. Jim and the undertaker helped them put the coffin in the hearse. It was an automobile hearse. Jim and Jeannie rode to the graveyard in the preacher's car. They went fast. The dust from the hearse was bad. Jeannie sat in a corner of the back seat, with the dirt settling on her, and cried. The baby was worried about riding in the car and hung around her neck and looked at Jim through the yellow cloud. Jim returned the stare and tried to fix in his mind just how the kid's red mouth, flat nose and blue eyes looked.

It was hot in the graveyard. The baby went to sleep on Jeannie's shoulder and she tried to keep his face out of the sun. The front of her dress was wet where she had been holding him.

The mound on Happy's grave had been fixed up so that it looked fresh. The Wellhof graves had been fixed up for Ned's funeral not long before and didn't look bad, but the other graves were overgrown with weeds and some of them had coyote holes in them.

Jim was afraid Jeannie would collapse in the graveyard, but she stood through the ceremony and walked to the car strong enough.

On the way home there was a young mule grazing in the road. The preacher honked and the mule locked up but didn't move. There was no getting out of the ruts, and the preacher didn't stop soon enough. The radiator bumped the mule and the mule struck back, smashing one of the headlights. "Oh, *shaw!*" the preacher yelled, so loud that he woke up the baby. He got out and looked at the light. The mule, unhurt, trotted off fifty yards and stood looking at them with interest. The preacher looked around for something to throw, and seeing nothing made a run at the mule, shouting angrily. The mule, his head high and cocked to one side, trotted on and turned down a side road.

The preacher, red-faced, got back in the car and drove on, saying nothing, but when they got to Jim's place and Jim paid him he looked at the money and said through his nose, "Well, what about the light that was broken on the trip?"

Jim looked at him in amazement. "Say," he said finally, "you git the hell down the road before I bust somepin' else."

The preacher snorted and slammed the car door and drove off.

"You hadn't ought to swear at him," Jeannie said. "Not on a day like this."

She held up until the evening work was done, then she broke down and was sick most of the night.

But Jim's hardest ordeal came one afternoon several days later. He was whittling down a little patch of wheat stubble with an old dry-land plow that had belonged to Mack. The plow was dull, and the ground wasn't dry enough to be powdery. The soil turned up like so much pavement, sometimes in chunks as big as a bucket. The three horses moseyed along fighting flies, and when the plow bucked very hard over some big hunk the horses would stop, thinking something was wrong. Jim usually didn't have the ambition to pound them on the back right away but let them stand for a minute or two, so their habit of stopping got worse.

The job was so slow that it seemed like a waste of time, but Jim had to be busy at something until he was called, and this was as good as anything he could do. If all this mess hadn't happened he would be sitting there on the plow half asleep and wishing something would happen, any damned thing for a change.

He wasn't afraid of going to war or of being killed. Better be dead and buried, he thought, than be dead and still ploddin' away on top of the ground, like farmers have to do.

He remembered a story he had heard about an island where the witch doctors or somebody gave the natives dope that would cause them to lose consciousness, and the family, thinking they were dead, would bury them; then the witch doctors would dig them up and revive them and sell them to white men in another part of the island, or somewhere else, to cut cane. After they were revived they had no will power, but would go about in a daze doing whatever they were told and eating almost nothing, as Jim remembered the story. They would cut cane for a month or two, and then drop down dead. That was the way the cane raisers got cheap labor.

But it was really no different from anywhere else. The rich gave the poor a shot of dope, and the poor went around in a daze all their lives doing what they were told. And if they developed any wills of their own the banker got a bunch of town loafers and the sheriff to shoot hell out of them and arrest them. Well, a change would have to come some time, but not soon enough to do Jim any good.

He saw three men come out of the blackjacks and wait for him at the end of the field. He wondered what they wanted of him, and began to feel excited because none of the farmers had spoken to him since they had come back from their trials, released on good behavior.

He recognized these fellows. One was Uncle Billy Turner, who had been sick during the rebellion and so hadn't taken any part. Another was a man by the name of McSlarrow, who had been on the hill. The third was one of the boys who had gone with him to burn the bridge.

He pulled up to where they were and swung the team around and stopped. They looked very solemn. "Perty dry, ain't it?" Uncle Billy said, hobbling toward him over the clods. The other two followed and stood a few yards from the plow.

"Pretty dry," Jim said.

Uncle Billy stooped over and broke off the end of a dry weed stalk that slanted up from the plowed ground. He scratched at it with his thumb nail and then put it between his teeth. Jim looked from one to the other and then looked at the horses. He waited a long time. The young man picked up a clod and threw it across the stubble.

"You fellers want to see me?" Jim asked at last, not impatiently but by way of encouraging them to begin. Uncle Billy rolled his red-rimmed eyes at McSlarrow, and McSlarrow leaned forward and released a ball of tobacco juice.

"Yeah," McSlarrow said. "We aimed to come over yesterday, but Uncle Billy wasn't feelin' any too pert, and I went around lookin' fer that heifer that I ain't seen since we cut the fences."

McSlarrow stopped as if he had said all that was necessary and looked over toward the timber. Uncle Billy studied his toothpick and threw it down.

"What was it you wanted to see me about?" Jim asked. His throat was so dry that he could hardly talk. McSlarrow kicked a clod for a while.

"Well," he said, "some of the boys had a little secret get-together the other night in my pasture for a sort of funeral for Mack. They talked things over then, and they decided that considerin' how everythin' was and all, and you're goin' off to the army perty soon, they thought you hadn't ought to come back any more to this here community."

Jim took a chew of tobacco, but it stayed dry and hard in his mouth because he didn't have any spit to mix with it.

"Well," he said at last, "why don't you boys come and git me out and horse-whip me some night?"

"Well, some of the boys talked about that," McSlarrow explained, "but you could complain to the law and all of us would be rounded up and sent to the pen, and maybe somebody else would be killed."

"You don't need to worry about that," Jim said. "You can beat hell out of me and they won't be no complaints. I ain't that low."

He wrapped the whip-lash around a lever and unwrapped it. "I guess I ought to tell you boys how I feel. They ain't no danger of me comin' back here. When the war is over I'm gonna be one of these God-damned dead heroes. I ain't changed my mind none about things—but I had to enlist. I don't blame you boys none for feelin' like you do about my joinin' the army."

"Well, hit hain't only joinin' the army," Uncle Billy put in. "Hit's—well—the boys feel like you was to blame about Mack's gal, an' I tol' 'em that was jist a lot of talk—" He stopped and reached for the weed again.

"Well, that there is the reason I went back on you boys and joined the army. My brother said he'd tell Mack, and I couldn't bear to have the old man know what a son-of-a-bitch I was."

"Well, hit's too bad they told him," Uncle Billy said.

"What d'you mean?"

"Hain't that what you said?" Uncle Billy asked McSlarrow.

"Why, yeah. Some of the boys was mighty sore at you, and when they was in jail with Mack before the trials one of them told him about you and his girl—and he wouldn't believe nothin'. And they all swore it was true, and he never would say he believed it, but after that he was jist in a daze and didn't really know what he was doin'."

"Well, he's daid now," Uncle Billy said, "and hit don't make no difference."

Jim turned about in his seat, preparing to drive on. "You fellers don't need to worry about ever layin' eye's on me after I leave. One thing I hope is that nobody won't talk to Jeannie about all this. It wouldn't do no good. I don't know whether I can get her to sell out and move out of this community or not, but if she stays here with the kid I hope you fellers don't talk about it to your kids so's they'll throw it up to my kid when he goes to school. That's the only God-damned thing I care about."

"Well, he won't hear nothin' about it so far's I'm concerned," McSlarrow said. "But you know how kids is, and I hope to God she don't stay around here. Maybe if she'd rent the place and move to town it'd be all right, because in town you're quite a hero, and if you git killed in the war your kid'll grow up proud of you."

"Well, if he knew the whole story," Jim said, "he wouldn't be much proud."

# THIRTY-EIGHT

Several weeks passed before Jim had to go to war. There was plenty to do getting the place ready for Jeannie to manage. By selling the farm she had inherited from her father she could have Jim's eighty free from debt and could probably live in town on the rent, but she refused to consider any such plan. She said she would go crazy living in town with nothing to do. "You'll be back maybe next spring," she said, "and then with 240 acres of our own and Ted's eighty leased we can soon get out of debt."

"Yeah," he agreed. "But if I don't come back you better take the kid to town. He'll have an easier time."

"What makes you talk like that?" she demanded. "Just want to make it harder for me? Of course you'll come back."

The only fun Jim had now was playing with the baby. When he came in at noon he would rush into the front room, and usually he found the kid there sitting on the floor in the midst of a damp spot that had been wiped free of dust by his wet diaper. The spot was fringed by finger trails.

Jim would start a big game. "You're spoiling him," Jeannie would say.

Once Jim defended himself for this practice. "This is about the only chance I'll have," he said.

She looked at him half angrily. "You know you'll be back here in a year or two," she said.

"Well, maybe."

What the baby had been doing was always the big topic of conversation. A fall, a bump on the nose, a poor appetite—these things were important. Jim wanted to know just how he had lost his temper trying to pick up a stick he was sitting on; how he had pulled the nipple from his bottle and spilled the milk on the floor, and then pulled the tails of the cats who came to lap it up; how he had been frightened at the sight of a flopping chicken.

For the first time in years Jim became a sort of hero to Jeannie. She urged him not to work too hard and worried because he ate and slept very little. One morning, because Jim had spent a sleepless night and had dropped off to sleep only a little while before daybreak, Jeannie crept out of bed without waking him and did the chores alone. Jim woke up with a start about eight o'clock, the latest he had slept in all the time he could remember.

On the last Sunday before Jim went to war Jeannie did what he had always wanted her to do: she fixed herself and the baby up and sat down in the front room to rest. There was no place they could go and nothing they could do except sit in the front room, where there was a little breeze.

Except for her brown hair she looked a lot like Happy. He realized that he had always been in love with the girl she used to be. He wasn't altogether to blame for getting excited about Happy.

But it wasn't Jeannie's fault either that she hadn't always looked good. If she hadn't worked so hard and kept his nose to the grindstone most of the time they would have been foreclosed long ago.

He wanted to tell her that he was in love with her, but he didn't know exactly how to do it. He was very tired, and nothing made very much difference anyway.

They talked about the baby, remembered when the various cows were to come fresh, estimated how much it would cost to paint the barn. Then they closed the door because the wind was getting so hot that it was more comfortable in the still air. Finally Jim and the baby fell asleep on the floor. Jeannie changed clothes and went out to fix a chicken coop.

The last day that he was at home was something like this: Jeannie cooked a big breakfast, but neither of them was hungry. It was the same with dinner, so Jeannie fixed a good lunch for Jim to eat on the train.

Jeannie wouldn't go to town with him because even her best clothes looked funny in town. The train didn't leave until five and Jim got ready hours too early. He was restless. "Guess I'll mosey along," he said. "I got to report beforehand."

He sat down in the front room, and the kid came crawling up to him at a great rate on his hands and feet. "God, he'll be walkin' in a couple of weeks," Jim said.

The kid pulled himself up at Jim's knee, and Jim said "boo" at him. The kid cackled and reached for Jim's face.

"Guess I better mosey on," he said. "Wouldn't want to be late." He was afraid Jeannie would start bawling; then he would break down, and that'd be damned foolishness.

He tossed the kid up to the ceiling, caught him, set him down, picked up the shoebox that had the lunch in it, and walked toward the door.

"You can just throw the shoebox out the window when you're through," Jeannie said. He kissed her then and started down the driveway, walking fast as if he didn't have much time. But when he was out of sight around the bend he stopped for a minute. It was really early. He could play with the kid for maybe an hour more and it seemed like a shame to run away. But if he went back now Jeannie would be crying and the kid would be tickled to see him, and he couldn't stand it. He walked on.

He saw one of the cows trying to push through the fence, and stopped to drive her back and fix the wire up the best he could without a hammer. He took a big chew of tobacco and walked on.

He went to the court-house, where he was supposed to report, and found quite a crowd there. About a dozen other fellows were going on the same call, and a lot of people had gathered for the send-off.

There was a little program. Jim and the town boys who were going to war were herded together on the court-house lawn, and the others crowded around. The postmaster made a little speech, and everybody cheered.

There was a bunch of high-school girls dressed up in red, white and blue, and they led the parade through Main Street to the station. Jim and the other heroes trudged along behind the girls.

Jim felt conspicuous because he was the tallest man in the crowd. And he got a lot of attention because he had been one of the rebels and had turned patriotic. He was the only one of the rebels who had turned patriotic. The crowd loved him for it, but all this bull made Jim mad. He wished to hell the train was there so they could get on and get out of this damned place.

They waited around on the station platform for half an hour, and the crowd milled around. He saw a high-school girl smiling at him and turned away. He probably got red in the face. He didn't know what to do with his shoeboxful of food. The butter was melting and making the sides of the box greasy and transparent.

But he caught sight of one of Ned Wellhof's orphans, who had been adopted by a family in town, and he managed to get the kid to one side and give him the lunch. "Take that some place and eat all of it you can," he said, "and then if you want to, take the rest of it home. Be sure and eat all you can before you divide it up with anybody else." The kid looked like he could eat it all without help.

Ted came up and shook hands with Jim. "By God, I'd give anything in the world to be in your shoes," Ted said. Ted meant it, the damned fool. Ted was kind of watery-eyed.

The train pulled in, and the high-school girls started kissing the departing heroes. Mothers started bawling. Jim crowded toward the train steps, and when a girl rushed toward him he couldn't see her at all. Looked right over her head.

But the heroes got on the train at last and the train pulled out, and the crowd broke into the *Star Spangled Banner*, and the high-school girls ran down the tracks waving flags and crying.

But Jim's troubles weren't quite over yet. The train went within a quarter of a mile of his place, and when it passed Jim saw Jeannie standing at the right-of-way fence holding up the kid on her shoulder. The kid was frightened by the train, and Jim could see his face twisted in the agony of crying.

Jim leaned out the window and waved his hat. Jeannie waved and smiled, then turned suddenly and ducked her head and started back toward home.

Jim remembered all at once something that Mack had said: "That kid of yours will maybe help finish up this job that we made such a mess of."

The news butch came down the aisle carrying a paper so Jim could see the headline. It read "Lenin and Trotsky Seize Power in Russia. Institute Bloody Reign. Democracy Temporarily Crushed."

Jim couldn't make up his mind to buy a paper, but one of the boys in the seat ahead bought one and turned to the sport page. Jim decided to watch his chance and when the boy threw the paper away he would get it and read about the bloody reign in Russia.